I HEARD THAT SONG BEFORE

I Heard That Song Before

Mary Higgins Clark

THORNDIKE
WINDSOR
PARAGON

This Large Print edition is published by Thorndike Press, Waterville, Maine USA and by BBC Audiobooks Ltd, Bath, England.

Copyright© 2007 by Mary Higgins Clark.

Thomson Gale is part of The Thomson Corporation.

Thomson and Star Logo and Thorndike are trademarks and Gale is a registered trademark used herein under license.

Thorndike Press® Large Print Basic.
The text of this Large Print edition is unabridged.
Other aspects of the book may vary from the original edition.
Set in 16 pt. Plantin.

LIBRARY OF CONGRESS CATALOGING-IN-PUBLICATION DATA

Clark, Mary Higgins.
  I heard that song before / by Mary Higgins Clark.
    p. cm. — (Thorndike Press large print basic)
  ISBN 978-0-7862-9448-0 (lg. print : alk. paper)
  ISBN 0-7862-9448-5 (lg. print : alk. paper)
  1. Rich people — Fiction. 2. Sleepwalking — Fiction. 3. Englewood (N.J.)
  — Fiction. 4. Large type books. I. Title.
  PS3553.L287I15 2007b
  813'.54—dc22
                                                              2007010639

BRITISH LIBRARY CATALOGUING-IN-PUBLICATION DATA AVAILABLE

Published in 2007 in the U.S. by arrangement with G. P. Putnam's Sons,
a member of Penguin Group (USA) Inc.
Published in 2007 in the U.K. by arrangement with Simon & Schuster UK Ltd.

U.K. Hardcover: 978 1 405 61786 4 (Windsor Large Print)
U.K. Softcover: 978 1 405 61787 1 (Paragon Large Print)

Printed in the United States of America on permanent paper
10 9 8 7 6 5 4 3 2 1

ACKNOWLEDGMENTS

Writing is essentially a lonely occupation. A writer is blessed who has people who support and encourage along the way. When I begin to tell the tale, my forever editor, Michael V. Korda, and senior editor Chuck Adams continue to cheer and advise me. My thanks always to them and to Lisl Cade my publicist, my agent Sam Pinkus, and Associate Director of Copyediting Gypsy da Silva and her special team: Joshua Cohen and Jonathan Evans.

Kudos and thanks to my family, children, and grandchildren, to Himself, the ever-perfect John Conheeney, to my closeknit supporters Agnes Newton, Nadine Petry, and Irene Clark. You're a grand group, and I love you all.

And now, my dear readers, I hope you enjoy this story.

For Marilyn
My Firstborn Child and Very Dear Friend
With love

PROLOGUE

My father was the landscaper for the Carrington estate. With fifty acres, it was one of the last remaining private properties of that size in Englewood, New Jersey, an upscale town three miles west of Manhattan via the George Washington Bridge.

One Saturday afternoon in August twenty-two years ago, when I was six years old, my father decided, even though it was his day off, that he had to go there to check on the newly installed outside lighting. The Carringtons were having a formal dinner party that evening for two hundred people. Already in trouble with his employers because of his drinking problem, Daddy knew that if the lights placed throughout the formal gardens did not function properly, it might mean the end of his job.

Because we lived alone, he had no choice except to take me with him. He settled me on a bench in the garden nearest the terrace

9

with strict instructions to stay right there until he came back. Then he added, "I may be a little while, so if you have to use the bathroom, go through the screen door around the corner. You'll see the staff powder room just inside it."

That sort of permission was exactly what I needed. I had heard my father describe the inside of the great stone mansion to my grandmother, and my imagination had gone wild visualizing it. It had been built in Wales in the seventeenth century and even had a hidden chapel where a priest could both live and celebrate Mass in secrecy during the era of Oliver Cromwell's bloody attempt to erase all traces of Catholicism from England. In 1848 the first Peter Carrington had the mansion taken down and reassembled stone by stone in Englewood.

I knew from my father's description that the chapel had a heavy wooden door and was located at the very end of the second floor.

I had to see it.

I waited five minutes after he disappeared into the gardens and then raced through the door he had pointed out. The back staircase was to my immediate right, and I silently made my way upstairs. If I did encounter anyone, I planned to say that I was looking for a bathroom, which I persuaded myself was partially true.

On the second floor, with rising anxiety I tiptoed down one carpeted hallway after another as I encountered a maze of unexpected turns. But then I saw it: the heavy wooden door my father had described, so out of place in the rest of the thoroughly modernized house.

Emboldened by my luck in having encountered no one in my adventure, I ran the last few steps and rushed to open the door. It squeaked as I tugged at it, but it opened just enough for me to squeeze through.

Being in the chapel was like going back in time. It was much smaller than I'd expected. I had pictured it as similar to the Lady Chapel in St. Patrick's Cathedral, where my grandmother always stopped to light a candle for my mother, on the rare occasions when we shopped in New York. She never failed to tell me how beautiful my mother had looked the day she and my father were married there.

The walls and floor of this chapel were built of stone, and the air I was breathing felt damp and cold.

A nicked and peeling statue of the Virgin Mary was the room's only religious artifact, and a battery-lit votive candle in front of it provided the only dim and shadowy lighting. Two rows of wooden pews faced the small wooden table that must have served as an altar.

As I was taking it all in, I heard the door begin to squeak and I knew someone was pushing it open. I did the only thing I could do — I ran between the pews and dropped to the ground, then ostrichlike buried my face in my hands.

From the voices I could tell that a man and a woman had entered the chapel. Their whispers, harsh and angry, echoed against the stone. They were arguing about money, a subject I knew well. My grandmother was always sniping at my father, telling him that if he kept up the drinking there wouldn't be a roof over his head or mine.

The woman was demanding money, and the man was saying that he already had paid her enough. Then she said, "This will be the last time, I swear," and he said, "I heard that song before."

I know my memory of that moment is accurate. From the time I could understand that, unlike my friends in kindergarten, I did not have a mother, I had begged my grandmother to tell me about her, every single thing she could remember. Among the memories my grandmother shared with me was one of my mother starring in the high school play and singing a song called "I Heard That Song Before." "Oh, Kathryn, she sang it so beautifully. She had a lovely voice. Everyone clapped so long and shouted, *'encore, encore.'* She had to sing it again." Then my grandmother would hum it for me.

Following the man's remark, I could not hear the rest of what was said except for her whispered, "Don't forget," as she left the chapel. The man had stayed; I could hear his agitated breathing. Then, very softly, he began to whistle the tune of the song my mother sang in the school play. Looking back, I think he may have been trying to calm himself. After a few bars, he broke off and left the chapel.

I waited for what seemed forever, then I left, too. I hurried down the stairs and back outside, and, of course, never told my father that I'd been in the house or what I had heard in the chapel. But the memory never faded, and I am sure of what I heard.

Who those people were, I don't know. Now, twenty-two years later, it is important to find out. The only thing that I have learned for certain, from all of the accounts of that evening, is that there were a number of overnight guests staying in the mansion, as well as five in household help, and the local caterer and his crew. But that knowledge may not be enough to save my husband's life, if indeed it deserves to be saved.

1

I grew up in the shadow of the Lindbergh baby kidnapping.

By that I mean I was born and raised in Englewood, New Jersey. In 1932, the grandson of Englewood's most prominent citizen, Ambassador Dwight Morrow, was kidnapped. Furthermore, the baby's father happened to be the most famous man in the world at the time, Col. Charles Lindbergh, who had flown the first solo flight across the Atlantic Ocean in his single-engine plane, the *Spirit of St. Louis*.

My grandmother, who was eight years old at that time, remembers the blazing headlines, the crowds of reporters who congregated outside Next Day Hill, the Morrow estate, the arrest and trial of Bruno Hauptmann.

Time passed, memories faded. Today Englewood's most prominent residence is the Carrington mansion, the stone-castlelike structure that I had stolen into as a child.

All these thoughts went through my mind as, for the second time in my life, I went inside the gates of the Carrington estate. Twenty-two years, I thought, remembering the inquisitive six-year-old I had been. Maybe it was the memory of my father being dismissed by the Carringtons only a few weeks later that made me suddenly feel self-conscious and awkward. The bright October morning had changed into a windy, damp afternoon, and I wished that I had worn a heavier jacket. The one I had chosen now seemed much too light both in color and fabric.

Instinctively, I parked my secondhand car to the side of the imposing driveway, not wanting it to be the object of anyone's scrutiny. One hundred and eight thousand miles on the speedometer takes a lot of starch out of a car, even one recently washed and mercifully free of dents.

I had twisted my hair into a bun, but the wind tore at it as I walked up the steps and rang the bell. A man who looked to be in his midfifties, with a receding hairline and narrow, unsmiling lips, opened the door. He was dressed in a dark suit, and I wasn't sure whether he was a butler or a secretary, but before I could speak, without introducing himself, he said that Mr. Carrington was expecting me and that I should come in.

The wide entrance hall was illuminated by light that filtered through leaded stained-glass windows. A statue of a knight in armor stood next to a medieval tapestry depicting a battle scene. I longed to examine the tapestry, but instead I dutifully followed my escort down a corridor to the library.

"Miss Lansing is here, Mr. Carrington," he said. "I'll be in the office." From that remark I guessed he was an assistant.

When I was little I used to draw pictures of the kind of home I'd love to live in. One of my favorite rooms to imagine was the one in which I would read away my afternoons. In that room there was always a fireplace and bookshelves. One version included a comfortable couch, and I'd draw myself curled up in the corner, a book in my hand. I'm not suggesting I'm any kind of artist because I'm not. I drew stick figures and the bookshelves were uneven, the carpet a splotched multicolored copy of one I'd seen in the window of an antique rug store. I could not put the exact image in my mind on paper, but I knew what I wanted. I wanted the kind of room I was standing in now.

Peter Carrington was seated in a wide leather chair, his feet on a hassock. The lamp on the table beside him not only illuminated the book he was reading but spotlighted his handsome profile.

He was wearing reading glasses, which sat on the bridge of his nose and slipped off when he looked up. Retrieving them, he laid them on the table, removed his feet from the hassock, and stood. I had caught occasional glimpses of him in town and had seen his picture in the papers, so I had an impression of him, but being in the same room with him was different. There was a quiet authority about Peter Carrington that he retained even as he smiled and extended his hand.

"You write a persuasive letter, Kathryn Lansing."

"Thank you for letting me stop in, Mr. Carrington."

His handshake was firm. I knew he was studying me just as I was studying him. He was taller than I had realized, with the narrow body of a runner. His eyes were more gray than blue. His thin, even-featured face was framed by dark brown hair that was a shade long but which suited him well. He was wearing a dark brown cardigan with a rust thread running through the weave. If I had been asked to guess his job from his appearance alone, I would have said college professor.

I knew he was forty-two years old. That meant he would have been about twenty the day that I crept into this house. I wondered if he had been home for that party. It was possible, of course — in late August he might not yet have gone back to Princeton, where he had been a student. Or, if he had already started school, he might have come home for the weekend. Princeton was only an hour-and-a-half drive away.

He invited me to sit down in one of the two matching armchairs near the fireplace. "I've been wanting an excuse to have a fire," he said. "This afternoon the weather cooperated."

I was more than ever conscious of the fact that my lime green jacket was more suitable to an August afternoon than to midautumn. I felt a strand of hair slip over my shoulder and tried to twist it back into the bun that was supposed to anchor it.

I have a master's in library science, my passion for books having made that a natural career choice. Since graduation five years ago, I've been working at the Englewood Public Library and am heavily involved in our community's literacy project.

Now I was in this impressive library, "with my hat in my hand," as my grandmother would say. I was planning a fundraiser for the literacy program and wanted to make it spectacular. There was one way I was sure I could get people to pay three hundred dollars for a cocktail reception, and that would be if it were held in this house. The Carrington mansion had become part of the folklore of Englewood and the surrounding communities. Everyone knew its history and that it had been transported from Wales. I was certain that the prospect of being inside it would make all the difference in whether or not we could have a sellout event.

I usually feel pretty comfortable in my own skin, but sitting there, sensing that those gray eyes were taking my measure, I felt flustered and ill at ease. Suddenly I felt, once again, like the daughter of the landscaper who drank too much.

Get over it, I told myself, and stop with the "gee-whiz" nonsense. Giving myself a brisk mental shake, I began my well-rehearsed solicitation. "Mr. Carrington, as I wrote you, there are many good causes, meaning many reasons for people to write checks. Of course it's impossible for anyone to support everything. Quite frankly, these days even well-off people feel tapped out. That's why it's essential to our event to find a way to get people to write a check for us."

That was when I launched into my plea for

him to allow us to have a cocktail party in this house. I watched as his expression changed, and I saw the "no" word forming on his lips.

He put it gracefully. "Miss Lansing," he began.

"Please call me Kay."

"I thought your name was Kathryn."

"On my birth certificate and to my grandmother."

He laughed. "I understand." Then he began his polite refusal. "Kay, I'd be happy to write a check . . ."

I interrupted him. "I'm sure you would. But as I wrote, this is more than just about money. We need volunteers to teach people how to read, and the best way to get them is to make them want to come to an affair, and then sign them up. I know a great caterer who has promised to reduce his price if the event is held here. It would just be for two hours, and it would mean so much to so many people."

"I have to think about it," Peter Carrington said as he stood up.

The meeting was over. I thought quickly and decided there was nothing to lose by adding one final thing: "Mr. Carrington, I've done of lot of research about your family. For generations this was one of the most hospitable homes in Bergen County. Your father and grandfather and great-grandfather supported local community activities and charities. By helping us now, you could do so much good, and it would be so easy for you."

I had no right to feel so terribly disappointed, but I did. He didn't respond, and without waiting for him or his assistant to show me out, I retraced my steps to the door. I did pause to take a quick glance to the back of the house, thinking of the staircase I had sneaked up all those years ago. Then I left, sure that I had made my second and final visit to the mansion.

Two days later Peter Carrington's picture was on the cover of *Celeb,* a national weekly gossip rag. It showed him coming out of the police station twenty-two years ago, after being questioned about the disappearance of eighteen-year-old Susan Althorp, who had vanished following the formal dinner dance she had attended at the Carrington mansion. The blaring headline, IS SUSAN ALTHORP STILL ALIVE?, was followed by the caption under Peter's picture: "Industrialist still a suspect in the disappearance of debutante Susan Althorp, who would be celebrating her fortieth birthday this week."

The magazine had a field day rehashing

details of the search for Susan and, since her father had been an ambassador, comparing the case to the kidnapping of the Lindbergh baby.

The article included a summary of the circumstances surrounding the death of Peter Carrington's pregnant wife, Grace, four years ago. Grace Carrington, known for drinking heavily, had given a birthday party for Carrington's stepbrother, Richard Walker. Carrington had arrived home after a twenty-three-hour flight from Australia, observed her condition, grabbed the glass out of her hand, dumped the contents on the carpet, and angrily demanded, "Can't you have a little mercy on the child you're carrying?" Then, claiming exhaustion, he went up to bed. In the morning, the housekeeper found the body of Grace Carrington, still dressed in a satin evening suit, at the bottom of the swimming pool. An autopsy showed that she was three times over the limit of being legally drunk. The article concluded, "Carrington claimed he went to sleep immediately and did not awaken until the police responded to the 911 call. MAYBE. We're conducting an opinion poll. Go to our Web site and let us know what you think."

A week later, at the library, I received a call

from Vincent Slater, who reminded me that I had met him when I had an appointment with Peter Carrington.

"Mr. Carrington," he said, "has decided to permit the use of his home for your fundraiser. He suggests that you coordinate the details of the event with me."

2

Vincent Slater put down the phone and leaned back, ignoring the faint squeak of his desk chair, a sound that had begun to annoy him and that several times he'd made a mental note to get fixed. His office in the mansion had originally been one of the seldom-used sitting rooms at the back of the house. In addition to its remoteness, he had chosen it because of the French doors that not only gave a view of the formal gardens but also served as a private entrance from which he could come and go without being observed.

The problem was that Peter's stepmother, Elaine, who lived in a house on the grounds, thought nothing of coming up to his office and entering without knocking. At that moment, she had done exactly that again.

She did not waste time on a greeting. "Vincent, I'm glad I caught you. Is there any way you can persuade Peter to give up the idea of having that charity reception here? One would think that after all the terrible publicity last week in that trashy *Celeb* magazine, rehashing Susan's disappearance and Grace's death, he would know enough to attract as little attention as possible."

Vincent stood up, a courtesy he wished he could forego when Elaine barged in on him. Now, even though he was intensely irritated by the intrusion, he could not resist noticing begrudgingly how exquisitely attractive she was. At sixty-six, Elaine Walker Carrington, with her ash-blond hair, sapphire blue eyes, classic features, and willowy body, could still turn heads. She moved with the grace of the fashion model she had once been, even as, uninvited, she settled herself in the antique armchair on the other side of Vincent's desk.

She was wearing a black suit that Slater guessed was an Armani, whom he knew to be her favorite designer. Her jewelry consisted of diamond earrings, a narrow strand of pearls, and the wide diamond wedding ring that she still wore even though her husband, Peter's father, had been dead for nearly twenty years. Her faithfulness to his memory, Vincent well knew, had everything to do with the terms of her prenuptial agreement, which allowed her to live here for the rest of her life, unless she remarried, and ensured her a million-dollar-a-year stipend.

26

And, of course, she liked to be referred to as Mrs. Carrington, with all the attendant privileges.

Which does not give her the right to walk in here and act as if I hadn't considered very carefully the pluses and minuses of having a public event in this house, Vincent thought. "Elaine, Peter and I have discussed this thoroughly," he began, his tone revealing his irritation. "Of course the publicity is terrible and embarrassing, which is why Peter has to make some move to show he's not in hiding. That is precisely the perception which must be changed."

"Do you really think that having strangers milling around in this house will change the perception most people have of Peter?" Elaine asked, her tone laced with sarcasm.

"Elaine, I suggest you stay out of this," Slater snapped. "May I remind you that the family company went public two years ago, and there is a negative side to having to answer to stockholders. Even though Peter is by far the largest stockholder, the fact remains that there's a growing opinion that he should step down as chairman and CEO. Being 'a person of interest' in the disappearance of one woman and the death of another is hardly a good image to have as the head of an international company. Peter may not talk about it, but I know he's deeply concerned. That's why, from now on, he's got to be seen as active in community affairs and, even if he hates it, his very generous philanthropies have got to be publicized."

"Really?" Elaine got up as she spoke. "Vincent, you're a fool. Mark my words, this won't work. What you're doing is exposing Peter, not protecting him. Socially, Peter comes across as a zero. He may be a genius at business, but as you certainly know, he isn't comfortable with small talk. Away from the office he's much happier with a book in his hand and the door of the library closed than at some cocktail party or dinner. 'Never less alone than when alone,' as the saying goes. When is this affair going to take place?"

"Thursday, December sixth. Kay Lansing, the woman who's running it, needed about seven weeks lead time to publicize it."

"Is there any limit to how many tickets can be sold?"

"Two hundred."

"I'll be sure to buy one of them. So will Richard. I'm on my way to the gallery. He's having a reception for one of his new artists." With a dismissive wave of her hand, she pulled open the French doors and walked out.

Slater watched her go, his mouth drawn in

a thin, tight line. Richard Walker was Elaine's son by her first marriage. She's paying for that reception, he thought. Carrington money has been supporting that loser son of hers since he was twenty years old. He remembered how it drove Grace crazy that Elaine assumed she could walk into the main house anytime she wanted. The one thing Peter was smart enough to do was to not let Elaine move back in here after Grace died.

Not for the first time, Vincent Slater wondered whether there was more to Peter Carrington's tolerance of his stepmother than met the eye.

3

I was at the library when I received the call from Vincent Slater. It was late Wednesday morning and I was about to commit to having our fund-raiser at the Glenpointe Hotel in Teaneck, a neighboring town to Englewood. I've attended affairs there, and they do a really good job, but I was still disappointed I'd been turned down by Peter Carrington. Needless to say, I was absolutely delighted by Slater's message and decided to share my excitement with Maggie, the maternal grandmother who raised me and who still lives in the same modest house in Englewood where I grew up.

I'm a reverse commuter. I live on West Seventy-ninth Street in Manhattan, in a small second-floor apartment in a converted town house. It's about as big as a minute, but it has a working fireplace, high ceilings, a bedroom large enough for a bed and dresser, and a kitchen area that is separate from the living room. I furnished it from garage sales held in the tonier parts of Englewood and I love the way it looks. I also love working at the library in Englewood, and, of course, that means I get to see a lot of my grandmother, Margaret O'Neil, whom my father and I have always called Maggie.

Her daughter, who was my mother, died when I was only two weeks old. It happened in the late afternoon. She was propped up in bed nursing me, when an embolism hit her heart. My father called shortly after and was alarmed she did not answer the phone. He rushed home to find her lifeless body, her arms still cradling me. I was asleep, my lips contentedly suckling her breast.

My father was an engineer who, after a year with a bridge-building company, had quit and made gardening, previously his avocation, his full-time career. He used his keen mind to achieve a different kind of engineering triumph in the local estates, creating gardens with rock walls, and waterfalls, and winding paths. Which is why he was hired by Peter Carrington's stepmother, Elaine, who disliked the unyielding rigidity of her predecessor's taste in landscaping.

Daddy was eight years older than my mother, thirty-two when she died. By then he had established a solid reputation in his

31

field. All might have been well enough except that after my mother's death, Daddy began to drink too much. Because of it, I began to spend more and more time with my grandmother. I can remember her pleading with him, "For God sake, Jonathan, you've got to get help. What would Annie think of what you are doing to yourself? And how about Kathryn? Doesn't she deserve better?"

Then one afternoon after Elaine Carrington fired him, he did not come to my grandmother's house to collect me. His car was found parked on a bank of the Hudson River, some twenty miles north of Englewood. His wallet and house keys and checkbook were on the front seat. No note. No good-bye. Nothing to indicate he knew how much I needed him. I wonder how much he blamed me for my mother's death, if he thought that somehow I sucked the life from her. But surely not. I had loved him fiercely, and he always had seemed to love me the same way. A child can tell. His body was never recovered.

I still remember how, when we got home from Maggie's, he and I would cook dinner together. He would reminisce about my mother. "As you well know, Maggie's no cook, Kathryn," he would say, "so your mother opened a cookbook and learned out

of sheer desperation. She and I used to try recipes together, and now it's you and me."

Then he would talk to me about my mother. "Always remember, she would have given anything to watch you grow up. She kept the bassinet by our bed for a month before you were born. You've missed so much by not having her, by not knowing her."

I still can't forgive him for not remembering all that when he decided to end his life.

All of these thoughts were going through my mind as I drove from the library to Maggie's house to tell her the news. She has a beautiful red maple tree on her small lawn. It gives a special air to the whole place. I was sorry to see the last of its leaves blowing away in the wind. Without their protection, the house looked somehow exposed, and a bit shabby. It is a one-story Cape Cod, with an unfinished attic where Maggie stores the accumulated paraphernalia of her eighty-three years. Boxes of pictures she's never gotten around to putting in photo albums, boxes of letters and treasured Christmas cards she will never live to wade through, the furniture that she replaced with the contents of my parents' home but couldn't bear to throw out, clothes that she hasn't worn in twenty or thirty years.

Downstairs isn't much better. Everything

is clean, but Maggie creates clutter just by walking into a room. Her sweater lies on one chair, the newspaper articles she always means to read on another; books are piled by her easy chair; the shades she pulled up in the morning are always uneven; the slippers she can't find are tucked between the chair and the hassock. It's a real home.

Maggie wouldn't meet Martha Stewart's idea of good housekeeping, but she's got plenty going for her. She retired from teaching to raise me, and still tutors three kids every week. As I found out through experience, she can make learning a joyful thing.

But when I went inside and told her my news, she let me down. I could see the look of disapproval on her face as soon as I mentioned the Carrington name.

"Kay, you never told me you were thinking of asking them to let you hold the literacy fund-raiser in that place."

Maggie has lost a couple of inches in height in the last few years. She jokes that she's disappearing, but as I looked down at her, she suddenly seemed very formidable. "Maggie, it's a great idea," I protested. "I've been to a couple of events in private homes, and they've been sellouts. The Carrington mansion is bound to be a big draw. We're going to charge three hundred dollars a

ticket. We wouldn't get that anywhere else."

Then I realized that Maggie was worried, genuinely worried. "Maggie, Peter Carrington couldn't have been nicer when I met with him to talk about the event."

"You didn't tell me you saw him."

Why hadn't I told her? Maybe because I knew instinctively that she would not approve of my going there, and then, when he turned me down, there was no need to talk about it. Maggie was convinced that Peter Carrington was responsible for Susan Althorp's disappearance, and that he may very well have been involved in his wife's drowning. "Maybe he didn't push his wife into the pool, Kay," she had told me, "but I bet if he saw her fall in, he didn't make it his business to save her. And as for Susan, he was the one who drove her home. I'd bet anything she sneaked out and met him after her parents thought she was going to bed."

Maggie was eight years old in 1932 when the Lindbergh baby was kidnapped, and she considers herself the world's leading expert on that subject, as well as on the disappearance of Susan Althorp. From the time I was little, she had talked to me about the Lindbergh kidnapping, pointing out that Anne Morrow Lindbergh, the baby's mother, was raised in Englewood, not a mile from our home, and that Anne's father, Dwight Morrow, had been ambassador to Mexico. Susan Althorp was also raised in Englewood, and her father had been ambassador to Belgium. To Maggie, the parallels were obvious — and scary.

The Lindbergh baby kidnapping was one of the most sensational crimes of the twentieth century. The golden child of the golden couple, and all the unanswered questions. How did Bruno Hauptmann learn that the Lindberghs had decided to stay in their new country home that evening because the baby had a cold, rather than return to the Morrow estate as initially planned? How did Hauptmann know exactly where to place the ladder to reach the open window of the baby's room? Maggie was always seeing similarities between the two cases. "The Lindbergh baby's body was found by accident," she would point out to me. "It was terrible, but at least it meant that the family didn't spend the rest of their lives wondering if he was growing up somewhere with someone who might be harming him. Susan Althorp's mother has to wake up every morning wondering if this is the day the phone will ring and it will be her daughter. I know that's the way I would feel if my child was missing. At least if her body had been found, Mrs. Althorp could visit her grave."

Maggie hadn't talked about the Althorp case in a long time, but I'll bet anything that if she was at the supermarket checkout and saw that *Celeb* magazine with Peter Carrington's picture on the cover, she would buy it. Which explains her sudden uneasiness at the thought of my being in his presence.

I kissed the top of her head. "Maggie, I'm hungry. Let's go out and have some pasta. My treat."

When I dropped her home an hour and a half later, she hesitated, then said, "Kay, come back inside. I want to go to that affair. I'll write you a check for a ticket."

"Maggie, that's crazy," I protested. "That's too much money for you."

"I'm going," she said. Her determined expression left no room for argument.

A few minutes later I was driving over the George Washington Bridge, back to my apartment, her check in my wallet. I knew the reason she had insisted on attending. Maggie had appointed herself as my personal bodyguard while I was under the roof of the Carrington mansion.

4

As she waited for her visitor to arrive, Gladys Althorp studied the picture of her missing daughter. It had been taken on the terrace of the Carrington mansion the night Susan disappeared. She was wearing a white chiffon evening gown that clung to her slender body. Her long blond hair, slightly tousled, tumbled onto her shoulders. She had been unaware the camera was on her, and her expression was serious, even pensive. What was she thinking at that moment? Gladys asked herself once again, as her fingers traced the outline of Susan's mouth. Did she have a premonition that something was going to happen to her?

Or did she finally realize that night that her father had been involved with Elaine Carrington?

Gladys sighed as she slowly stood, resting one hand on the armchair for support. Brenda, the new housekeeper, had served her dinner on a tray and then headed back to her apartment over the garage. Unfortunately, Brenda wasn't much of a cook. Not that I'm really hungry, Gladys thought as she carried the tray to the kitchen. The sight of the uneaten food made her feel slightly nauseous, and she quickly scraped it into the compactor, rinsed the dishes, and placed them in the dishwasher.

"Just leave it for me, Mrs. Althorp," she knew Brenda would protest in the morning. And I'll say it only takes a minute to tidy up, Gladys thought. Tidy. That was the way to describe what I'm doing now. Trying to tidy up the most important piece of business in my life before I leave it.

"Maybe six months," the doctors had agreed when they delivered the verdict that she hadn't yet shared with anyone.

She went back into the study, her favorite of the seventeen rooms in the house. I've been wanting to downsize for years, and I know Charles will once I'm gone. She knew the reason she hadn't. Susan's room was here, everything still exactly as it had been when she left that night after knocking on the bedroom door to let Charles know she was home.

I let her sleep late the next morning, Gladys thought, once again replaying that day in her mind. Then, finally, at noon I looked in on her. The bed was still made. The towels in her bathroom hadn't been touched. She must have gone right back out after announcing she was home.

Before I die, I have to try to learn what happened to her, she vowed. Maybe this investigator can find some answers. Nicholas Greco was his name. She had seen him on television talking about the crimes he had solved. After retiring as a detective from the New York City Police Department, he'd opened his own agency and become well known for solving crimes that initially had seemed unsolvable.

"The families of victims need closure," he had said in an interview. "There's no peace for them until they have it. Fortunately, there are new tools and new methods being developed every day that make it possible to take a fresh look at cases that are still open."

She had asked him to come at eight o'clock tonight for two reasons. That she knew Charles would be out was one of them. The second was that she didn't want Brenda to be around when he was there. Two weeks ago, Brenda had come into the study when she was watching a tape of Greco on television. "Mrs. Althorp, I think the true cases he talks about are more interesting than the ones they make up," Brenda had said. "Just looking at him you can tell he's smart."

The front door chimes pealed promptly at eight o'clock. Gladys hurried to open the door. Her first impression of Nicholas Greco was both comforting and reassuring. From his television appearances, she knew he was a conservatively dressed man in his late fifties, of average height, with sandy hair and dark brown eyes. But meeting him, she liked the fact that his handshake was firm and that he looked her directly in the eye. Everything about him invited trust.

She wondered what his impression of her might be. Probably he'd just see a woman in her midsixties, far too thin, with the pallor of terminal illness on her face. "Thank you for coming," she said. "I know you must have many requests from someone like me."

"I have two daughters," Greco said. "If one of them disappeared, I wouldn't be at peace until I found her." He waited, then added quietly, "Even if what I learned was not what I was hoping to hear."

"I believe that Susan is dead," Gladys Althorp said, her voice calm, but the expression in her eyes suddenly bleak and sad. "But she would not have disappeared on her own. Something happened to her, and I believe that Peter Carrington was responsible for her death. Whatever the truth is, I have got to know it. Are you interested in helping me?"

"Yes, I am."

"I have put together for you all my files about Susan's disappearance. They're in my study."

As Nicholas Greco followed Gladys Althorp down the wide hallway, he managed quick glances of the paintings along the way. Someone in this family is a collector, he thought. I don't know if these are museum-quality, but they certainly are pretty fine.

Everything that he could see in the house had an air of good taste and quality. The emerald green carpet was thick and soft underfoot. The crown molding on the stark white walls provided an added frame for the paintings. The area rug in the study where Gladys Althorp led him contained a mellow red and blue pattern. The shade of blue in the couch and chairs matched the blue in the rug. He saw the picture of Susan Althorp on the desk. To the side was a decorative shopping bag, bulging with legal-sized documents.

He walked over to the desk and picked up the picture. Since deciding to take on the case, he had done some preliminary research and had seen this picture on the Internet.

"This is what Susan was wearing when she disappeared?" he asked.

"It was what she was wearing at the Carrington dinner. I was not feeling well and my husband and I left the party before it broke up. Peter promised to drive her home."

"You were still awake when she came in?"

"Yes, about an hour later. Charles had the twelve o'clock news on in his room. I heard her call to him."

"Isn't that a bit early for an eighteen-year-old to be home?"

Greco did not miss the tightening of Gladys Althorp's lips. The question had evoked anger in her.

"Charles was an overprotective father. He insisted that Susan wake him up whenever she came home."

Gladys Althorp was one of many grief-stricken parents Nicholas Greco had encountered in his career. But unlike many of the others, he suspected that she had always managed to keep her emotions rigidly private. He sensed that, for her, hiring him was a difficult step, a quantum leap into frightening territory.

With a professional eye, he observed the extreme pallor of her complexion, the air of fragility about her entire body. He had a strong suspicion that she might be terminally ill, and that that was the reason for her decision to contact him.

When he left half an hour later, Greco was carrying the shopping bag containing files with all the information Gladys Althorp could give him about the circumstances surrounding her daughter's disappearance: the follow-up stories in the newspapers, the journal she had kept as the investigation continued, and the recent copy of *Celeb* magazine with a picture of Peter Carrington on the cover.

In his preliminary research, Greco had taken down the address of the Carrington estate. On impulse, he decided to swing past it. Even though he knew it was not far from where the Althorps lived, he was surprised at how very close the two homes were. It couldn't have taken Peter Carrington more than five minutes to drop her off that night, if that's what he did, and not more than five minutes to get back home. As he drove back to Manhattan, he realized that this case had hooked him already. He was anxious to get started. A classic "corpus delicti," he thought, then remembered the pain in Gladys Althorp's eyes and felt ashamed.

I'm going to solve it for her, he thought grimly as he experienced the familiar rush of energy that came when he knew he was about to begin working on a case that would prove to be fascinating.

5

Gladys Althorp waited in the study for her husband to come in. She heard him opening and closing the front door shortly after the eleven o'clock news began. She switched off the television and hurried down the hallway. He was already halfway up the stairs.

"Charles, I have something to tell you."

His already ruddy face became flushed and his voice kept rising as, after hearing that she had hired Nicholas Greco, he demanded, "Without consulting me? Without considering that our sons will also be forced to relive that terrible time? Without understanding that any new investigation attracts media attention from the rags? Wasn't that disgusting story last week enough for you?"

"I have consulted our sons, and they agree with my decision," Gladys said calmly. "I absolutely must learn the truth about what happened to Susan. Does that worry you, Charles?"

6

The first week of November was balmy, but after that the weather turned sharply cold and drizzly, the kind of clammy days that make you want either to stay in bed or go back to bed with the newspapers and a cup of coffee — neither of which I had time to do. Just about every day, I work out early in a gym on Broadway, then shower, dress, and head for the library in New Jersey. Meetings about the fund-raiser were held after working hours.

Needless to say, the tickets to the event sold fast, which was gratifying, but the rehashed story of Susan Althorp's disappearance had triggered renewed interest in the case. Then, when Nicholas Greco, the private investigator, disclosed on *Imus in the Morning* that he had been hired by the Althorp family to look into their daughter's disappearance, it became hot news. On the heels of Greco's statement, Barbara Krause, the formidable Bergen County prosecutor, told the press that she would welcome any new evidence that would bring closure to the case. When asked about Peter Carrington, she said cryptically, "Peter Carrington has always been a person of interest in the disappearance of Susan Althorp."

On the heels of that statement, the gossip columns began to print reports that the board of directors of Carrington Enterprises was urging Peter to resign as chairman and CEO, even though he was by far the largest stockholder. According to the reports, the other directors felt that since it was now a publicly traded company, it was not appropriate for anyone designated as a "person of interest" in two potential homicides to continue to head a worldwide multibillion-dollar organization.

Pictures of Peter began appearing regularly in the business sections of major newspapers, as well as in the more sensational magazines.

As a result, all through November, I kept my fingers crossed, expecting to get a call from Vincent Slater any day to tell me that the cocktail reception was off and that they would send a check to compensate for our lost revenue.

But the call never came. The day after

Thanksgiving I went to the mansion with the caterer we had hired to go over details for the affair. Slater met us and turned us over to the couple who were housekeepers for the mansion, Jane and Gary Barr. They appeared to be in their early sixties, and it was obvious that they had been with the Carringtons for a long time. I wondered if they had been working at the mansion the night of the infamous dinner, but I didn't have the nerve to ask. I learned later that they had come to work for Peter's father after his first wife, Peter's mother, had died, but then left after Elaine Walker Carrington came on the scene. They were coaxed back, however, after Peter's wife, Grace, drowned. They seemed to know everything about the place.

They told us that the living room was actually divided into two rooms, and that when the pocket doors were opened, the space was sufficient to accommodate two hundred people. The buffet should be laid out in the formal dining room. Small tables and chairs would be set up throughout the ground floor so that people would not have to balance plates. Before we left, Vincent Slater joined us again to say that Mr. Carrington was underwriting all the expenses of the reception. Before I even had time to thank him, Slater added, "We have a photographer who will take pictures. We do ask that your guests refrain from using their own cameras."

"As you probably guessed, we'll give a brief report about the literacy campaign," I told him. "It would mean a lot if Mr. Carrington would say a few words of greeting."

"He's planning to do that," Slater said. Then he added, "Before I forget, it goes without saying that the staircases leading upstairs will be roped off."

I had been hoping to slip upstairs for an adult view of the chapel. Sometimes, over the years, I'd wondered if I should have revealed to Maggie the angry conversation I heard there, but she would have been angry at me for going into the house, and besides, what could I tell her? I had heard a man and a woman quarreling about money. If I thought that quarrel had anything to do with Susan Althorp's disappearance, I certainly would have reported it, even years later. But if there was one thing Susan Althorp would never have had to do, it was to plead for money from anyone. So the only thing my revelation would establish was that I'd been a curious six-year-old.

Before the caterer and I left that day, I did glance down the corridor, hoping to see the door to the library open and Peter Carrington come out. For all I knew, he was halfway around the world. But because many executives take the Friday after Thanksgiving off, I fantasized that if he was in the house, I'd run into him.

It didn't happen. I contented myself with the knowledge that December 6th was less than two weeks away, and I'd get to see him then. Then I tried to push away the realization that if for any reason Peter didn't attend the reception, I would be desperately disappointed. I've been dating Glenn Taylor, Ph.D., associate dean of science at Columbia University, with increasing regularity. We had met while having coffee in a Starbucks, helping that establishment to live up to its reputation as a great place for singles to make friends.

Glenn is thirty-two, transplanted from Santa Barbara, and is about as laid back as any Californian ever born. He even looks as though he's from there — after six years of living on the Upper West Side in Manhattan, his hair still retains a sun-streaked look. He's just tall enough to let me be not quite eye level when I'm wearing heels, and he shares my passion for the theatre. I think in the past couple of years we've gone to most of the Broadway and off-Broadway shows, using discounted tickets of course. No business-page editor ever wrote a story about the

51

year-end bonus a librarian received, and Glenn is still paying off his school loans.

In a way, we love each other and certainly we count on each other. Sometimes Glenn even speculates that, with my side of the brain into literature and his into science, we'd have a chance at producing awesome offspring. But I know that we're not anywhere near the emotional level of Jane Eyre and Mr. Rochester, or Cathy and Heathcliff.

It may be that I've set my standards too high, but ever since I was young, I've been into the classic love stories of the Brontë sisters.

From the beginning, something about Peter Carrington had intrigued me, and I think I began to understand what it was. Seeing him sitting there alone in that crazy castlelike mansion was a haunting image. I wished I had had the chance to see what book he was reading. If it was one I had read myself, maybe I could have lingered for a few minutes to discuss it.

"Oh, I see you have the new biography of Isaac Bashevis Singer," I might have said. "Do you agree with the author's interpretation of his personality? I thought he was a little unfair because . . ."

You can see the way my mind was going.

Then, the night before the reception, I

went to Maggie's house to pick her up for one of our regular pasta dinners. When I arrived, she was powdering her nose in the hall mirror, humming cheerfully. When I asked her what was up, she blithely told me that Nicholas Greco, the investigator who was delving into Susan Althorp's disappearance, had called and was coming to see her. She was expecting him any minute.

I was dumbfounded. "Maggie, why in the name of God would that guy want to talk to you?" But even before she had answered, I knew that Greco was coming here because my father had worked for the Carringtons at the time of the Althorp disappearance.

Automatically I began to straighten up the living room. I adjusted the window shades so that they were at the same level, picked up the newspapers that were scattered around, hung up her sweater in the hall closet, and carried the teacup and plate of cookies that were on the coffee table into the kitchen.

Greco arrived as I was putting some loose strands of silver hair into the bun at the back of Maggie's head.

I'm a Dashiell Hammett fan, and Sam Spade, especially in *The Maltese Falcon,* is the prototype for my mental image of a private investigator. Applying that yardstick, Nicholas Greco was a disappointment. In his appearance and manner he reminded me of the insurance adjuster who came to see me when a pipe broke in the apartment above mine.

That illusion was quickly shattered, however, when, after Maggie had introduced me as her granddaughter, he said, "You must be the one who accompanied your father to the Carrington estate the same day that Susan Althorp disappeared."

When I stared at him, he smiled. "I've been going through the files on the case. Twenty-two years ago your father told the prosecutor's office that he had gone to the estate unexpectedly that day because of a problem with the lighting, and that he took you with him. One of the caterer's workers also mentioned seeing you sitting on a bench in the garden."

Had anyone seen me sneak into the house? I hoped I didn't look as guilty as I felt when I invited Greco to sit down.

It irritated me to see that Maggie was obviously enjoying herself. I knew that this man — who no longer reminded me of an insurance adjuster — had been hired to prove Peter Carrington had been responsible for Susan Althorp's disappearance, and that upset me.

But his next question startled me. It was

not about the Carringtons or the Althorps; it was about my father. He asked Maggie, "Had your son-in-law shown signs of depression?"

"If you call hitting the bottle a sign of depression, I would say so," Maggie said, then glanced at me as though afraid I'd be upset by her answer. She hurried to qualify it. "I mean, he never got over Annie's death. She was my daughter, but when a couple of years had passed after her death, I begged Jonathan to start dating. Let me tell you, there were plenty of women around here who would have jumped at the chance to go out with him. But he never would. He'd say, 'Kathryn's the only girl I need.'" Then she added, somewhat unnecessarily, "When she was ten, Kathryn decided she wanted to be called Kay."

"Then you feel that the excessive drinking was a sign of his depression, and that it led to his taking his own life?"

"He'd lost out on a number of landscaping jobs. I think that being fired by the Carringtons may have pushed him over the edge. His insurance policy was about to expire. After he was declared legally dead, it paid for Kay's education."

"But he did not leave a suicide note, and his body was never recovered. I've seen his picture. He was a strikingly handsome man."

I could see where that line of questioning was going. "Are you suggesting that my father did not commit suicide, Mr. Greco?" I asked.

"Miss Lansing, I'm not suggesting anything. Anytime a body is not recovered, there is always an open question about the manner of death. There are numerous documented cases of people who were believed to be dead, and who showed up or were tracked down twenty or thirty years later. These people simply walked away from a life that had become in some way unbearable. It happens often."

"Then I assume you believe that Susan Althorp may have done the same thing?" I shot back at him. "Her body was never found. Maybe her life was suddenly unbearable."

"Susan was a beautiful, healthy young woman, a gifted student pursuing a fine arts degree at Princeton, and the recipient of a trust fund that meant she would lead a life of wealth and privilege. She was very popular and attracted men easily. I'm afraid I don't see the comparison."

"Peter Carrington did something to that girl. I bet he was jealous of her." Now Maggie sounded like the Lord Chief Justice of the United Kingdom pronouncing a verdict.

"I gave him the benefit of the doubt until his wife drowned, but it just goes to show that if you kill someone, you're capable of doing it again. As for my son-in-law, I think he was depressed enough to believe he was doing Kay a favor by insuring her education."

That night the pasta stuck in my throat, and it wasn't any comfort when Maggie rehashed Greco's visit. "He's supposed to be smart, but he was way off the mark in even thinking that your dad would just walk out on you."

No, he wouldn't just walk out on me, I thought, but that's not where Greco is going. He's wondering if Daddy had to stage his own disappearance because of what happened to Susan Althorp.

7

It had begun to snow. Nicholas Greco was barely aware of the light wet flakes that drifted onto his face as he looked up at the windows of the second-floor art gallery on West Fifty-seventh Street, the one that bore the name of Richard Walker.

Greco had done his homework on Walker. Forty-six years old, twice divorced, the son of Elaine Walker Carrington, an indifferent reputation in the art world, and undoubtedly supported by the luck of having his mother marry into the Carrington family fortune. Walker had been at the formal dinner the night Susan Althorp vanished. According to the reports in the prosecutor's files, he had left for his apartment in Manhattan when the party ended.

Greco opened the door to the building, was checked by a security guard, and walked up the single flight of stairs to the gallery. He was immediately clicked inside by a smiling receptionist.

"Mr. Walker is expecting you," she said. "It will be just a few minutes since he's on a conference call at the moment. Why don't you look at our new exhibit? We're displaying a wonderful young artist the critics are raving about."

If ever I heard a canned speech, I'm listening to one now, Greco thought. Walker is probably doing the crossword puzzle in his office. The gallery, dreary to him with its stark white walls and dark gray carpeting, was devoid of visitors. He walked from painting to painting, pretending to study them, all scenes of urban blight. He was at the next to the last of the twenty or so paintings when a voice at his shoulder asked, "Doesn't this one particularly remind you of an Edward Hopper?"

Not even remotely, Greco thought, and with a grunt that could be taken as assent, he turned to face Richard Walker. He looks younger than forty-six — was Greco's first thought. Walker's eyes were his most remarkable feature — sapphire, and set far apart. His features were rugged. He was medium in height, with a boxer's solid body and thick arms. He would not have looked out of place in a gym, Greco decided. Walker's dark blue suit was obviously expensive but with his thick frame was not shown off to advantage.

When it was clear that Greco had no intention of discussing art, Walker suggested they go into his private office. On the way he kept up a running commentary on how many family fortunes were based on people having the ability to spot genius in an unknown painter. "Of course, you hear it in every field," he said as he went around to his desk and waved Greco to a chair opposite it. "My grandfather used to tell the story of how Max Hirsch, the legendary horse trainer, turned down the chance to buy the greatest racehorse in history, Man O' War, for one hundred dollars. Do you enjoy racing, Mr. Greco?"

"I'm afraid I don't have much time for hobbies," Greco said, his voice sounding regretful.

Walker smiled amiably. "Nor for small talk, either, I would gather. Very well. What can I do for you?"

"First I want to thank you for agreeing to let me drop in. As you may know, Susan Althorp's mother has hired me to investigate her daughter's disappearance."

"I'd guess that, at least in Englewood, everybody's heard about it," Walker replied.

"Do you spend much time in Englewood, Mr. Walker?"

"I don't know what 'much time' means. I live in Manhattan, on East Seventy-third Street. As you certainly know, my mother, Elaine Carrington, has a home on the Carrington estate, and I visit her there. She also comes into Manhattan frequently."

"You were at the estate the night Susan Althorp disappeared?"

"I was at the party with some two hundred other people. My mother had married the present Peter Carrington's father three years earlier. The real purpose of the party was that Carrington senior had turned seventy that year. He was very sensitive about the fact that my mother was so much younger, twenty-six years to be exact, so the party wasn't called a birthday celebration." Walker raised an eyebrow. "If you do your arithmetic, you'll see that old man Carrington specialized in young women. He was forty-nine when Peter was born. Peter's mother was much younger as well."

Greco nodded and looked around. Walker's office was not large, but it was tastefully furnished with a striped blue and red love seat, creamy-white walls, and a deep-blue carpet. He found the painting over the couch of old men gathered around a table playing cards more interesting than the scenes of squalor he'd seen in the gallery exhibit. A corner cabinet held several photos of Walker on the polo field, as well as a golf ball on an engraved silver tray. "A hole in one?" he asked, pointing to the ball.

"At Saint Andrew's," Walker said, not attempting to conceal the pride in his voice.

Greco could see that the memory of that achievement had relaxed Walker, which was what he had hoped to achieve. Leaning back in his chair, he said, "I'm trying to form a kind of overall picture of Susan Althorp. What were your impressions of her?"

"Let's start with the fact that I knew her only slightly. She was eighteen or nineteen. I was twenty-four, had a full-time job at Sotheby's, and lived in the city. Besides that, to be perfectly blunt, I was not particularly fond of my mother's husband, Peter Carrington IV, nor was he of me."

"Why did you clash?"

"We didn't exactly clash. He offered me a trainee job in a brokerage firm he owned, where, as he put it, I could eventually make real money and not live on a shoestring. He was contemptuous of me when I declined the offer."

"I see. But you did visit your mother frequently at his home?"

"Of course. That summer, twenty-two years ago, was very warm, and there were frequent pool parties. My mother loved to entertain. She would have their friends over regularly. Peter and Susan both attended Princeton, and their Princeton friends were around a lot. I was usually invited to bring a guest or two. It was very pleasant."

"Were Peter and Susan considered a couple?"

"They'd been dating quite a lot. From what I saw, I thought they were falling in love, or, at least, that he was falling in love with her."

"You mean it was one-sided?" Greco asked, his voice mild.

"I don't mean anything. She was very outgoing. Peter was always quiet. But whenever I stopped by on weekends it seemed as though she was on the estate, playing tennis or lounging by the pool."

"Did you stay at the Carrington home the night of the party?"

"No. I was scheduled to play in a golf foursome early the next morning, and left when the dinner ended. I didn't stay around for the dancing."

"Susan's mother is convinced that your stepbrother was responsible for Susan's death. Do you believe that?"

There was a hint of anger in Richard Walker's eyes when he looked directly at

Greco. "No, I do not," he said crisply.

"What about Grace Carrington? You were at dinner at the estate the night she drowned. Actually the dinner was in your honor, wasn't it?"

"Peter traveled a great deal. Grace was the sort of outgoing woman who didn't like to be alone. She was always inviting people to dinner. When she realized my birthday was coming up, she decided that dinner that night would be a birthday celebration for me. There were just six of us there. Peter didn't arrive until nearly the end. His plane was delayed coming home from Australia."

"I understand that Grace drank a lot that evening."

"Grace always drank a lot. She was in rehab several times, but could never quite make it stick. Then, when she was finally able to sustain a pregnancy after several miscarriages, we were all worried about fetal alcohol syndrome."

"Did anyone try to stop her from drinking that evening?"

"She was great at faking it. People thought she was drinking club soda, but it was straight vodka. She was really bombed when Peter got home, and, of course, it drove him crazy to find her in that condition. But when he grabbed the drink out of her hand,

poured it on the carpet, and had that outburst, it sort of shook her up. When he
stormed upstairs, I remember she said, 'I
guess the party's over.' "

" 'The party's over' can mean the end of
more than a party," Greco said.

"I suppose so. Grace looked very sad. My
mother and I were the last to leave. I was
staying at Mother's house that night. Grace
said she was going to lie down on the couch
for a while. I don't think she wanted to face
Peter."

"You and your mother left together?"

"We walked to Mother's house. The next
morning the housekeeper phoned, hysteri-
cal. She had found the body."

"Do you believe that Grace Carrington either fell into the pool accidentally or committed suicide?"

"I can only answer that question one way."
Grace wanted that baby, and she knew Peter
wanted it. Would she have deliberately taken
her own life? No, unless she felt overwhelmed by her inability to stop drinking,
and was panicked at the possibility that she
had already damaged the fetus."

Nicholas Greco's manner became even
friendlier as he casually asked, "Do you
think Peter Carrington was angry enough to
have helped his wife to end her life, perhaps

after she passed out on the couch?"

This time, it was obvious to him that Richard Walker's angry reply was both phony and forced: "That's utterly ridiculous, Mr. Greco."

That's not what he believes, Greco thought as he got up to leave. But it's what he wants me to *think* he believes.

8

Peter Carrington and I were married in the Lady Chapel of St. Patrick's Cathedral where thirty years ago my mother and father exchanged their vows.

The irony for Maggie was that she had been the catalyst that brought us together.

The literacy reception at the estate was a complete success. The housekeeping couple, Jane and Gary Barr, had worked with me and the caterer to be sure that everything was perfect.

Elaine Walker Carrington and Peter's stepbrother, Richard, were very much present, oozing genteel charm as they greeted guests. Except for those beautiful eyes, I was startled at how unalike mother and son were physically. Somehow I had expected that Elaine Carrington's son would resemble Douglas Fairbanks Jr., but nothing could be further from the truth.

Vincent Slater was omnipresent but remained in the background. With my usual need to figure everything out, I played guessing games with myself as to how he had entered Peter's life. The son of someone who worked for Peter's father? I wondered. After all, I'm the daughter of someone who worked for Peter's father. Or perhaps he was a college friend invited to join the family business? Nelson Rockefeller invited his roommate at Dartmouth, a scholarship student from the Midwest, to work for the family. That man ended up a multimillionaire.

When the brief program began, I introduced Peter. There was nothing in his demeanor to suggest the pressure he was under when he welcomed the guests and talked about the importance of our literacy program. "It's fine to give money to help," he said, "but it's equally important to have people — people like all of you — to volunteer a little time, on a one-to-one basis, in helping others learn to read. As you all probably know, I travel a lot, but I'd like to be a literacy volunteer in a different way. So let's make this an annual event at my home." Then, as the crowd applauded, he turned to me. "Is that all right with you, Kathryn?"

Was that the moment I fell in love with him, or was I already there? "That would be wonderful," I said, as my heart melted. Just that day there'd been another item in the business section of the *New York Times* that asked the question. "Is it time for Peter Carrington to go?"

Peter gave me a thumbs-up, and then, smiling at people and shaking hands with a few of them, he walked down the corridor toward his library. I noticed he didn't go into it, though. I thought he either escaped up the back staircase or even left the house completely.

I had been in and out of the house all day to oversee the caterer and the florist, and to make sure that the people who were rearranging furniture didn't break or scratch anything. The Barrs became my friends that day. At lunchtime, over a cup of tea and a quick sandwich in the kitchen, they made me see the Peter Carrington they knew: the twelve-year-old boy who was sent to Choate after his mother died, the twenty-year-old Princeton senior who was relentlessly questioned about Susan Althorp's death, the thirty-eight-year-old husband whose pregnant wife was found dead in a pool.

Thanks in no small part to the couple's help, everything went perfectly. I waited to be sure the last of the guests were on their way, the cleanup complete, and the furniture put back in place before I left. Though I kept hoping he would, Peter didn't reappear, and in my head I was already trying to frame a way to see him again soon. I didn't want to wait until it was time to plan a reception next year.

But then, inadvertently, and certainly unwillingly, Maggie brought us together. I had driven her to the reception, so of course she waited for me to drive her home. Then, as Gary Barr opened the front door for us, Maggie caught the tip of her shoe in the slightly elevated rim of the door frame and fell hard, almost bouncing off the marble floor of the entrance hall.

I screamed. Maggie is my mother and father and grandmother and friend and mentor, all in one. She is all I have. And she's eighty-three years old. As the years pass, I worry more and more, facing the inevitable fact that she is not immortal, even though I know that she will put up a fight before she goes gentle into that good night.

Then, from the floor, Maggie snapped, "Oh, for heaven's sake, Kay, be quiet. I didn't do any damage except maybe to my dignity." She raised herself on one elbow and began to struggle up, then she fainted.

The events of the next hour are a blur. The Barrs called an ambulance, and I guess they let Peter Carrington know what had happened because suddenly he was there, kneeling beside Maggie, his fingers feeling for the pulse in her throat, his voice reassuring. "Kathryn, her heart seems strong. I think her forehead took the impact. It's swelling."

He followed the ambulance to the hospital, and waited with me in the emergency room until I was reassured by the doctor that Maggie had only a mild concussion, though they wanted to keep her overnight. After she was settled in a room, Peter drove me home to Maggie's house. I guess I was trembling so much from both relief and shock that he had to take the key from my hand and open the door. Then he came in with me, found the light switch, and said, "You look as though you could use a drink. Does your grandmother keep any liquor in the house?"

That question made me start to laugh, a little hysterically, I think. "Maggie claims if everyone followed her regimen of a nightly hot toddy, Ambien would be out of business."

That was when I felt myself trying to blink back tears of relief. Peter handed me his handkerchief and said, "I can understand how you feel."

We both had a scotch. The next day he sent flowers to Maggie and called me to suggest we have dinner together. After that I saw him every day. I was in love and so was he. Maggie, though, was heartsick. She was still sure he was a murderer. Peter's stepmother suggested we wait, warning us that it was much too soon to be sure of ourselves. Gary and Jane Barr, however, were delighted for us. Vincent Slater brought up the subject of a prenuptial agreement and was obviously relieved when I told him that I would sign one. Peter became furious, and Slater stalked out. I told Peter that I had read about agreements where, if the marriage was brief, the settlement would be very limited. I said that was fine with me. I also told him that I wasn't worried about it, because I knew that we would always be together and that we would have a family.

Later, of course, Peter and Slater made peace, and Peter's lawyer drew up a generous agreement. Peter insisted that I have a lawyer of my own review it so that I could be sure that it was fair. This was done, and, a few days later, I signed the document.

The following day, we went to New York and quietly made our wedding arrangements. On January 8th, we were married in the Lady Chapel of St. Patrick's Cathedral, where we solemnly vowed to love, honor, and cherish each other until death do us part.

9

Prosecutor Barbara Krause studied the picture the paparazzi had snapped of Peter Carrington and his new wife, Kay, walking on a beach in the Dominican Republic. *Happy is the bride the sun shines on today,* she thought sarcastically as she pushed aside the newspaper.

Now fifty-two years old, Barbara had graduated from law school and began her career as a clerk for a Bergen County criminal judge; after one year she moved across the courthouse to become an assistant prosecutor. For the next twenty-seven years, she worked her way up in that office, becoming trial chief, first assistant, and finally, upon the retirement of her predecessor three years ago, was named prosecutor. It was a world she loved, an enthusiasm she shared with her husband, a civil court judge in nearby Essex County.

Susan Althorp had disappeared when Barbara had only been in the office a few years. Because of the prominence of both the Althorp and the Carrington families, the case had been investigated from every possible angle. The inability to solve it or even to be able to indict the number one suspect, Peter Carrington, had been a bone in the throat to Barbara's predecessors, as it was to her.

From time to time, over the years, she had taken out the Susan Althorp file and reviewed it, trying to take a fresh look, circling some testimony, putting a question mark after certain statements. Unfortunately, none of it had ever led anywhere. Now, as she sat at her desk, some of Peter Carrington's statements ran through her mind.

He claimed that he had dropped Susan at her door that night: "She didn't wait for me to open the car door. She ran up the steps to the porch, turned the handle, waved to me, and went inside."

"That was the last time you saw her?"

"Yes."

"What did you do then?"

"I went home. There were still some people dancing on the terrace. I'd been playing tennis all afternoon and was tired. I parked my car in the garage and went into the house through the side door, straight upstairs to my room and to bed. I fell asleep instantly."

See no evil, hear no evil, Barbara thought. Interestingly enough, he used the same story the night his wife drowned in the pool.

She glanced at her watch. It was time to go. She had been sitting in on a homicide trial, just observing. Closing arguments were about to begin. In this case, the identity of the killer was not in question; rather it was a matter of whether the jury would find the defendant guilty of murder or of manslaughter. A domestic quarrel had turned violent, and now the father of three young children would probably spend at least the next twenty-five to thirty years in prison for killing their mother.

Let him! Because of him, these kids have nothing, Barbara thought as she stood up to head back to the courtroom. He should have taken the twenty-year plea we offered him. Nearly six feet tall, and always fighting a weight problem, she knew her nickname around the courthouse was "the linebacker." She reached for a final sip of coffee from the cup on her desk.

As she did, the newspaper picture of Peter Carrington and his new wife again came into her line of vision. "You've had twenty-two years of freedom since Susan Althorp disappeared, Mr. Carrington," she said aloud. "If I ever get a chance to get my hands on you,

I can promise you one thing: There won't be any plea to manslaughter. I'll try you for murder and I'll get a conviction."

10

The two weeks we spent on our honeymoon were idyllic. We had married so quickly that we were finding out new things about each other every day, little things, like me always wanting a midmorning cup of coffee, or the fact that he loves truffles and I hate them. I hadn't realized how basically lonely I had been until Peter was there with me all the time. Sometimes I would wake up at night and listen to his even breathing, and think how incredible it was that I was now his wife.

I had fallen so intensely in love with him, and Peter seemed to feel exactly the same way about me. When we'd started to see each other daily, he had asked, "Are you sure you can be interested in a man who is a 'person of interest' in two deaths?"

My answer was that long before I knew him, I absolutely believed that he was a victim of circumstances, and I knew how horrible that must have been, and, of course, continued to be for him.

"It is," he said, "but let's not talk about it. Kay, you give me so much joy that I can really believe there is a future, a time when the answer to Susan's disappearance will be solved and people will know with certainty that I had nothing to do with it." And so, during our courtship, we never talked about either Susan Althorp or Peter's first wife, Grace. He did talk lovingly about his mother — it was obvious they had been very close. "My father was constantly traveling on business. My mother had always accompanied him. But after I was born she stayed home with me," he reminisced.

I wondered if it was after he lost her that the look of pain had settled into his eyes.

On our honeymoon I was somewhat surprised that there were no calls to or from his office. Later I learned the reason.

The paparazzi hung around the gates of the villa he had rented, and, except for one brief walk on the public beach, we stayed on the grounds. I called to check on Maggie every day, and she grudgingly admitted that the stories about Peter had disappeared from the tabloid magazines. I began to hope that Nicholas Greco had run into a blank wall in his investigation of the Susan Althorp disappearance; a blank wall at least as far as Peter was concerned.

I found out soon enough that I was living on false hope.

Home: It seemed impossible to me that I would ever call the Carrington mansion home. As we were driven through the gates on the return from our honeymoon, I thought of the child I had been when I crept upstairs to the chapel, and the trepidation I had felt in late October when I came to ask Peter to allow me to hold a reception here.

I was uneasy when, on the flight back, Peter had become more and more quiet, but I thought I knew the reason. He would once again be in the glare of publicity, and with the demands of his position would not be able to avoid it. I had resigned from the library regretfully, because I loved my job. On the other hand, I had done some serious thinking about how best I could help Peter. I was going to suggest to him that he plan to do a lot of traveling for his company. There would be less interest in Greco's ongoing investigation if the prime target was not around to be followed all the time by the media. Of course I would travel with him.

"Does one still carry a bride over the threshold?" Peter asked as the car stopped at the front door.

I sensed immediately that he would be very

uncomfortable if the answer was yes, and wondered if he had carried Grace over the threshold when they were married twelve years ago. "I'd rather walk in hand in hand," I said, and I knew my answer pleased him.

After our blissful two weeks in the Caribbean, that first evening in the mansion was oddly uncomfortable. In a mistaken gesture of "welcome home," Elaine had ordered a gourmet dinner served by a caterer, relegating the Barrs to the kitchen. Instead of the small dining room that looked out over the terrace, she had ordered it served in the large formal one. Even though she had been wise enough to have us placed opposite each other in the center of the banquet-sized table, with the two waiters hovering around us the dinner felt stilted and awkward.

We were both glad when it was over and we could go upstairs. Peter's suite consisted of two very large bedrooms, each with its own bathroom, divided by a beautiful sitting room. Everything about the bedroom to the right of the parlor made it unmistakably a man's domain. It had two massive hand-carved dressers, a handsome maroon leather couch and matching chairs by the fireplace, a king-sized bed with bookshelves over it, and a television screen that could be lowered from the ceiling at the push of a button. The walls were white, the coverlet had black and white squares, the carpet was charcoal gray. Several paintings depicting different scenes from fox hunting in the English countryside adorned the walls.

The bedroom on the other side of the parlor had always been occupied by the Carrington lady of the house. Peter's wife, Grace, had been the last one to use it. Before that, Elaine had slept there, and before that, Peter's mother, and all his maternal ancestors back to 1848. It was very feminine, with pale peach walls and peach and green draperies, headboard, and bedspread. A love seat and lady chairs near the fireplace made the room look cozy and welcoming. A truly beautiful painting of a garden scene was above the mantel of the fireplace. I knew that soon I would want to put my own stamp on the room because I like more vibrant colors, but it amused me to think that I could have tucked my little studio into it.

Peter had already warned me that he had frequent spells of insomnia, and that when that was happening he would slip over to the other room to read. Since I am sure I will sleep through Gabriel's horn when it finally sounds, I told him that wasn't necessary, but whatever made him more comfortable and more likely to sleep was fine with me.

That night we went to sleep in my room, I with sugarplums dancing in my head at the prospect of really beginning my life as Peter's wife. I don't know what woke me up during the night, but something did. Peter was gone. Even though I knew he was probably in his room reading, I suddenly felt a tremendous sense of anxiety. I slipped my feet into slippers, pulled on a robe, and padded through the sitting room. His door was closed. I opened it very quietly. It was dark, but there was enough early-morning light flickering around the window shades to see that the room was empty.

I don't know what made me do it, but I hurried over to the window and looked down. From there the pool was clearly visible. Of course, in February the pool was covered, but Peter was there, kneeling beside it, resting one hand on the edge, and slipping the other hand under the heavy vinyl covering into the water. His whole arm was moving back and forth as if he was either trying to push something into the pool or drag something out of it.

Why? What was he doing? I wondered. Then, as I watched, he stood up, turned, and came slowly back toward the house. A few minutes later he opened the door to the bedroom, went into the bathroom, turned on the light, dried his arm and hand on a towel, and rolled down the sleeve of his pajama top. He then turned out the light, walked back into the bedroom, and stood facing me. It was obvious he was not aware of my presence, and I realized what was happening. Peter was walking in his sleep. A girl in our dormitory in college had been a sleepwalker, and we'd been warned never to wake her suddenly.

As Peter made his way through the sitting room, I followed him silently. He got back into bed in my room. I slipped off my robe, kicked off my slippers, and gently got in beside him. A few minutes later, his arm went around me and his drowsy voice murmured, "Kay."

"I'm here, dear," I said.

I could feel his body relax, and soon his even breathing told me that he was asleep. But for the rest of the night I lay awake. Peter was a sleepwalker, I now realized, but how often did that happen? And far more important, why, in that altered state, did he go through the motions of trying to push something into the pool or pull something from it?

Something — or *someone?*

11

Nicholas Greco drove through Cresskill, a town near Englewood, watching for street signs and reminding himself once again that it was time to get a navigation system for his car. *Frances always tells me that for someone who is so good at solving crimes, I can't make it to the grocery store without getting lost,* he thought. *She's right.*

Nice town, he thought as, following the directions he had taken from MapQuest, he turned right on County Road. He was on his way to interview Vincent Slater, the man who had been called "indispensable" by Peter Carrington's father.

Greco had done exhaustive research on Slater before he'd requested the meeting, but there hadn't been much of interest to learn from it. Slater was now fifty-four years old, a bachelor, still living in the childhood home he had bought from his parents when they moved to Florida. He had commuted to a local college. His first and only job was with Carrington Enterprises. Within a couple years of his employment he had gained the attention of Peter's father and had become a kind of aide-de-camp to him. After Peter's mother died, Slater became a combination of trusted employee and surrogate parent for Peter. A dozen years older than Peter, during the Carrington heir's adolescent years Slater would drive him to Choate, his prep school in Connecticut, and visit him there regularly, stay in the mansion with him on vacations, and take him skiing and sailing during holidays.

Slater's background was interesting, but it was the fact that he had been a guest at the party the night Susan Althorp disappeared that was of primary interest to Greco. He had grudgingly consented to the interview but insisted that it be conducted at his home. He doesn't want any part of me at the mansion, Greco thought. He should know that I've already been there, at least to the guesthouse to talk to the Barrs.

He watched the house numbers and stopped in front of Slater's house, which turned out to be a split-level, the kind so popular in the fifties. When he rang the bell, Slater answered the door instantly. I wonder if he was standing behind it, Greco thought.

And without having laid eyes on him before, why do I think he's that kind of guy? "Very good of you to see me, Mr. Slater," he said mildly, reaching out his hand.

Slater ignored it. "Come in," he said curtly.

I could make my way around here blind-folded, Greco thought. Kitchen straight ahead at the end of the foyer. Living room to the right of the entrance, opening into a small dining room. Three bedrooms up-stairs. The family room a half level below the kitchen. Greco knew because he had been brought up in the mirror image of this house in Hempstead, Long Island.

It was immediately obvious that Slater's taste ran to the minimal. The beige walls were dull above the brown carpet. Greco fol-lowed Slater into the sparsely furnished liv-ing room. A modernistic couch and chairs were arranged in a seating group around a wide glass coffee table with steel legs.

Nothing warm and fuzzy about this place or this guy, Greco thought as he sat down in the chair Slater had indicated.

It was too low for his taste. A subtle way of putting me at a disadvantage, he thought.

Before he could make his usual remarks thanking Slater for agreeing to meet him, Slater said, "Mr. Greco, I know why you are here. You are investigating the disappearance of Susan Althorp at the request of her mother. That is praiseworthy, except for one serious problem — your mandate is to somehow prove that Peter Carrington is criminally responsible for Susan's disappearance."

"My mandate is to find out what happened to Susan, and if possible to give her mother peace," Greco said. "I recognize that because he was the last known person to see her before her disappearance, Peter Carrington has lived under a cloud of suspicion for twenty-two years. As his friend and assistant, I would think you would be interested in dispelling that cloud if it were at all possible to do so."

"That obviously goes without saying."

"Then help me. What is your recollection of the events of that evening?"

"I am certain that by now you know exactly what testimony I gave when the investigation was opened initially. I was a guest at the dinner. It was a very pleasant affair. Susan arrived with her parents."

"She arrived with them, but Peter drove her home."

"Yes."

"What time did you leave the party?"

"As you surely know, I stayed over that night. For years I have had my own room in the mansion. Ninety-nine percent of the time I come home to this house, but that night I decided to stay over, as did a number of other guests. Elaine, Peter's stepmother, was planning a ten A.M. brunch, and it was easier to stay there than to drive back and forth."

"When did you retire to your room?"

"When Peter left to drive Susan home."

"How would you describe your relationship with the Carrington family?"

"Exactly as you must have gathered from your various interviews. I never forget the fact that I am their employee, but I am also, I hope, a trusted friend."

"So trusted that you would do anything to help them, especially Peter, who is almost a surrogate son or brother to you?"

"I have never had to worry about doing anything for Peter that would not stand the light of day, Mr. Greco. Now, if you have no more questions, I need to get to Englewood now."

"Just one. You were also present the night Grace Carrington died, weren't you?"

"The night Grace died in an accident, you mean. Yes. Peter had been away in Australia for several weeks. He was expected home in time for dinner, and his wife, Grace, had asked Elaine, her son, Richard, a few local friends, and myself for dinner. Because Richard's birthday was coming up, Grace called it a birthday party for him."

"When Peter came in, he was quite angry at what he saw?"

"Mr. Greco, there is nothing more to add to what you obviously already know about that situation. Peter was understandably upset to see that Grace had been drinking heavily."

"He was very angry."

"I would say upset rather than angry."

"Did you stay over at the mansion that night?"

"No. It was about eleven o'clock when Peter arrived. We were all about to leave any-how. Peter went upstairs. Elaine and Richard stayed with Grace."

"Were there servants in the house?"

"Jane and Gary Barr had been hired after Peter's mother died. Elaine let them go when she married Peter's father. After his father's death, however, Elaine moved to the smaller house on the grounds, and Peter rehired the Barrs. They've been there ever since."

"But if they had been fired, why were they at the mansion the night Susan disap-peared? Peter's father was still alive. In fact, the dinner was really to celebrate his seven-tieth birthday."

"Elaine Walker Carrington has no hesitation in using people to suit her convenience. Even though she had let the Barrs go because she wanted to hire a fancy chef and butler and a couple of maids, she asked them to help with the serving that evening, and then work the brunch the next morning. They were ten times more efficient than the new staff, and I'm sure she paid them very well."

"Then they were rehired and I presume they served the dinner the night of Grace Carrington's death. Would they still have been up when Peter returned?"

"Both Peter and Grace were very considerate. After coffee had been served, and the cups collected, the Barrs retired to their own place. They had moved back to the former gatehouse on the estate."

"Mr. Slater, I spoke with Gary and Jane Barr last week. We went over their recollection of the dinner party and the brunch the next day. I discussed with Gary something I had noticed in the files. Twenty-two years ago he told investigators that the morning of the brunch, he overheard Peter Carrington tell you that Susan had left her handbag in his car the night before and he asked you to deliver it to her because there might be something she needed in it. He remembered

91

making that statement and having heard that exchange between you and Peter."

"He may remember it, but if you continued to look in the notes, you'd know that at that time I said his recollection was only partially true," Vincent Slater said evenly. "Peter did not tell me Susan had left her purse in the car. He said that she *might* have left her purse there. It wasn't in the car, so obviously he was mistaken. In any case, I don't get your point."

"It's only a comment. Mrs. Althorp is sure she heard Susan close the door of her room that night. Obviously she didn't intend to stay there long. But by then if she had realized her purse was in Peter's car, and she was planning to meet him, she wouldn't be concerned. Otherwise, if she were meeting someone else, wouldn't it seem natural for her to select another purse, get a compact and handkerchief, the usual things women carry?"

"You're wasting my time, Mr. Greco. You're not seriously suggesting that Susan's mother knew exactly how many handkerchiefs, or, for that matter, how many evening purses were in her daughter's room?"

Nicholas Greco got up. "Thank you for your time, Mr. Slater. I'm afraid there is a development you need to know about. Mrs.

Althorp has been interviewed by *Celeb* magazine; the issue will be on the stands tomorrow. In it, Mrs. Althorp specifically accuses Peter Carrington of the murder of her daughter, Susan."

He watched as Vincent Slater's complexion took on a sickly yellow tint.

"That's libel," Slater snapped. "Slander and out-and-out libel."

"Exactly. And the normal reaction of an innocent man like Peter Carrington will be to instruct his lawyers to sue Gladys Althorp. This would be followed by the usual process of interrogatories and depositions until there was either a retraction, settlement, or public trial. In your opinion, will Peter Carrington demand an immediate retraction from Gladys Althorp and, if it is not received, institute a suit against her to clear his name?"

Slater's eyes had turned icy, but not before Greco caught a sudden look of fear in them. "You were about to leave, Mr. Greco," he said.

Neither man exchanged another word as Nicholas Greco left the house. Greco walked down the path, got into his car, and started it. Who is Slater on the phone with now? he wondered as he drove down the street. Carrington? The lawyers? The new Mrs. Carrington?

An image of Kay's heated defense of Peter Carrington when he met her in her grandmother's home came into his mind. Kay, you should have listened to your grandmother, he thought.

12

In the morning, Peter showed no sign of being aware that he had been sleepwalking during the night. I wasn't sure whether or not to bring it up to him. What could I say? That it looked as if he was trying to push something or someone into the pool or pull something or someone from it?

I thought I had the explanation. He was having a nightmare about Grace drowning in the pool. He was trying to rescue her. It made sense, but talking to him about it seemed pointless. He wouldn't remember any of it.

We got up at seven. The Barrs would come in at eight to prepare breakfast, but I squeezed juice and made coffee because we decided to take a quick jog through the grounds of the estate. Oddly enough, up until now we had spoken very little about my father's role as landscaper here. I had told Peter how hard my mother's death must have been on Daddy, and how his suicide had devastated me. I did not, of course, mention the appalling things Nicholas Greco had said. I was infuriated by his suggestion that Daddy might have chosen to disappear because he had something to do with Susan Althorp's disappearance.

As we jogged, Peter began to talk about my father. "My mother never changed the landscaping after my grandmother died," he said. "Then, in fairness to Elaine, when she married my father, she said the whole place looked as if it had been designed as a cemetery. She said it had everything but a sign reading 'rest in peace.' Your father did a beautiful job in creating the gardens that are here now."

"Elaine fired him because of his drinking," I said, trying to sound matter-of-fact.

"That's her story," Peter said mildly. "Elaine always fooled around, even when my father was alive. She made a play for your dad and he brushed her off. *That*'s really why she fired him."

I stopped so suddenly that he was six strides ahead of me before he slowed and came back. "I'm sorry, Kay. You were a child. How could you possibly have known?"

It had been Maggie, of course, who told me that it was Daddy's drinking that cost

96

him the job. She blamed everything that happened on Daddy's drinking: the loss of the job here, even his suicide. I realized I was suddenly furious at her. My father had been too much of a gentleman to give her the real reason he'd been fired, and then, being a know-it-all, she'd decided she knew the reason. Not fair, Maggie, I thought, not fair.

"Kay, I didn't mean to upset you." Peter's hand was in mine and our fingers intertwined.

I looked up at him. Peter's aristocratic face was strengthened by his firm jaw, but always it was his eyes that I saw when I looked at him. Now they were concerned, troubled that he had inadvertently hurt me.

"No, you didn't upset me, not at all. In fact, you've cleared up something important. All these years I've had a mental image of my father stumbling around this place in a drunken stupor, and I've been embarrassed for him. Now I can erase it forever."

Peter could tell that I didn't want to discuss the subject any further.

"Okay, then," he said. "Shall we pick up the pace?"

By running down the stone walks that wind through the gardens, and then reversing a couple of times, we got in a mile, then decided to do a final loop to the end of the west path that ended at the street. High hedges had been planted there. Peter explained that the state had installed a gas line near the curb many years ago, and when my father had prepared the landscaping design, he had suggested moving the fences fifty feet back. Then, if repairs were ever needed, it wouldn't damage any of the plantings.

When we reached the hedges we could hear voices and the sound of machinery beyond the fence. By peeking through we could make out that a Public Service crew was creating a detour on the road and unloading equipment out of trucks. "I guess this is exactly what my father anticipated," I said.

Peter said, "I guess so," then turned and began to run again. "Race you to the house?" he called over his shoulder.

"Not fair," I yelled, as he took off. A few minutes later, out of breath but feeling good about ourselves — at least so I thought — we went back into the house.

The Barrs were in the kitchen, and I could smell corn muffins baking. For someone whose normal breakfast is black coffee and half a toasted bagel minus either butter or cream cheese, I realized that firm discipline would be in order if I was going to stay in shape. But I wouldn't worry about it today, our first breakfast at home.

There's one thing about a mansion: You do get your choice of locations. The breakfast room is like a cozy indoor garden, with painted green and white lattice walls, a round glass top table, cushioned wicker chairs, and a breakfront filled with lovely green and white china. Glancing at the china made me realize again that there were so many treasures in this house, collected since the early nineteenth century. I had a fleeting thought of wondering who, if anyone, kept track of them.

I could tell that there was something troubling Jane Barr. Her warm greeting did not conceal the worry in her eyes. Something was wrong, but I did not want to ask her what it was in front of Peter. I know that he sensed it, too.

The *New York Times* was on the table next to his place. He started to pick it up, then pushed it aside. "Kay, I've been so used to reading the newspapers at breakfast that I forgot for a moment that now I have a very good reason to let them wait."

"You don't have to," I said. "You can have the first section. I'll take the Metro section."

It was after she had poured our second cup of coffee that Jane Barr came back into the breakfast room. This time she did not attempt to hide the concern she was feeling. She addressed Peter. "Mr. Carrington, I'm not one to be the bearer of bad news, but when I stopped at the supermarket this morning they were delivering copies of *Celeb* magazine. The cover story is about you. I know you'll be getting calls, so I wanted to warn you, but I also wanted you to have your breakfast in peace first."

I saw that she was holding the copy of the magazine, still folded in half, under her arm. She handed it to Peter.

He unfolded it, looked at the front page, then his eyes closed as though he was turning away from a sight that was too painful to watch. I reached across the table and grabbed the tabloid. The banner-sized headline read, PETER CARRINGTON MURDERED MY DAUGHTER. There were two side-by-side pictures beneath it. One was a formal picture of Peter, the kind of stock photo newspapers use when they're running a story on an executive. He was unsmiling, which didn't surprise me. My innately shy Peter is not the kind of man who smiles for a camera. Nevertheless, in this particular unfortunate shot, he did look cold, even haughty and disdainful.

Susan Althorp's picture was next to his, a radiant Susan in her debutante gown, her long blond hair spilling over her shoulders, her eyes sparkling, her beautiful young face joyous. Not daring to look at Peter, I turned the page. The double spread inside pages were just as bad. DYING MOTHER DEMANDS JUSTICE. There was a photo of an emaciated, grief-stricken Gladys Althorp, surrounded by pictures of her daughter at every stage of Susan's brief life.

I know enough about the law to understand that if Peter did not demand a retraction and get it, his only alternative would be to sue Gladys Althorp. I looked at him and now could not read his expression. But I was sure that the last thing he wanted was to hear useless cries of outrage from me. "What are you going to do?" I asked.

Jane Barr vanished into the kitchen.

Peter looked as if he were in pain, as if he'd been physically attacked. His eyes glistened and his voice was agonized when he said, "Kay, for twenty-two years I have answered every question they ever asked about Susan's disappearance. Only hours after they realized she was missing, the prosecutor's office descended upon us, questioning me. Twenty-four hours later, even before they asked, my father gave permission to have bloodhounds sniff the grounds. He allowed a search of the house. They impounded my car. They couldn't come up with one single iota of evidence that suggested I knew what happened to Susan after I dropped her off that night. Have you any idea what a nightmare it would be if I demand a retraction from Susan's mother, don't get it, and institute a suit? I'll tell you what will happen. It will be a three-ring circus for the media and that poor woman will be dead long before it even gets near a court date."

He stood up. He was shaking and fighting back tears. I rushed around the table and put my arms around him. The only way I could possibly help was to tell him how much I loved him.

I think my words gave him some comfort, so that at least he didn't feel totally alone. But then, in a voice that was sad, even a little remote, he said, "I've done you no favor by marrying you, Kay. You don't need this mess."

"Neither do you," I said. "Peter, I think that, horrible as it is, you've got to demand a retraction from Mrs. Althorp, and if necessary file suit against her for libel and slander. I'm sorry for her, but she's done it to herself."

"I don't know," he said. "I just don't know."

Vincent Slater came in as Peter was showering. I knew they were going to Peter's office together that morning. "You've got to convince Peter that he must demand a retraction," I told him.

"That's a subject we'll take up with our lawyers, Kay," he said, his tone dismissive.

We looked at each other. From the first minute I met him, when I came here begging to have the reception in the mansion, I had sensed Slater's animosity toward me. But I knew I had to be careful. He was an important part of Peter's life.

"Peter has been given the chance to clear his name, to show that there isn't a shred of evidence to tie him to Susan's disappearance," I told Vincent. "If he doesn't demand a retraction, he might as well hang a sign around his neck saying, 'I did it. I'm guilty.'"

He did not answer. Then Peter came downstairs, kissed me good-bye, and they were gone.

That afternoon, as they were digging to lay new underground cables, the Public Service crew unearthed the skeleton of a woman, tightly wrapped in plastic bags, buried in the unfenced area at the edge of the Carrington estate. Traces of what appeared to be blood were visible on the front of her decaying white chiffon gown.

Gary Barr was the one who rushed in to tell me what was happening. On his way back from a shopping trip, he had passed the excavation site and was there when the first shout came from the workman whose equipment uncovered the body. Gary told me that he had parked and watched as police cars began to arrive on the scene, sirens blaring.

From the security cameras outside the mansion, I could see a crowd gathering. I don't think that for a minute I doubted that the body would be identified as that of Susan Althorp.

The ringing of the front door reminded me of the pealing of the church bells at the memorial Mass for my father. I can still remember the mournful sound as, my hand in Maggie's, we left the church and stood with friends on the steps of St. Cecilia's. I remember Maggie saying something like, "When and if they find Jonathan's remains, there will be a proper burial, of course." But it had never happened.

As a flustered Jane Barr rushed in to inform us that detectives were here to speak to Mr. Carrington, I had the incongruous thought that soon there would be a proper burial for Susan Althorp.

13

"We know he did it, but do we have enough to indict him?" Barbara Krause threw the question out to Assistant Prosecutor Tom Moran, the head of her homicide squad. Six days had passed since the remains of Susan Althorp had been found on the unfenced grounds of the Carrington estate. An autopsy had been performed and positive identification had been established. The cause of death was strangulation.

Moran, a balding and somewhat overweight twenty-five-year veteran of the prosecutor's office, shared his boss's frustration. Since the body had been discovered, the wealth and power of the Carrington family had become evident. Carrington had lined up a team of nationally known criminal defense attorneys, and they were already at work preparing to defend a possible indictment. The cold hard facts were that the Bergen County prosecutor did have enough evidence to establish probable cause to file a murder complaint against Carrington, and a grand jury would almost certainly indict him. But the odds were that a trial jury, with the burden of proof being beyond a reasonable doubt, would either acquit him or end up a hung jury.

Nicholas Greco was expected at the prosecutor's office momentarily. He had called and requested an appointment with Barbara Krause, and she had invited Moran to sit in on it.

"He says he may have come across something useful," Krause told Moran. "Let's hope so. I'm not crazy about outsiders involved in our cases, but in this instance I'll be happy to give him any credit he wants if he helps us convict Carrington."

She and Moran had spent the morning discussing the strengths and weaknesses of the case, and found nothing new. The fact that Carrington had driven Susan home and had been the last person known to see her was diminished by the fact that both her mother and father heard her come into the house, and that she had called out "good night" to them. When foul play was suspected, Carrington, then twenty years old, had answered all of the questions their office had thrown at him. When he realized that his son was a suspect, Carrington's father had allowed, even demanded, a thorough search of the mansion, the grounds, and Peter's car. The search had yielded nothing.

By the end of the first day that Susan had not contacted her family, Carrington's summer tuxedo and shoes had been tested for any possible evidence, with negative results. The formal shirt he had been wearing could not be found. He claimed he had put it in the hamper as usual and the new maid had sworn that she had given it to the dry cleaner's pickup service the next morning. The cleaner claimed to have received only one dress shirt, the one belonging to Carrington's father, but that lead had gone nowhere. Investigation showed that the particular cleaner had a long history of mishandling clothing and mixing up orders.

"In fact, the delivery they made when they supposedly picked up the shirt had a neighbor's jacket in it," Krause said, exasperation evident in her voice. "That shirt Carrington was wearing is the piece of evidence we've always needed. Dollars to donuts it had blood on it."

The buzzer on Krause's intercom sounded. Nicholas Greco had arrived.

Greco had met Tom Moran when he initially reviewed the files of the Althorp case.

Now he wasted no time in getting to the reason for his visit. "You can imagine how Mrs. Althorp is feeling," he said. "She told me that at least she knows that before too long she and Susan will be lying side by side in the cemetery. But of course the discovery of the body on Carrington property has reinforced her need to see Peter Carrington brought to justice."

"Exactly our reaction," Krause said bitterly.

"As you know, I have been interviewing people close to the Carringtons, including some of the staff. Sometimes memories can be jogged long after the excitement of the initial investigation has taken place. I saw in your files that at the time of the disappearance, you questioned Gary and Jane Barr, the former and present Carrington housekeepers."

"Of course we did." Barbara Krause leaned forward slightly, an indication that she sensed she was about to hear something of interest.

"It's noted in your files that Barr mentioned that the morning of the brunch he overheard Carrington tell Vincent Slater that Susan had left her pocketbook in his car, and he asked Slater to run it over to her home in case she needed anything from it. It seemed to me to be a very unusual request, since Susan was expected at the brunch, and her mother remembers that she was carrying a very small evening bag at the dinner. Slater reported that he looked in the car; the purse was not there. When I pressed Barr, he told me he recalled that when Carrington got that response from Slater, he said, 'That's impossible. It *has* to be there.' "

"The purse was found with Susan's body," Barbara Krause said. "Are you suggesting that Carrington returned it to her after he supposedly went to bed, then forgot that he had done so? That doesn't make sense."

"Was there anything found in the purse that might have been significant?"

"The material was rotted through. A comb, a handkerchief, lip gloss, a compact." Barbara Krause's eyes narrowed. "Do you believe this sudden spurt of precise memory from Gary Barr?"

Greco shrugged. "I do, because I spoke to Slater. He verified the conversation, although with different emphasis. He insists that Carrington told him that Susan *may* have forgotten her purse. I might add two personal observations: The question upset Slater, and Barr seemed very nervous to me. Don't forget, I talked to Barr *before* the body was found. I know that he and his wife helped out at parties at the Althorp home from time to time. So he would have been in contact with Susan there as well as at the Carrington estate."

"Jane Barr swears that after the dinner party she and Gary went directly to their condominium, which was not on the grounds of the estate," Tom Moran told Greco.

"Barr is hiding something," Greco said flatly. "And, I'll bet you anything you want to wager that whether or not Susan Althorp had her purse with her when she got out of Peter Carrington's car is significant, and may have a lot to do with solving this case."

"I'm even more interested in the missing dress shirt Carrington was wearing the night of the dinner party," Barbara Krause said.

"That was the other thing I wanted to discuss. I have a stringer in the Philippines. He managed to track down Maria Valdez, the maid who gave that statement about the shirt."

"You know where she is!" Krause exclaimed. "About one month after our initial investigation, she quit the job, went back to the Philippines, and got married. We know that much. She had promised to keep us informed of any address change, but then we lost track of her. The most we could find out is that she had gotten a divorce and disappeared."

"Maria Valdez is remarried and has three children. She lives in Lancaster, Pennsylvania. I saw her yesterday. I would suggest that someone authorized to make a deal with her accompany me back to Lancaster tomorrow. By that I mean a guarantee in writing that she would never be prosecuted for lying when she was questioned years ago."

"She was lying about the shirt!" Krause and Moran shouted at the same time.

Greco smiled. "Let's say that as a mature woman she can no longer live with the knowledge that her statement twenty-two years ago has kept a murderer from being punished."

14

The funeral for Susan Althorp was front-page news around the country. The picture of the flower-covered casket, followed into St. Cecelia's by her grieving parents, must have sold tons of newspapers and improved the ratings of television stations around the country. Maggie went to the service along with a group of her friends. An alert Channel 2 reporter spotted her and rushed to get an interview.

"Your granddaughter recently married Peter Carrington. Do you believe in his innocence and stand by him now that the body was discovered on his property?"

Maggie's honest answer was fodder for the press. She looked straight into the camera as she said, "I stand by my granddaughter."

"I'm sorry," I told Peter when I heard about it.

"Don't be," he said. "I always valued honesty. Besides, if she hadn't fallen at that reception, you wouldn't be sitting here with me now." He smiled that quizzical smile of his, one with warmth but no mirth in it. "Oh, Kay, for heaven's sake, don't worry. Your grandmother made it clear from the start that she wanted no part of me and didn't want me in your life, either. Maybe she was right. Anyhow, we're doing our best to prove she was wrong, aren't we?"

We'd had dinner and gone upstairs to the parlor between the bedrooms. The suite had become more and more of a retreat for us. With the media constantly camped at the gates, and grim-faced lawyers coming and going, I felt as if we were in a war zone. To go out without being followed by the press was impossible.

There had been a debate this past week between Peter and Vincent Slater and the lawyers as to whether or not Peter should issue some kind of statement expressing sympathy to Susan's family. "No matter what is put out in my name, it's going to be misunderstood," Peter had said. In the end, his brief statement expressing profound sorrow was scorned and torn apart by both Gladys Althorp and the media.

I had talked to Maggie, but hadn't seen her since we'd come home from our honeymoon. I was both angry at her and worried about her. Before we were married, she hadn't budged an inch in her opinion that Peter had killed both Susan and his wife; now she was practically announcing that belief on television.

But there was something else bothering me. The poison that Nicholas Greco had injected into my consciousness by suggesting that my father might have had something to do with Susan's death had been festering inside me. Then Peter's revelation the morning we jogged through the grounds had only made it worse. My father hadn't been fired because he was drinking. He had been let go because he hadn't responded to Elaine Walker Carrington's advances. And that begged the question: What had driven him to suicide?

I knew I had to find a way to sneak out and visit Maggie without being hounded by the press. I had to talk to her. I knew with all my heart and soul that Peter was not capable of hurting anyone — it was the kind of primal knowledge that is part of our being. But I also knew with equal certainty that my father would never have vanished willingly, and I was more convinced than ever that he had not committed suicide.

It was incredible to me that Peter and I had known such an idyllic time for two weeks, and now, married only three weeks, had been thrown headlong into this nightmare.

We had been watching the ten o'clock news, and I was about to switch off the television when for some reason I decided to check the headline on the eleven o'clock broadcast.

The anchor began, "A source inside the Bergen County prosecutor's office tells us that Maria Valdez Cruz, a former maid at the Carrington mansion, has admitted she lied when she stated that she gave the cleaner a formal shirt Peter Carrington was wearing the night he escorted Susan Althorp home twenty-two years ago, a shirt that prosecutors at the time thought was a key to the case."

"She's lying," Peter said flatly, "but she's just sealed my fate. Kay, there isn't a chance in hell that I won't be indicted now."

15

At age thirty-eight, Conner Banks was the youngest lawyer in the Carrington dream team of top defense attorneys, but no one, not even his more celebrated — and publicized — peers, could deny his brilliance in criminal court. The son, grandson, and nephew of wealthy corporate lawyers, he had made it clear during his undergraduate years at Yale, to his relatives' collective horror, that he intended to be a criminal defense attorney. When he graduated from Harvard Law School, he clerked for a criminal court judge in Manhattan, then was hired by Walter Markinson, a renowned defense attorney who had defended all types of accused and was especially famous for keeping high-profile celebrities out of prison.

One of Banks's earliest court cases for the Markinson firm had required him to convince a jury that the exotic wife of a billionaire had been mentally ill when she shot her husband's longtime girlfriend. The verdict of not guilty by reason of insanity had been handed down after less than two hours of deliberation, a near-record for any jury deciding a murder case with that defense.

That case had made the reputation of Conner Banks, and in the next ten years that reputation had continued to grow. With his genial manner, large frame, and Celtic good looks, he had become something of a celebrity in his own right, known for his quick wit and for the beautiful women he escorted to high-profile events.

When Gladys Althorp directly accused Peter Carrington of murdering her daughter, Vincent Slater had called Walter Markinson and asked him to assemble a team of top lawyers to weigh the strategy of suing Mrs. Althorp, and then to handle the case if we decided to do it.

Peter Carrington had decided that he wanted the lawyers to hold their meetings in his home rather than in Manhattan, so that he could be present without having to run the press gauntlet outside his home. Now, a week later, Conner Banks had become a regular visitor to the Carrington estate.

The first time they were driven through the gates and they saw the mansion, Conner's senior partner had remarked disdainfully,

"Who in the name of God would want to cope with anything that big?"

A passionate student of history, Banks replied, "As a matter of fact, I would. It's magnificent."

When the lawyers reached the formal dining room where the conferences were to be held, Slater was already there. Coffee, tea, bottles of water, and small pastries were laid out on the sideboard. Pads and pens were in place on the table. The other two defense attorneys, Saul Abramson from Chicago and Arthur Robbins from Boston, both in their early sixties and with formidable track records in criminal cases, arrived minutes after Conner Banks and Markinson.

Then Peter Carrington entered the room. To Banks's surprise, he was accompanied by his wife.

Banks was not given to trusting first impressions, but it was impossible not to recognize that Peter Carrington had an aura about him. Unlike his defense team and Slater, all dressed in typically conservative suits, he was wearing an open-necked shirt and a cardigan. Introduced to the lawyers, he immediately said, "Forget 'Mr. Carrington.' It's Peter. My wife is Kay. I have a feeling we're going to be meeting with each other for a long time, so let's dispense with the formalities."

Conner Banks hadn't known what to expect of Carrington's bride. He had already somewhat prejudged her — the librarian who had married a billionaire after a whirlwind romance — as just another very lucky fortune hunter.

He saw immediately that Kay Lansing Carrington did not fit that profile at all. Like her husband, she was dressed casually in a sweater and slacks. But the crimson shade of her high-necked sweater framed a face dominated by eyes such a dark shade of blue that they seemed almost as black as the long hair that was gathered at the nape of her neck and fell loosely past her shoulders.

During that first meeting and the ones that followed, she always sat to the right of Peter, who was at the head of the table. Slater's place was the chair to the left of Peter. By sitting next to Slater, Conner Banks was able to witness the byplay between Peter Carrington and his wife. Their hands often touched tenderly, and the expression of affection in their eyes when they looked at each other made him wonder if it was really all that great to be footloose and fancy-free, as he was.

Out of curiosity, Banks had done some research on the case even before he was hired to help consider the lawsuit. His interest had been piqued because he had met former ambassador Charles Althorp socially on a number of occasions and had noted that he never was accompanied by his wife.

In the first two conferences, which took place prior to Susan Althorp's body being found, the discussion focused on the need for Peter to file suit for libel and slander against Gladys Althorp. "She's never going to retract that accusation," Markinson said. "This is their way to force your hand. You'll have to answer interrogatories and give a deposition. They're hoping to trip you up when you're under oath. As of now, the prosecutor doesn't have enough evidence to indict you. Peter, you were dating Susan, casually. You were longtime family friends. You drove her home that night. Unfortunately, by returning home through the side door, you don't have anyone to support your statement that you went upstairs."

No one? Conner Banks asked himself. A guy, twenty years old, a little after midnight, a party in full swing, and you go to bed? Our client is innocent, he thought, sarcastically. Of course he is. It's my job to defend him. But that doesn't mean I have to believe him.

"I would say that what has helped to keep this case alive is the fact that your dress shirt was missing," Markinson stated. "The fact that the maid said she took it out of the hamper and gave it to the dry cleaner pickup service means that if they try to use the missing shirt as evidence of guilt, it will backfire on them. You don't have anything to lose by filing the suit, and, if it comes to trial, to let the public realize that this case is all about baseless accusations."

The third meeting took place the day after Susan Althorp's funeral, following also the stunning revelation that Maria Valdez, the maid who had claimed to have given Peter's dress shirt to the cleaner, was now retracting her story.

This time, when the Carringtons came into the dining room, the strain on both their faces was obvious. Without bothering to greet the lawyers, Peter said, "She's lying. I can't prove it, but I know she's lying. I put that shirt in the hamper. I have no idea why she's doing this to me."

"We'll try to prove she's lying, Peter," Markinson told him. "We'll look into everything she's been doing for the past twenty-two years. Maybe it will turn out that she's pulled some stuff that would make her a less than credible witness."

Conner Banks initially had strongly suspected that Peter Carrington was guilty of the death of Susan Althorp. Now, adding up the evidence, he was virtually certain. No one had seen Carrington return to the house the night of the party. Twenty years old, he goes straight to bed when there are still guests in the house dancing on the terrace. Nobody sees him park the car. Nobody sees him come in. Susan is missing the next morning, and so is the dress shirt Carrington was wearing. Now her body has been found on his property. The prosecutor is bound to arrest him. Peter, I'll do my best to help get you off, he thought as he looked at the man who was now holding hands with his wife, but I saw some of the footage of that funeral on the news last night. In a way, I wish that I was *prosecuting* this case. And I know that my colleagues feel the same way.

Kay was blinking back tears. She'll stand by her man, Banks thought. That's good. But if he's responsible for Susan Althorp's death, then maybe everyone is right to be suspicious about his first wife's drowning. Is he a psychopath, and, if so, will his new bride get in his way?

Why did he also feel that there was something odd — and perhaps oddly suspicious — about Carrington's rush to the altar with a woman he'd known for such a short time?

16

He's nervous, Pat Jennings decided, as she looked at her boss, Richard Walker. I'll bet anything he's been playing the horses again. For all the money he makes on this place — or *doesn't* make on this place — he might just at well try his luck on the ponies.

Pat had been working six months as receptionist and secretary at the Walker Art Gallery. When she took the job, it seemed like the perfect part-time situation for a woman with two kids in elementary school. Her hours were from nine until three, with the understanding that if a cocktail party was given for a new exhibit, she would come back later. There had been only one such event since she'd been working there, and it had been poorly attended.

The problem was that the gallery wasn't selling enough to even cover the overhead. Richard would be sunk without his mother, Pat thought, as she watched him go restlessly from one painting to another, straightening them.

He's really jumpy today, she decided. I heard him placing bets these last few days; he must have lost a lot of money. Of course, the business of that girl's body being found on his stepbrother's property is pretty upsetting. Yesterday, Richard had turned on the TV to watch live coverage of Susan Althorp's funeral. He knew her, too, Pat thought. Even though it's been a long time, seeing her casket carried into church must bring back a lot of painful memories.

That morning she asked Walker how his stepbrother was reacting to all the publicity.

"I haven't seen Peter," he told her. "I did call and let him know I was thinking about him. All this is happening with him just back from his honeymoon. It's got to be difficult."

Later it had been so quiet in the gallery that when the phone rang, Pat jumped. This place is getting on my nerves, she thought as she reached for the receiver.

"Walker Art Gallery. Good afternoon."

She looked up to see Richard Walker running toward her, waving his arms. She could read his lips: "I'm not here. I'm not here."

"Put Walker on." It was a command not a request.

"I'm afraid he's out on an appointment. I

don't expect him back this afternoon."

"Give me his cell phone number."

Pat knew what to say: "When he's at a meeting, he won't turn it on. If you give me your name and number, I'll —"

The slamming of the phone at the other end of the connection made her yank the receiver from her ear. Walker was standing next to her desk, perspiration on his forehead, his hands trembling. Before he asked, Pat volunteered, "He didn't give a name, but I can tell you this, Richard. He sounds awfully angry." Then, because she felt sorry for him, she offered some unsolicited advice: "Richard, your mother has a lot of money. If I were you, I'd tell her to give you what you need. That guy was scary. And then, a final piece of advice — quit playing the ponies."

Two hours later, Richard Walker was in his mother's home at the Carrington estate. "You've got to help me," he pleaded. "They'll kill me if I don't pay. You know they will. This is the last time, I swear it."

Elaine Carrington looked at her son, fury in her eyes. "Richard, you've drained me dry. I get one million dollars a year from the estate. Last year, between your gambling and the expense of the gallery, you got nearly half of it."

"Mother, I'm begging you."

She looked away. He knows I have to give it to him, Elaine thought. And he knows where, if I'm desperate, I can get whatever amount I need.

17

Former ambassador Charles Althorp knocked at the door of his wife's bedroom. Yesterday, after the funeral, she had come home and gone straight to bed. He did not yet know whether or not she had heard that Maria Valdez, the former maid at the Carrington estate, had recanted the version of events she had given at the time of Susan's disappearance.

He found her propped up in bed. Even though it was nearly noon, Gladys Althorp had clearly not attempted to get up. Her breakfast tray, virtually untouched, was on the bedside table. The television was on, although the sound was turned down so low it was only a murmur.

Looking at the emaciated woman from whom he had been estranged for years, Althorp felt an unexpected and overwhelming wave of tenderness toward her. At the funeral parlor, the casket had been surrounded by pictures showing moments from Susan's nearly nineteen years. I traveled so much, he thought. So many of the pictures, especially the later ones, were just of Gladys and Susan.

He pointed to the television. "You've obviously heard about Maria Valdez."

"Nicholas Greco phoned me, and then I saw it on CNN. He said that her testimony could be the key to convict Peter Carrington of Susan's death. I only wish I could be in court to see him led away in handcuffs."

"I hope you are there, my dear. And I can assure you that I will be."

Gladys Althorp shook her head. "You know perfectly well that I am dying, Charles, but it doesn't matter anymore. Now that I know where Susan is, and that I'll be with her soon, I have to confess something. I've always believed that Peter took Susan's life, but there's also been one tiny doubt in my mind. Did you hear her go out that night? Did you follow her? You were very angry with her. Had the two of you quarreled because she learned that you were involved with Elaine? Susan was so protective of me."

"Elaine was a mistake, and it was over by the time she married Peter's father," Charles said bitterly. "When I saw her, she was divorced and unattached, and that is the truth."

"*She* may have been unattached, but *you* weren't, Charles."

"Isn't it a bit late in the game to discuss that, Gladys?"

"You still haven't answered me. What did you and Susan quarrel about that night?"

"Try to rest, Gladys," Charles Althorp said as he turned and left his wife's room.

18

For the first time, the lawyers were staying for lunch. With skilled fingers, Jane Barr prepared a tray of sandwiches and made fresh coffee. Aghast, she had watched the television reports that Maria Valdez had changed her story. It's all Elaine's fault, she thought. If she hadn't let us go, I'd have been here to pick up the laundry that morning. I would have known *exactly* what was or wasn't in the hamper, and what did or didn't go to the cleaner. How can that Valdez woman dare to change her story now? Who is paying her? she wondered.

It's too bad that I wasn't here when that detective, Nicholas Greco, came by and spoke to Gary. He's been nervous ever since. He thinks he may have done some harm to Peter by telling Greco that Peter was shocked when he learned Susan's purse wasn't in his car.

"What harm can that do?" she had asked

Gary at the time, but now she wondered. Maybe that bit of information did have significance. But she knew Peter Carrington, and it wasn't as though he could ever hurt anyone.

She and Gary had attended Susan Althorp's funeral Mass. Such a sweet, pretty girl she was, Jane thought as she took plates and cups from the cupboard. I used to love to see her dressed up and going out when we would work the dinner parties for Mrs. Althorp.

Outside the church, before the hearse and family limousines left for the private burial, the Althorps had stood in the vestry and accepted the condolences of their friends. Why did Gary duck around behind the crowd instead of speaking to them? Jane wondered. Susan was always so nice to him. At least a half dozen times that last year he chauffeured her to parties when the ambassador didn't want her or her friends to be driving home late on their own. But she knew her husband was not one to show emotion, and perhaps he felt it wasn't his place to be talking to the Althorps with all the dignitaries in the church around them.

Gary had been vacuuming the upstairs hallways while Jane was preparing the lunch. He came into the kitchen in time to save her the trouble of getting him. "Good timing," Jane said. "You can take the plates and cups and silverware inside now. But be sure to knock before you open the door."

"I think I know enough to do that," he said sarcastically.

"Of course you do," she said, sighing. "I'm sorry. I don't have my wits about me. I keep thinking about yesterday and the funeral. Susan was such a beautiful girl, wasn't she?"

As she watched, her husband's face turned a deep shade of red and he turned away. "Yes, she was," he mumbled as he took the tray and left the kitchen.

19

The lawyers didn't leave until three o'clock, following five straight hours of questioning Peter in preparation for what seemed to be the inevitable — a charge of murder in the death of Susan Althorp. We didn't even take a break for lunch, only pausing to nibble on sandwiches and to sip coffee. All the while, every detail of the dinner party and the brunch all those years ago was dragged out.

Occasionally Vincent Slater contradicted Peter about some detail. One in particular surprised me. "Peter, Susan was sitting next to you at the dinner and Grace was at another table."

Until then I hadn't realized that Grace Meredith, the woman Peter married when he was thirty years old, had been at that party. But then, why not? Some twenty of Peter's friends from Princeton had been there. Peter explained that she had come as someone else's date.

"Who was that someone else?" Conner Banks asked.

"Gregg Haverly, an eating-club brother at Princeton."

"Had you met Grace Meredith at any point before that evening?" Banks asked.

I could tell by then that Peter was getting worn down by the constant barrage of questions. "I never met Grace before that evening," he said, his tone frosty. "In fact, I didn't see her again for over nine years. I bumped into her at a Princeton-Yale game. We were both with a group of friends, but neither one of us had a specific date and we paired off."

"Are there other people who know that you hadn't seen her in all those years?" Banks asked.

I guess that Banks saw the expression on Peter's face because he added, "Peter, I'm trying to anticipate the prosecutor. This is the kind of question they'll be asking you. Since your first wife was at the party, they could think that maybe you became interested in her and Susan noticed. Then maybe you and Susan had a fight about it later on and it turned violent."

That was when Peter pushed his chair back from the table and stood up. "Gentlemen," he said, "I think it's time to call it a day." I noticed that he was deliberately cool to Conner Banks when good-byes were being exchanged.

After the lawyers were gone, Peter said, "I don't think I want that Banks character on my defense team. Get rid of him, Vince."

I knew Peter was making a mistake, and fortunately Vincent did, too. He understood that Banks was only preparing Peter for the kind of stinging questions that were coming his way. "Peter, they'll question you about everything," he said. "And they'll make insinuations. You have to get used to it."

"What you're telling me is that the fact that I met Grace that night can be used against me, that maybe I fell madly in love with her and decided to kill Susan?" He obviously didn't expect an answer.

I hoped Vincent Slater would go home; I wanted some quiet time, alone with Peter. We both needed it. But then Peter announced that he was going into the office. "Kay, I have to step aside as CEO and chairman of the company although I will continue to have a major voice in decisions. All my attention has to be given to trying to stay out of prison." Then he added almost helplessly, "That woman is lying. I swear to you, I remember putting my dress shirt in that hamper."

He came over to kiss me. I guess I looked pretty worn out myself because he suggested, "Why don't you try to take a nap, Kay? It's been one hell of a day."

Resting was the last thing on my mind. "No," I said. "I'm going to see Maggie."

I guess the day had really gotten to Peter, because he said, "Be sure to give her my best, and ask her if she'd like to be a character witness for me at my trial."

20

Joining Nicholas Greco and Tom Moran, Barbara Krause flew to Lancaster, Pennsylvania, where they rented a car and drove to Maria Valdez Cruz's home, a modest ranch-style house not far from the airport. It had been snowing there and the roads were slippery, but Greco, because he had already visited the former maid, did the driving. Krause was furious that information about Maria Valdez recanting her previous statement had been leaked to the press. She had vowed to discover the source of the leak and fire the person responsible for it.

"When I was here two days ago, I advised Maria to have her own attorney with her when we come to see her," Greco reminded them as they rang the doorbell.

And it was that lawyer, Duncan Armstrong, a tall, thin man in his early seventies, who answered the door. Once the visitors were inside, he stood protectively next to his petite client and immediately expressed outrage at the leak to the press.

Moran had been present when they questioned Maria Valdez twenty-two years ago. She was a kid then, he thought, nineteen or so, the same age as Susan Althorp. But she had been stubborn, and wouldn't budge from her story that she gave that shirt to the cleaner.

Oddly, the firmness and determination she had shown then was missing now. She seemed nervous as she invited her visitors to sit down in the cozy, spotlessly clean living room. "My husband took our daughters to the movies," she said. "They're teenagers. I told them you were coming, and explained to them that I had made a mistake and lied to the authorities when I was a young girl, but that it's never too late to set the record straight."

"Maria means that she may have been mistaken when you questioned her at the time Susan Althorp disappeared," Armstrong interjected. "Before we do any further talking, I must see what papers you have prepared."

"We are offering Mrs. Cruz immunity from prosecution for her full and truthful cooperation regarding this investigation," Barbara Krause said firmly.

"I'll take a look at those papers," Armstrong said. He read them carefully. "Now, Maria, you know this means that at a trial you'll be called to testify, and the defense attorneys will argue that you're lying now. But the important thing is that you will not be prosecuted on a charge of giving a false statement originally."

"I have three daughters," Cruz replied. "If one of them disappeared and then was found dead, my heart would be broken. When I heard that girl's body had been found, I felt terrible that my statement may have helped her murderer go free. I admit, though, that I would not have had the courage to speak up if Mr. Greco had not found me."

"Are you saying you never saw that shirt, and that you did not give it to the cleaner?" Moran asked.

"I never saw the shirt. I knew Mr. Peter Carrington had said it was in the hamper, and I was afraid to contradict him. I was new in the country, and I didn't want to lose my job. I sent the shirts that were in the hamper to the cleaners, but I was almost certain that his dress shirt had not been there. At that time the police were questioning me, and I thought I could be wrong, but deep down I knew I wasn't. There was no dress shirt in his hamper. But I told the police that it was there, and that it must have been lost by the cleaner."

"The man who owned the laundry always swore they never received that shirt," Barbara Krause said. "Let's hope he's still around."

"If I have to testify, will they think I'm lying now?" Maria asked timidly. "Because I can prove I'm not."

"Prove? What do you mean prove?" Moran asked.

"I quit the job about a month after I was questioned by the police. I went back to Manila because my mother was very sick. Mr. Carrington senior knew that, and gave me a five thousand dollars 'bonus,' as he called it, before I left. He was so grateful I had backed up his son's story. In fairness to him, I believe he really thought I was telling the truth."

"I think you're being too charitable," Krause said. "That money was a payoff."

"I cashed the check, but I was afraid that when I came home with so much money, people might say that I had stolen it, so I made a copy of the check, front and back, before I took it to the bank." Maria reached into the pocket of her jacket. "Here it is," she said.

Barbara Krause took the copy of the check, reviewed it intently, then handed it to

Moran. It was obvious to Greco that they believed it to be bombshell evidence. "Now we know that shirt never went into the hamper," Krause said. "It's time to arrest him and go to the grand jury."

21

For the first time in days, there was no media hanging around the main gate when I left. I guess if there had been, they had seen Peter and Vincent leave, maybe even had followed them. I had called Maggie and told her I was on my way to see her. She sounded chastened, probably having realized that what she said to the reporter was a low blow, and that I'd be furious.

But it had been over three weeks now since I'd seen her, and the minute I walked in the door I realized how much I'd missed her. The living room was even more cluttered than usual, but Maggie looked great. She was sitting in her favorite chair, watching Judge Judy, nodding in agreement with the just-rendered verdict, a smile on her face. She loved Judge Judy's outbursts to defendants. The TV was loud because Maggie never will put in her hearing aid, but she heard the door close behind me and sprang up so we could hug each other.

Of course, being Maggie, she got in the first word. "How is he?" she asked.

"By 'he,' I assume you mean my husband, Peter. He's under a great deal of stress and handling it beautifully."

"Kay, I'm worried about you. He's a . . ."

I interrupted her. "Maggie, if you ever use the word to describe Peter that I think you were about to use, I'm out of here, for good."

She knew I meant what I said. "Let's have a cup of tea," she suggested.

A few minutes later I was propped up on the couch and she was back in her chair. We were both holding teacups, and it felt familiar and comfortable and good. I asked about her friends and told her about our honeymoon.

We didn't talk about Gladys Althorp's accusation, or the fact that the former maid had changed her story. I was sure Maggie would be on top of those facts. But I did lead the conversation where I wanted it to go. "Maggie, as awful as it is for the Althorps, I'm glad Susan's body was found. At least it will give her mother some measure of peace."

"It was found on Carrington property." Maggie couldn't resist that one.

"Technically on the property, but outside the fence. Anyone could have put it there." I didn't give Maggie a chance to respond before I said, "Did you know it was Daddy's idea to move the fence back so that none of the landscaping would be affected if there was any public work in that area?"

"Yes. I remember your dad talking about that at the time. He intended to do something with that property outside the fence, but he never got to do it."

"Maggie, you were wrong about something. Daddy was not fired because he had a drinking problem. He was fired because Elaine Carrington started flirting with him, and when he didn't respond she got rid of him. Peter told me that. Where did you get the idea that it was because of his drinking?"

"I don't care what your husband told you. Your father had a drinking problem, Kay."

"Well, according to Peter, he certainly wasn't drinking when he was working."

"Kay, when your father told me that he'd been fired, he was upset, terribly upset."

"That was only a few weeks after Susan Althorp disappeared, wasn't it?"

"Yes, as I remember it was exactly fifteen days later."

"Then the police must have questioned Daddy as well. He was still working there."

"They questioned everybody who worked on the estate or even visited it. You were staying here with me the night Susan disappeared. Your father had some of his friends in for a poker game at your house. They were at it till midnight, and I gather when it broke up they were all feeling pretty good. That Greco fellow was way off base insinuating your father's suicide had anything to do with Susan Althorp."

"I'm sure of that, but he did have a point. Daddy's body was never recovered. Why were you so sure he committed suicide?"

"Kay, I went with him to the cemetery on the sixth anniversary of your mother's death. That was only a month before he killed himself. Six years and still he broke down and cried like a baby. He told me he missed her every single day, and it wasn't letting up. Something else. He loved working on the Carrington estate. Sure, he had other families up there he worked for, but the Carringtons were the only one who would let him do exactly what he wanted. It was a terrible blow to be thrown out of that job."

Maggie got up from her chair, walked over, and put her arms around me. "Kay, he loved you like crazy, but your dad was in serious depression, and when you drink and are depressed, terrible things happen."

We cried together. "Maggie, I'm so scared," I admitted. "I'm so scared of what may happen to Peter."

She didn't answer, but she might just as well have shouted what she was thinking: Kay, I'm scared of what may happen to *you*.

I called Peter on his cell phone. He was still in the city and wasn't going to be home until at least ten o'clock. "Take Maggie out for dinner," he said. Then he even laughed when he added, "Tell her it's on me."

Maggie and I went out for "a plate of pasta," as she puts it. Our conversation led her to reminiscences about my mother, and once again she told me the story about how she had stopped the show when she sang that song. She sounded so poignant when she sang that last line, "I heard that song before," Maggie said, her eyes glistening as she hummed the tune, off-key. It was on the tip of my tongue to tell her about my visit to the chapel that afternoon long ago, but I held back. I didn't want a lecture about how foolish I'd been.

Following dinner, I dropped her off at her door, watched until she was inside, then drove home. There were some lights on in the gatehouse, so I assumed that the Barrs were there. I never can tell if Elaine is in, though. Her house is too far away from either the front gate or the mansion to see any lights coming from it.

It was only nine o'clock. The mansion felt really scary to go into alone. I could almost imagine someone hiding inside the suit of armor in the entrance hall. The outside lights sent muted shadows through the stained-glass windows. For an instant I wondered if they were the same lights my father had installed, the ones he'd rushed over here to check that afternoon when he brought me with him.

I got comfortable in a robe and slippers and waited for Peter to get home. I was reluctant to turn on the television, afraid I'd come across another story about the Althorp case and the newest development, the maid who had changed her testimony. I had started a book on the plane coming home and picked it up again. It was no use; the words were meaningless.

I was thinking about my father. All the good memories were flooding my mind. I still missed him.

Peter came in a little after eleven. He looked exhausted. "As of today, I've resigned from the board," he said. "I'll maintain an office at the company."

He said that Vincent had ordered dinner brought into the office, but admitted he hadn't touched it. We went down to the kitchen, and I got some of Jane Barr's home-made chicken soup out of the refrigerator and heated it for him. He seemed to perk up a bit and got up and brought a bottle of red wine and two glasses from the bar. He poured the wine and held up his glass. "Let's offer each other the same toast every night," he said. "We will get through this. The truth will come out."

"Amen," I said fervently.

Then Peter looked directly at me, and his eyes were thoughtful and sad. "Here we are alone, Kay," he said. "If anything happened to you tonight, they'd be sure to blame it on me, wouldn't they?"

"Nothing's going to happen to me," I told him. "Whatever would make you say that?"

"Kay, do you know if I have been sleep-walking since we've been home?"

His question surprised me. "Yes, you were, that first night. You've never told me that you knew you were a sleepwalker, Peter."

"I was as a kid. It started after my mother died. The doctor gave me some medicine, and for a while it pretty much stopped. But I had a nightmare about putting my arm in the pool and trying to get at something, and it keeps sticking in my mind. You wouldn't know if that happened, would you?"

"It *did* happen, Peter. I woke up at about five o'clock and you weren't there. I looked for you in the other bedroom and happened to glance out the window. I could see you at the pool. You were kneeling beside it and your arm was in the water. Then you came back into the house and got into bed. I knew enough not to wake you."

"Kay," he began, his voice hesitant. Then he said something in so low a tone that I could not hear him clearly. His voice broke, and he bit his lip. I could tell he was close to tears.

I got up, went around the table, and cradled him in my arms. "What is it, Peter? What do you want to tell me?"

"No . . . it's nothing."

But it *was* something, and it was terribly important. I could swear that Peter had whispered, "I've had other nightmares, and maybe they really happened . . ."

22

Barbara Krause, Tom Moran, and Nicholas Greco did not arrive back from Lancaster until late afternoon. Krause and Moran went directly to their offices in the Bergen County Courthouse and spent the next several hours preparing an affidavit that summarized the evidence gathered so far in the investigation. The affidavit would be submitted in support of their request that a criminal complaint be docketed and a search warrant be issued. The criminal complaint would charge Peter Carrington with the murder of Susan Althorp, and the warrant would authorize the search of the homes and grounds of the Carrington estate.

"I want them to scour the grounds with the cadaver dogs," Krause told Moran. "How could they have missed finding her twenty-two years ago, when the scent would have been much stronger? Could he have buried her somewhere else and then moved her to the grounds when he believed they would never be searched again?"

"Maybe," Moran said. "I was standing there when those dogs went through the area where she was just found. I don't see how the dogs would have missed the scent, and I can't imagine how our guys, and I include myself, would have missed freshly disturbed soil."

"I'll alert Judge Smith right now," Barbara Krause said, "and request that we be permitted to go to his home at five o'clock tomorrow morning, so he can review the warrants."

"The judge will love that," Moran commented, "but it will give us time to assemble our team tonight and get over there with the warrant by 6:30 A.M., when we're pretty sure Carrington will be snuggled in bed with his new bride. I'll enjoy being his wake-up call."

It was after two A.M. when they completed the paperwork. Moran stood up and stretched. "I don't think we remembered to get any dinner," he said.

"We've both had about eight cups of coffee," Krause told him. "I'll buy you dinner tomorrow night, after we get this guy in custody."

23

I don't think I closed my eyes that night. Peter was so tired that he went to sleep immediately, but I lay beside him, my arm around him, trying to make sense of what I believed I had heard him say. Did he mean that events that he thought were nightmares were actually things that had happened while he was sleepwalking?

Peter woke at six o'clock. I suggested we go for an early-morning jog. I almost never get headaches but was feeling the beginning of one. He agreed, and we dressed quickly. We went down to the kitchen, and he squeezed fresh juice while I made coffee and put a slice of bread in the toaster for Peter. We didn't bother to sit at the table, just stood while we sipped the juice and coffee.

That was the last somewhat normal minute we were to have together.

The insistent pealing of the doorbell made

both of us jump. We looked at each other; we both knew what was going to happen. The police were here to arrest him.

It's crazy what you do when something catastrophic happens. I ran to the toaster and grabbed the toast as it popped up. I wanted Peter to eat something before they took him away.

He shook his head when I handed it to him. "Peter, you may not get to eat anything for a long time," I said. "You had almost nothing yesterday."

The door chimes were echoing through the house, and we were talking about food. But he did take the slice of toast from me and began to eat it. With the other hand he refilled his coffee cup and, hot as the coffee was, began to gulp it down.

I ran to open the door. There were at least six men and a woman standing there. I could hear the sound of dogs barking from inside one of the fleet of cars and vans parked in the driveway.

"Mrs. Carrington?"

"Yes."

"I am Assistant Prosecutor Tom Moran. Is Mr. Carrington here?"

"Yes, I am." Peter had followed me into the entrance hall.

"Mr. Carrington, I have a warrant authorizing the search of the houses and grounds of this estate." Moran handed it to Peter and then continued. "You are also under arrest for the murder of Susan Althorp. You have the right to remain silent. Anything you say can and will be used against you in a court of law. You have a right to have an attorney present while you are being questioned. If you choose to answer questions, you can stop the questions at any time. I know you can afford an attorney, so I won't go into the details of having an attorney appointed by the court to represent you."

Intellectually, I had known since yesterday that this probably would happen. But to anticipate something, and then to see it actually take place, is the difference between nightmare and reality. Two detectives walked past me to stand on either side of Peter. Realizing what they were going to do, Peter gave me the search warrant, then brought his hands forward. I heard the click of the handcuffs. Peter's face was dead white, but he was calm.

One of the detectives opened the front door again. It was clear that they were going to take Peter away immediately. "Let me get his coat," I told Moran. "It's cold out."

Jane and Gary Barr had just arrived. "I'll

get it, Mrs. Carrington," Jane said, her voice trembling.

"Where are you taking my husband?" I asked Moran.

"To the Bergen County Jail."

"I'll follow you in my car," I told Peter.

"Mrs. Carrington, I would suggest you wait," Moran said. "Mr. Carrington will be fingerprinted and photographed. During that time you will not be allowed to see him. An arraignment before Judge Harvey Smith is scheduled for three P.M. this afternoon in the Bergen County Courthouse. At that time, bail will be set."

"Kay, call Vincent and tell him to be ready to post bail," Peter said. As the detectives urged Peter forward, Gary Barr put a coat over his shoulders, and Peter leaned down to kiss me. His lips were cold on my cheek, and his voice was husky as he said, "Three o'-clock. I'll see you there, Kay. I love you."

Moran and one of the detectives went out with him. When the door closed behind them, I stood there, unable to move.

The atmosphere changed. There were at least six detectives still in the foyer. As I watched, all but the female officer put on plastic gloves — the search of the house was beginning. From outside, the barking of the dogs was getting louder; they were starting the search of the grounds. I felt Jane Barr take my arm. "Mrs. Carrington, come back to the kitchen with me," she said.

"I've got to call Vincent. I've got to call the lawyers." My voice sounded odd to me, low, but shrill.

"I'm Detective Carla Sepetti," the officer said pleasantly enough. "I'll need the three of you to stay together, and I'll stay with you. If you wish, we can wait in the kitchen until they are finished searching the rest of the house. Then, we'll have to move. They will want to look through the kitchen, also."

"Let Jane fix you something to eat, Mrs. Carrington," Gary Barr urged.

Food is perceived to be a comfort, to give strength in time of trial, I thought wildly. They're trying to feed me for the same reason I shoved a piece of toast at Peter. I nodded and walked with the Barrs down the long corridor to the kitchen; Detective Sepetti was right behind us. We passed Peter's library. Two of the detectives were there — one of them was pulling books off the shelves, the other rummaging through his desk. I thought of how content Peter had looked that day less than four months ago when I sat in that room with him, admiring its ambiance.

In the kitchen, I tried to drink a cup of coffee, but my hand was trembling so much that the coffee spilled into the saucer. Jane put her hand on my shoulder for a quick second as she removed the saucer and replaced it with a clean one. I knew how much she loved Peter. She had known him since he was a motherless boy. I was sure her heart was breaking, too.

I phoned Vincent Slater. He took the news calmly. "It was inevitable," he said quietly. "But he'll be home tonight, I can promise you that. In New Jersey a judge has to give bail. I'm sure they'll set it in the millions, but we'll have it available."

The lawyers were due to arrive at nine o'clock. For no particular reason, I called Conner Banks rather than any of the other three. "We did expect this, Kay," he said, "but I know it's awful for both of you. We'll get a copy of the arrest warrant, and Markinson and I will be in court at three o'clock. We'll see you then."

When I hung up, I walked over to the window. Rain and sleet had been predicted by noon, but as I watched, I saw the first drops of rain begin to fall. Then pellets of sleet began to hit the window. "Didn't I read somewhere that police dogs don't work if it's raining?" I asked Detective Sepetti.

"It depends on what they're looking for,"

she said. "If it keeps up like this, I'd guess they'll bring them in."

"What *are* they looking for?" I asked her. I knew there was anger in my voice. The question I really wanted to ask was if they thought Peter was a serial killer and were expecting to find bodies buried all over the estate.

"I don't know, Mrs. Carrington," she said quietly, and I looked at her. She was in her late forties, I would guess. Her chin-length brown hair had a natural wave that softened her somewhat round face. She was wearing a dark blue jacket and black slacks. Earrings in the shape of X's were the only jewelry I could see, although I'm sure she must have been wearing a watch that was covered by her sleeve.

It was so crazy to focus on details like that, of absolutely no importance to anyone. I turned away from the window. There was a small television in the kitchen, and I turned it on just in time to see Peter leaving the police car and being led into the Bergen County Jail.

"As Carrington is arrested on a charge of murder, evidence continues to pile up against him, our sources tell us," the reporter was saying. "The former maid, Maria Valdez Cruz, has not only confessed that she lied when she claimed she saw Carrington's dress shirt in the hamper, but also has proof that Carrington's father paid her off with a five-thousand-dollar bribe."

I snapped off the television. "Oh, my God," Jane Barr was saying. "I don't believe it. It would never have happened. Mr. Carrington senior was an honorable man. He'd never bribe *anyone*."

Even to save his son's life? I asked myself. What would I have done if I were in his place?

I wasn't sure I knew the answer.

24

Elaine Carrington was still in bed when detectives from the prosecutor's office rang the doorbell of her home shortly after 6:30 A.M. Startled, she threw on a robe and rushed to answer it. Had something happened to Richard? she wondered frantically. Hadn't he satisfied those gambling debts in time? Terrified at what she might hear, she yanked open the door.

When she was handed the search warrant, her immediate reaction was something approaching relief. Then, accompanied by a detective whose presence she ignored, she went to the study and turned on the television.

A few minutes later, the sight of Peter getting out of a car in handcuffs at the Bergen County Jail made her cringe. He's always been good to me, she reflected as she watched him trying to turn his face away from the photographers.

"At age twenty-two, upon his father's sudden death, Peter Carrington became head of the family empire," the TV anchor was saying.

A picture of father and son, taken shortly before the elder man's fatal heart attack, flashed on the screen, immediately triggering an angry reaction from Elaine. Young as Peter was, he understood what it was like for me to live with that miserable tightwad, she thought. One of the richest men in the world, yet we even argued about money the day of his own birthday party. He was always threatening not to pay bills. "You run them up. You figure out a way to pay them." That was his big speech. In the five years I was married to him, he complained about every nickel I spent, she thought bitterly.

When the segment of the program about Peter was over, Elaine pushed the power button on the remote control. When I married him, everything about this place had been let go for years, she remembered. The only thing he didn't begrudge was the landscaping. Nature boy himself.

She realized that whenever she was nervous or upset, her mind flooded with anger at the stinginess of the prenuptial agreement she had been pressured to sign. Then, a sound from outside made her hurry to the

161

window. Sleet was starting to pound against the panes, but she was hearing something else. "Are there dogs out there?" she asked incredulously of the young detective who was sitting on a chair in the doorway of the study.

"Those are the dogs searching the grounds, Mrs. Carrington," he answered, his tone businesslike.

"They already found Susan Althorp's body. What are they looking for now? Do they think this place is a cemetery?" she snapped.

The detective did not respond.

By noon, the search team had left her house, and Elaine went upstairs to her bedroom. As she showered and dressed, her mind raced with the possibilities raised by Peter's arrest. What will happen if Peter goes to prison for the rest of his life? she asked herself. Would he and Kay decide to sell this place? Can they do it while I'm alive? That might violate my prenup, or at the very least they'd have to buy me out.

The prenuptial she had signed had been the best her lawyer could do. Ten million dollars when Carrington senior died; lifetime residency both on the estate and in the smaller of the two Carrington Park Avenue apartments. Income of a million dollars a year for the rest of her life. But of course there was a catch: the availability of the house and apartment as well as the income would cease upon her remarriage. The ten million has been gone for years, most of it lost in that one lousy investment, Elaine thought bitterly. I should have gotten millions more.

I was wrong to try to talk Peter out of marrying Kay, she worried as she pulled slacks and a cashmere sweater from the closet. She's bound to be holding that against me. I guess I should have called them when they got back from the honeymoon, but I just didn't feel like looking at her strutting around the mansion.

She turned on the television again. According to the news reports, Peter was going to be arraigned in the courthouse at three o'clock. She picked up the phone. When Kay answered, she began, "Kay, darling, I'm absolutely heartsick for you and for Peter. I want to be with you at the arraignment."

Kay responded instantly to her expressions of concern. "No, don't come to the arraignment," she said, "but assuming Peter is able to come home after bail is posted, it would be nice if you and Richard were here for dinner. I'm going to ask Vincent to be with us, too. I think that Peter needs to look around the table tonight and have the reassurance of being with people who love and support him."

Then Kay broke down and sobbed. "I'm so scared for him, Elaine. I'm so scared for him. I know you are, too."

"Kay, I would do anything, anything, anything in the world to help Peter. I'll see you tonight, dear."

Elaine replaced the receiver. Kay, if only you knew what I've already done to help Peter, she thought.

25

"Are you sure you want to do this, Mrs. Al-thorp?" Nicholas Greco asked. "It's absolutely terrible outside."

"That's what I told her, Mr. Greco." Brenda, the housekeeper, her face creased with worry, was helping Gladys Althorp on with her coat.

"I am going to the arraignment of Susan's murderer, and there will be no further discussion about it. Mr. Greco, we will go in my car. I assume that my driver will be able to leave us near the door of the courthouse."

When she says no more discussion, she means it, Greco thought. He saw that Brenda was about to continue to protest, and he shook his head to warn her off.

The driver was waiting outside, holding an open umbrella. Without speaking, Greco and the driver each took an arm of the frail woman and helped her into the car. When they were on their way, Gladys Althorp asked, "Mr. Greco, tell me how an arraignment is conducted. Does it take very long?"

"No, Peter Carrington will appear with his attorney before the judge. He will have been waiting in a holding cell next to the courtroom. The prosecutor will read the charges that have been filed."

"How will he be dressed?"

"In a prisoner's jumpsuit."

"Will he be wearing handcuffs?"

"Yes. After the charge is read, the judge will ask him how he pleads. His attorney will answer for him. Of course, he will say, 'not guilty.' "

"I would certainly expect him to plead that way," Gladys said bitterly.

Greco could see that his client was biting her lip to keep it from trembling. "Mrs. Althorp," he said, "this isn't going to be easy for you. I wish you had someone in your family with you now."

"My sons could not have made it in time. They both live in California. My husband was already on his way to Chicago this morning when the word came that Peter Carrington had been arrested. But you know something, Mr. Greco, in a way, I'm not sorry to be the only one in my family here today. No one has grieved for Susan as I have all these years. We were so very close.

We did so many things together. From the time she was a child, she loved to go to museums and the ballet and opera with me. She was a fine arts major in college, just as I had been. When she chose that major, she joked that it would give us even more in common, as if we needed it. She was beautiful and intelligent and sweet and loving, a perfect, perfect human being. Charles and the boys will attend Peter Carrington's trial. I won't be around to see it. Today is my day in court to represent her. I feel almost as though Susan will be there in spirit, too. Does that sound silly to you?"

"No, it does not," Greco said. "I have attended many trials, and the presence of the victim is always felt as their relatives and friends give testimony about them. Today, when the formal charge of murder is read, everyone in that courtroom will be thinking of the pictures they have seen in the papers of Susan. She will come alive in their minds."

"You'll never know how grateful I am to you for locating Maria Valdez. Her testimony, and the copy of that check from Peter's father, will surely be enough evidence to convict Carrington."

"I believe that ultimately Carrington will be convicted," Greco replied. "It has been an honor to be of service to you, Mrs. Althorp, and I do hope that after today you will find some measure of peace."

"I hope so, too." She leaned back and closed her eyes, obviously exhausted. Twenty minutes later, the car pulled up to the courthouse.

26

Even though he was wearing an overcoat, Conner Banks felt chilled as he hurried from the parking lot to the Bergen County Courthouse in Hackensack, New Jersey. The lot was crowded, and the space he finally had found was about as far away from the courthouse as it was possible to get.

He began to walk faster, and Walter Markinson, his face already wet from the sleet, snapped, "Take it easy. I don't run two miles every morning the way you do."

"Sorry."

"It wouldn't have hurt you to have brought an umbrella."

"Sorry."

On the drive from Manhattan, they had debated the exact wording of the statement they would make to the media. "Mr. Carrington is innocent of this charge, and his innocence will be demonstrated in court." Or, "Our client has steadily maintained his inno-

169

cence. The case against him is based on supposition, innuendo, and a woman who, after twenty-two years, is recanting her sworn statement."

The way this case is developing, we might as well be defending Jack the Ripper, Conner thought grimly. He had never before been involved in a media circus quite like this one.

There have been some pretty sensational cases tried in this courthouse, he thought, as they finally reached the shelter of the building. There was the so-called Shoemaker, that guy from Philadelphia who marched through Bergen County, attacking women, with his twelve-year-old son in tow. His last victim, the one he killed, was a twenty-one-year-old nurse who had stopped by the house he was robbing to help out with an invalid who lived there. Then there were the Robert Reldan killings. That guy, handsome and from a good family, was reminiscent of Peter Carrington. He abducted and killed two young women. During his trial, he slugged the officer on guard who was taking off his cuffs out of sight of the jury, jumped out the window, stole a car, and had about thirty minutes of freedom. Now, twenty or thirty years later, the Shoemaker is dead, and Reldon is still rotting in prison.

And it is very likely Peter Carrington will spend the rest of his life with him, he thought.

The arraignment was to be held in the courtroom of the Honorable Harvey Smith, the judge who had signed the arrest warrant for Peter Carrington. As Banks had expected, when he and Markinson got there, the courtroom was already crowded with both spectators and the media. The cameramen were focused on a woman seated in the middle section of the room. To his dismay, he realized that she was Gladys Althorp, the mother of the victim.

He and Markinson darted to the front of the room.

It was only twenty of three, but Kay Carrington was already there, sitting in the front spectator row with Vincent Slater at her side. Somewhat to Banks's surprise, he noted that she was wearing a jogging suit. Then he realized, or thought he realized, the reason for it: Slater had told him that Carrington was about to go jogging when the arrest warrant was served. That's what he'll be wearing when he posts bail and leaves for home, Banks thought. She's presenting a united front.

Markinson's grumpy expression had

changed to a benevolent father-figure look. His brow furrowed, his eyes filled with understanding, he patted Kay's shoulder as he said in a reassuring voice, "Don't worry. We are going to take that Valdez woman apart when we get her on the stand."

Kay knows how bad this is, Banks thought. Walter should give her more credit. He caught a flash of anger in Kay's eyes as she looked up at Markinson.

In a voice that was low and strained, she said, "Walter, I don't need reassurances. I know what we're facing. What I also know is that there is someone out there who took that girl's life and who should be in this courtroom right now instead of my husband. Peter is innocent. He is incapable of hurting anyone. I want to feel that that is exactly what you believe, too."

"Blessed are they who have not seen and have believed." The words of scripture ran through Conner Banks's mind as he greeted Kay and Vincent. "He'll be home tonight, Kay," Conner told her. "*That* I can promise you." He and Markinson took their seats. Behind them, Banks could hear the courtroom filling up. It was to be expected — this was the kind of high-profile case that many courthouse personnel stopped in to observe.

"All rise for the court," the clerk announced.

They stood as the judge walked briskly into the courtroom from his chambers and took his seat on the bench. Banks had done his homework as soon as he learned who would be handling the arraignment. He'd learned that the Honorable Harvey Smith was known as very fair, but tough when it came to handing out sentences. *The best we may be able to do for Carrington is to drag out the proceedings as long as possible, because once he's convicted, he goes straight to jail,* Banks thought. *After he is released on bail, at least he can sleep in his own bed until the trial is over.*

Peter Carrington's case was not the only one on the docket: there were other detainees awaiting arraignment. The clerk read the charges as, one by one, the others came before the bench. *Comparatively petty stuff,* Banks thought. The first one was accused of passing bad checks. The second was a shoplifter.

Peter Carrington was the third to be arraigned. When he was led into court, wearing an orange jumpsuit and handcuffs, Banks and Markinson stood and placed themselves on either side of him.

Prosecutor Krause read the charge against

173

him. Cameras clicked and whirred noisily as, looking straight at the judge, his expression grave, his voice firm, Peter entered his plea: "Not guilty."

It was obvious to Conner Banks that Barbara Krause was salivating at the prospect of personally trying this case. When bail was about to be set, she addressed the judge: "Your Honor, this is a defendant with unlimited means at his disposal. He is a very high risk for forfeiting bail and leaving the country. We ask that bail be set in proportion to his resources; that his passport be taken from him; that he be ordered to wear an electronic wrist bracelet at all times, that he be confined to his home and the gated grounds around it; and that his leaving the grounds be confined to attending religious services, visiting his doctor, or conferring with his lawyers, and that these visits take place only after notification to and permission from the monitor of his electronic bracelet."

She's going to be one tough cookie at trial, Banks thought as he looked at Krause.

The judge addressed Peter. "I realize, Mr. Carrington, that with your great wealth, it doesn't matter whether I set bail at one dollar or twenty-five million dollars. Bail is hereby set at ten million dollars." He reviewed the list of conditions the prosecutor had requested and approved all of them.

"Your Honor," Peter said, his voice loud and clear, "I will absolutely abide by all conditions of bail. I can assure you that I look forward to clearing my name at trial and ending this horror for myself and my wife."

"Your wife! What about the wife you drowned? What about her?" The words were shouted, passion in every syllable.

Like everyone else in the courtroom, Banks turned around quickly. A well-dressed man was on his feet in the middle of the courtroom. His face twisted with anger, he slammed his fist on the seat in front of him. "Grace was my sister! She was seven-and-a-half-months pregnant. You killed the child our family will never know. Grace wasn't a drinker when she married you. You drove her into depression. Then you got rid of her because you didn't want to take the chance of having a damaged baby. Murderer! Murderer! Murderer!"

"Remove that man!" Judge Smith ordered. "Remove him at once!" He rapped his gavel sharply. "Silence in this court."

"You killed my sister!" Grace Carrington's brother shouted defiantly as he was rushed from the courtroom.

A hushed silence followed his exit. Then it was broken by the agonized sobs of Gladys Althorp, who sat with her face buried in her hands.

27

It was six o'clock and pitch dark before we finally got home. Outside it was still raining heavily. A police officer stood guard by the roped-off area of the grounds that the dogs had not yet searched.

Thanks to Vincent's quick action, Peter did not have to spend the night in jail. As soon as I phoned to tell him that Peter had been arrested, he had arranged to have whatever amount of bail the judge set wired to a bank near the courthouse in Hackensack. As soon as the arraignment was over, he rushed to that bank, got a check certified in the amount of ten million dollars, and returned to the courthouse to post it with the bail unit.

While he was gone and we waited for Peter to be released, I was allowed to stay with Conner Banks and Walter Markinson in the empty jury room off Judge Smith's courtroom. I think that they were almost as startled and shaken by the attack from Grace's brother, Philip Meredith, as I was. Then, to have it followed by the pitiful tears of Susan Althorp's mother made it all seem surreal. I watched Peter as he heard Meredith's accusations and Gladys Althorp's sobs. I don't think the expression on his face could have conveyed more pain if he were being flayed alive.

I said that to Markinson and Banks.

They expressed concern that, in the eyes of everyone in the courtroom, everything that happened was prejudicial to Peter, and they acknowledged that the media coverage of the event was going to be absolutely terrible. Even Markinson did not offer his usual conciliatory pats on the shoulder to me.

Then Conner Banks asked a question that absolutely threw me: "To your knowledge, did any member of the Meredith family ever threaten to file a civil suit for wrongful death against Peter?"

I was shocked. "No," I responded immediately. Then I amended my answer: "At least, Peter never told me about one."

"I'm going to be cynical," he said. "Philip Meredith may be a brother lusting for what he perceives to be justice, or he may be looking to extract a settlement from Peter. Actually, it's probably both. He certainly knows that the last thing Peter needs is to have another legal battle going on at the same time as his murder trial."

When Peter was released, Markinson and Banks spoke to him for a few minutes before they headed back to New York. They suggested he try to get as much rest as possible and told him that they would be at the house the next day, early in the afternoon.

Holding Peter's hand, I was aware suddenly of the electronic bracelet on his wrist. We walked down the long corridor toward the car waiting outside. I had hoped naïvely that there wouldn't be any media around when we finally left the courthouse. I was wrong, of course. They were there in force. I found myself wondering if they were the same people who had filmed Peter this morning on his way into jail, or if this was a fresh batch of reporters and photographers.

They began to hurl questions at both of us: "Mr. Carrington, have you anything to say about — ?" "Kay, did you ever meet — ?"

Vince was standing beside the car, the door open. We rushed into the backseat, ignoring the questions. When we were finally out of sight of the reporters, Peter and I wrapped our arms around each other. We hardly exchanged a word on the drive home.

Peter went straight upstairs. He didn't have

to tell me that he wanted to shower and change. I'm sure that after the experience of being in a cell, it was a physical need to have gallons of hot water splash over him.

Vincent was staying for dinner. Saying he had business phone calls to make, he went to his office in the back of the house.

I headed to the kitchen. I would have thought that nothing could lift my spirits, but the heartwarming smell of pot roast simmering on the stove gave me a genuine pickup, if for no other reason than the fact that Peter had told me it was his favorite meal. I was grateful for Jane Barr's thoughtfulness in remembering that and preparing it tonight.

Gary Barr was in the kitchen, watching television. He turned it off as soon as he saw me, but not soon enough. On the screen I could see that Philip Meredith was being interviewed. For a moment I was tempted to find out what he was saying, but I quickly changed my mind. Whatever it was, I had heard enough from him today.

"Where would you like me to serve cocktails, Mrs. Carrington?" Gary asked.

I had almost forgotten that I'd invited Elaine and Richard for dinner. "In the front parlor, I guess."

Elaine and I hadn't discussed time for the

simple reason we hadn't known what time Peter would be home, but when I'd been at the house for dinner before Peter and I were married, cocktails were always served around seven.

I hurried upstairs to shower and dress. I wondered briefly why Peter had closed the door leading from the parlor to the other bedroom, then decided he must have wanted to lie down for a few minutes. It was late, but I took the time to wash my hair. The mirror told me that my face looked pale and tired, so I took special care with makeup, adding eye shadow, mascara, a touch of blush, and lip gloss. I know Peter likes my hair loose on my shoulders so I decided to wear it that way tonight. I thought my black velvet pants with a print silk shirt would seem a little upbeat, although in reality there was nothing to be upbeat about.

When I was ready, I still hadn't heard a sound from Peter. Wondering if he had fallen asleep, I went through the parlor and quietly opened the door of the other bedroom. I gasped when I saw Peter standing at the side of the bed, a bewildered expression on his face, staring down at an open suitcase.

"Peter, what is it?" I ran to him.

He clutched my arms. "Kay, when I got up here, I lay down. I just wanted to rest for a few minutes. I must have fallen asleep. I know I was dreaming that I was going somewhere, and then I woke up. And look."

He pointed to the interior of the suitcase. Underwear and socks were neatly stacked inside.

In the forty minutes since we had been home, he had been sleepwalking again.

28

At seven o'clock, Nicholas Greco was contentedly enjoying dinner with his wife, Frances, in their home in Syosset, Long Island. Normally she would not have asked him about the case he was working on, but after having watched the six o'clock news with the story of the Peter Carrington arraignment, she wanted to know every single detail of what had taken place in court.

She had prepared his favorite meal, a green salad, macaroni and cheese casserole, and baked ham. Greco realized that even though he wanted to put the wrenching day behind him, he owed it to his wife to reflect aloud on his impressions of the day's events.

"If I were Carrington's lawyers, I'd be talking a plea bargain," he said. "That outburst in court made a tremendous impression on people. From what I understand, Philip Meredith isn't given to emotional demonstrations. I had Beth at the office check on him while I was driving home. He lives in Philadelphia, which is where the Merediths have lived for generations. Nice family background, but no real money. He and his sister, Grace, had academic scholarships when they went to college. Philip's a midlevel executive with a marketing company, married to his childhood sweetheart; three kids, two of them in college. He's forty-eight now, his sister was six years younger."

Frances passed the macaroni casserole to him. "Have a second helping. Running back and forth to Lancaster, you haven't been eating properly."

Greco smiled at her and, against his better judgment, reached for the serving spoon. At fifty-five, Frances weighed exactly the same as she had at twenty-five. Her hair was the same shade of ash-blond, but now, of course, was helped along by regular trips to the beauty salon. Even so, in his fond eyes, she hadn't changed much at all in the last thirty years.

"I read about how Grace Carrington's body was found in the pool," Frances said, as she bit into a bread stick. "There were a lot of stories about it four years ago when it happened. *People* magazine did a big spread on it. I remember that they brought up the fact that Peter Carrington had been 'a person of interest' in the disappearance of Susan Althorp. But at the time, I'm almost certain that the Meredith family made a statement to the effect that 'Grace's death is not a mystery. It is a tragedy.' Why do you think the brother is starting to make accusations now?"

Nicholas Greco would have loved to steer the conversation in another direction, but he reminded himself that, as with her figure and her hair color, Frances had retained her lively curiosity.

"From what I understand, Grace Carrington's parents were upset themselves about her drinking, and they also liked Peter very much. They didn't suspect foul play at the time, but now that the father's dead, and the mother is in a nursing home suffering from Alzheimer's, Philip Meredith may have decided that it's time to express his own feelings."

"Well, if you hadn't tracked down Maria Valdez, there wouldn't have been an arraignment today," Frances observed. "I hope Mrs. Althorp appreciates that you were able to do what no one else could."

"Maria had absolutely dropped out of sight when the prosecutor's office was looking to talk to her again. The guy we work with in the Philippines went over her old connections, and it just so happened that she was back in touch with a distant cousin. It took a lot of luck to find her."

"Even so, it was your idea to have Mrs. Althorp accuse Peter Carrington in *Celeb* magazine. All my friends agreed he would sue her for that. If you hadn't located Maria Valdez, you still would have made Peter Carrington answer questions under oath. And I'm sure he would have tripped himself up somehow."

Would he have tripped himself up? Greco wondered. There was still a nagging and unanswered part of the puzzle: the missing evening purse. Did Susan take it with her when she got out of Carrington's car? For some reason, that question wouldn't go away.

"Thank you for being my number one fan, dear," he told his wife. "Now, if you don't mind, let's talk about something else."

The telephone rang. Frances ran to get it and was back with the receiver on the third ring. "I don't recognize the number," she told him.

"Then let the answering machine pick it up," Greco said.

The message began: "Mr. Greco, this is Philip Meredith. I know you were in court today with Mrs. Althorp. I have been speaking with her. I would very much like to engage you to investigate the death of my sister, Grace Meredith Carrington. I have always believed she was murdered by her husband, Peter Carrington, and if it is at all possible, I want you to find evidence to support that fact. I hope you will return my call. My number is — ."

Greco took the phone from his wife's hand and pushed TALK. "This is Nicholas Greco, Mr. Meredith," he said.

29

If anyone had peered into the window that evening and observed us having cocktails in the parlor of the mansion, I am sure they would have thought how lucky we were. Of course Peter and I said nothing about the brief sleepwalking episode but sat side by side on the couch that faced the fireplace. Elaine and her son, Richard Walker, were in the fireside chairs, and Vincent Slater, who always preferred a straight chair, had pulled one over to join the group.

Gary Barr was serving drinks. Peter and I had a glass of wine, the others cocktails. Without being asked, Gary had drawn the doors that separated the parlor into two rooms, making our half more intimate, if you can call a twenty-seven-foot-long room intimate.

On our honeymoon, Peter had told me that he wanted me to hire a decorator to do anything I wanted to refurbish the house. He seldom talked about Grace, but I did re-member one comment about her, apropos of decorating: "When Elaine was married to my father, she did a lot of redecorating, and I must say she knew what she was doing. She had a great decorator working with her. Of course she hemorrhaged money in the process. You should have heard my father complain about it. Grace really didn't change anything. She preferred staying in the New York apartment. During the eight years we were married, she spent most of her time there."

All of that was going through my mind as we sat in that lovely room, staring at the fire in the fireplace. Elaine was beautiful as al-ways, carefully made up, her sapphire eyes sympathetic and loving as she looked at Peter.

I liked Richard Walker. He was not good-looking in the traditional sense, but there was magnetism about him that I am sure at-tracted women. Except for his eyes, you would never have dreamt that, given his rugged features and stocky frame, he had come from the womb of Elaine Walker Car-rington. Peter had told me that Richard's fa-ther, Elaine's first husband, had been born in Romania and moved to the United States with his parents when he was five or six years old. He anglicized his name when he went to college and was a successful entrepreneur by the time she married him.

"Elaine would never have married a guy without big bucks," Peter had told me, "but in a way she lucked out both times. I gather Richard's father was smart and rather charming but gambled everything away. The marriage didn't last long, and he died when Richard was a teenager. Then Elaine married my father, who was so frugal, the joke about him among his friends was that he still had his First Holy Communion money."

Obviously, Richard must have gotten most of his physical traits from his father, and something of his charm, too, I suppose. Over cocktails, he told us about the first time he had come to the mansion for dinner, and how formidable Peter's father had seemed to him. "Peter was a freshman at Princeton, Kay," he told me, "so he was away at school. I had just graduated from Columbia and had my first job as a trainee at Sotheby's. Peter's father was not impressed. He offered me a trainee job in one of the divisions of Carrington's. I forget which one."

Vincent Slater, who certainly is no conversationalist, began to laugh. "It was probably in the brokerage division. That's where I started."

"Anyhow, I turned him down," Richard said, "and that was the beginning of the end of a beautiful relationship. Your dad always thought I was wasting my time, Peter."

"I know." Peter smiled, too, and I could see that Richard's attempt to divert him from the grim reality of the day was working at least a little.

We went into dinner, and I was grateful to see that Peter responded to Jane Barr's pot roast by saying, "I didn't think I was hungry, but this looks awfully good."

As we ate, Richard talked about his first tour of the mansion. "Your father told me to have a look around," he said. "He told me about the chapel, and I went up to see it. It's unbelievable to think that a priest actually lived in it in the seventeenth century. I remember wondering if it was haunted. What do you think, Kay?"

"The first time I saw it, I was six years old," I said. Noting his astonished expression, I explained, "I told Peter about it the night my grandmother fell at the reception, and he stayed with me at the hospital and brought me home."

"Yes, Kay was an adventurous child," Peter said.

He hesitated, and I sensed he didn't want to talk about my father. I made it easy for him. "My dad had come back on a Saturday to check on the lighting. There were a lot of guests coming that night for a formal dinner party. I was left on my own for awhile, so I went exploring."

The atmosphere at the table changed. I had stumbled into talking about the night Susan Althorp disappeared. Trying to divert the subject, I rushed on: "It was so cold and damp in the chapel, and then I heard some people coming so I hid between the pews."

"You did?" Vincent Slater exclaimed. "Did you get caught?"

"No. I knelt down. I hid my face in my hands. You know how dopey kids are. 'If I can't see you, you can't see me.'"

"Did you catch a pair of lovers?" Vincent asked.

"No, the people were arguing about money."

Elaine began to laugh, a harsh, sarcastic sound. "Peter, your father and I were arguing about money all over the house that day," she said. "I don't particularly remember that we were in the chapel, though."

"The woman was promising him that it would be the last time." I was desperate to change the subject.

"That sounds like me, too," Elaine said.

"Well, it's certainly not important. I

wouldn't have thought about it, except that you began talking about the chapel, Richard," I said.

Gary Barr was standing behind me about to pour wine into my glass. An instant later, to our mutual dismay, the wine was cascading down my neck.

30

As Barbara Krause had promised Tom Moran, the evening of the arraignment they had a celebration dinner at the Stony Hill Inn, one of their favorite restaurants in Hackensack. Over rack of lamb, they discussed the sudden appearance and emotional tirade of Philip Meredith.

"You know, if we could get Carrington to admit to his wife's murder as well as to murdering Susan Althorp, I'd be tempted to offer him a plea," Krause said suddenly.

"I thought that was the last thing you said you'd do, boss," Moran protested.

"I know. But much as I think we'll get a conviction in the Althorp case, it's not a slam dunk by any means. The fact remains that Maria Valdez did flip-flop on her testimony. And Carrington's got the best defense counsel money can buy. It'll get rough."

Moran nodded. "I know. I saw the two of them with Carrington today. What they're getting paid for one day's work would pay for the braces on my kids' teeth."

"Let's talk about it," Krause said. "If he pled to both Susan's case and to killing his wife, we could offer him thirty years, without parole, on concurrent sentences. Let's face it, we don't have enough to charge him with his wife's death now, but he knows other evidence could develop. He would be released in his early seventies and still have plenty of money. If he took this offer, we would get the convictions and, assuming he lives that long, he'd have the hope of getting out.

"You know perfectly well that I'd love to try this case," Krause said. "But there's another issue. Right now, I'm thinking of the victims' families. You saw and heard both of them today. Mrs. Althorp won't live to see the trial, but if Carrington confesses, she'll probably live to see him sentenced. And there's another angle. If he confesses, it opens the door to civil suits."

"I don't think the Althorps need money," Moran said flatly.

"They're poor millionaires," Barbara Krause said. "Don't you love that designation? It applies to anyone with under five million. I read it in one of the magazines. A civil settlement would mean they could make a significant contribution in Susan's name to a hospital or her college. From what we know about Philip Meredith, he's never set the world on fire, and he has three kids to support."

"Then you are serious about offering a plea to Carrington's lawyers?" Moran asked.

"Let us say I'm turning it over in my mind. Kind of like being 'engaged to be engaged.' Anyhow, the lamb was delicious. Damn the calories. Full speed ahead. Let's have dessert."

31

I know that dinner relaxed Peter somewhat. As soon as it was over, and we'd had coffee in his library, the others got up to leave. Sometimes Richard stayed over at Elaine's house, but he told us that he was on his way to Manhattan for an after-theatre drink at the Carlyle with a young artist. "She's very gifted I think," Richard told us, "and very pretty, I might add. It so seldom goes together."

"Just don't fall in love, Richard," Elaine said tartly. "And if you decide to have a party for her at the gallery, let *her* pay for the champagne."

When she said that, Vincent raised his eyebrows to Peter and he responded with a trace of a smile. Peter and I walked with the three of them to the door. Both Richard's and Vincent's cars were parked directly in front of the mansion. The men opened umbrellas, and Elaine held on to her son's arm as they dashed down the steps to the cars.

Peter locked the door behind them, then, as we turned to the staircase, Gary Barr appeared. "Mrs. Carrington, we're leaving now. I had to tell you again how sorry I am about your blouse. I can't believe I was so clumsy. I don't think I've ever had an accident like that in all the years I've been serving."

Of course, when the wine spilled on me, I had accepted his apologies, gone upstairs, and quickly changed to another blouse. I think Peter had had enough of the apologizing, because before I could once again reassure Gary, he said brusquely, "I think Mrs. Carrington has made it clear that she understands it was an unfortunate accident. I don't really care to hear any more about it. Good night, Gary."

I had only seen glimpses so far of the formal — make that formidable — side of Peter, and in a way I was glad to witness it. These next months, until the trial, were going to be so humiliating and frightening for him. He had exposed his vulnerability to me because he trusted me. But in that moment I realized that the role I was assuming, less wife than protector, was unworthy of the essence of the man.

As we walked up the stairs, for some incongruous reason, I thought about an evening, maybe ten years ago, when I was home from college. Maggie and I had watched the old movie *To Catch a Thief,* starring Grace Kelly and Cary Grant, on television. During one of the commercials, she told me that Grace Kelly met Prince Rainier when she was making that movie in Monaco.

"Kay, I read about the time the prince came to visit her at her parents' home in Philadelphia. That was when he asked her father for her hand in marriage. The next day her mother told a reporter what a very nice person Rainier was and how easy it was to forget that he was a prince. A society reporter sniffed, " 'Doesn't Mrs. Kelly understand that marrying a reigning monarch is not like marrying someone who's just another prince?' "

Today I had seen the hounded Peter in court, followed by the frightened Peter standing over a suitcase that he could not remember having begun to pack. Just now, I had seen an imperial Peter who had heard enough of an employee's explanations. Who is the complete Peter? I asked myself when we were getting ready for bed.

I realized I did not have an answer.

32

The weather the next morning was almost unchanged. The temperature had risen so it was no longer sleeting, but the rain continued, a steady, dismal downpour.

"Looks as though our dogs get another day off," Moran observed when he went into Krause's office a few minutes after nine A.M. "No use having them sniffing around the Carrington estate today."

"I know. It would only be a waste of the taxpayers' money," Krause agreed. "Besides, we're not going to find anything there. I've been going over the little evidence they took from the mansion and the stepmother's house. The entire search seems to have resulted in a big nothing. But I don't suppose we really expected to find much after twenty-two years. If Peter Carrington was smart enough to get rid of his formal shirt right after he killed Susan, the odds are that there was nothing else for him to worry about."

"I'd guess if there had been anything, we would have found it the first time around," Moran shrugged.

"Just one thing kind of interests me. Take a look at this." Krause handed a sheet of paper to Moran. It was a landscaping design sketch.

Moran looked at it carefully. "What about it?"

"It was in a file drawer in a room on the top floor of the mansion. Apparently, over the years, the family has treated a couple of rooms there as an attic, the place where you stick things that you don't want to be bothered going through. The guys tell me that you could furnish a house with the stuff that's up there, from couches and chairs and carpets and china and silverware and pictures and bric-a-brac, to family letters that go back to the nineteenth century."

"I guess they never heard of yard sales or eBay," Moran commented. "Wait a minute, I see what this is. It's a drawing of the outside area of the Carrington estate, the place where the girl's body was found, except that there are plantings on it."

"That's right. Actually, it's a copy of an original sketch."

"What about it?"

"Look at the name in the corner."

Moran held it closer to the lamp on Barbara Krause's desk. "Jonathan Lansing! That was the landscaper, the guy who took a dive into the Hudson not long after Susan Althorp disappeared. He was the present Mrs. Carrington's father."

"That's right. He was fired by the Carringtons a few weeks after Susan went missing, and he apparently committed suicide. I say 'apparently,' because his body was never recovered."

Moran stared at his boss. "You're not suggesting there's a connection between him and Susan Althorp?"

"No, I'm not. We've got the guy who killed her. What I'm seeing is that Lansing was the one who suggested that the fence be moved those fifty feet back from the street. Looking at this, it would seem as though he didn't intend to leave the area between the fence and the curb untended. This sketch is a design for some perennials to be planted on the outer side of the fence."

"Then he was fired, and the family didn't bother to do anything but throw some grass seed on it," Moran said matter-of-factly.

"Looks like it," Barbara Krause agreed.

She put the sketch back in the file folder. . . . "I don't know," she said, more to herself than to Moran. "I just don't know. . . ."

33

On Tuesday morning, the day after the arraignment, Philip Meredith took the train from Philadelphia to New York. Aware that his picture might be splashed on the front page of the tabloids, he took the precaution of wearing dark sunglasses. He had no desire to be recognized and perhaps spoken to by strangers. He did not want sympathy from anyone. He had not laid eyes on Peter Carrington since his sister's funeral. He had gone to court simply for the pleasure of seeing him in handcuffs and charged with murder. His outburst had startled him as much as anyone else in court.

But now that it had happened he intended to follow through on his accusation. If Nicholas Greco had managed to find a key witness against Peter Carrington in the Althorp case, maybe he could find a key piece of evidence that would prove Grace had been murdered as well.

He got off the train at Penn Station on Thirty-third street and Seventh Avenue and would have preferred to walk the distance to Greco's office on Madison Avenue between Forty-eighth and Forty-ninth streets. But the fact that it was pouring rain dictated that he get in the taxi line. Weather such as this made him think of the day Grace was buried. It hadn't been cold, of course, because it was early September, but it had been raining. She was lying now in the Carrington family plot in Gate of Heaven Cemetery in Westchester County. That was something else he wanted, to bring her remains back to Philadelphia. She should be with the people who loved her, he thought — our parents and grandparents.

Finally he was at the head of the cab line. He got into the next available one and gave the address. He hadn't been to Manhattan in a long time, and was surprised at the traffic congestion. The ride cost nearly nine dollars and he could see that the cabby wasn't satisfied when he didn't add any money to the ten-dollar bill he handed him.

Between the price of the train and cabs back and forth, this day is getting expensive, even before I talk to Greco, Philip thought. He and his wife, Lisa, had already had a blowup about it. "I nearly died when I heard how you carried on in court," she told him. "You know that I loved Grace, but you've been obsessing about this for four years. Hiring a private detective costs money that we don't have, but for God's sake do it. Take out a loan if necessary, but one way or the other be finished with all this."

A narrow building, 342 Madison had only eight floors; Greco's office was on the fourth floor, a suite with a small reception area. The receptionist told Meredith he was expected and promptly escorted him to Greco's private office.

After a cordial greeting and a brief comment about the weather, Greco got down to business. "When you called me at home last night, you said that you may have some proof that your sister's death was not an accident. Tell me about that."

"Proof may be too strong a word," Meredith admitted. "The word I should have used was 'motive.' It went beyond Peter worrying about Grace giving birth to a damaged baby. We're talking about a lot of money as the motive to kill Grace."

"I'm listening," Greco said.

"The marriage was never one of those love matches made in heaven. Peter and Grace were different people. She loved New York society life; he did not. By the terms of their premarital agreement, Grace would have received a flat twenty million dollars if they divorced, *unless* — and this is a *big* unless — she gave birth to his child. Then, in the event they divorced, she would have received twenty million dollars a year so that the child could be raised in a way suitable to a Carrington."

"At the time of your sister's death, Peter Carrington offered to take a lie detector test and passed it," Greco said. "His income has been estimated at eight million dollars a week. Such exorbitant numbers seem incredible to you and me. Nevertheless, even a very large yearly sum payable by the terms of his prenuptial agreement to a divorced wife still is not a compelling motive to kill his unborn child. Even if fetal alcohol syndrome occurred, there would have been plenty of resources to take good care of a child with a problem."

"My sister was murdered," Philip Meredith said. "In the eight years she was married to Peter, she had three miscarriages. She desperately wanted a baby. She would never have committed suicide while she was carrying one. She knew she was an alcoholic and had quietly started going to AA. She was determined to stop drinking."

"Tests of her blood alcohol level showed

that she had three times the legal limit in her system when she was found. Many people fall off the wagon, Mr. Meredith. Surely you know that."

Philip Meredith hesitated, then shrugged. "I'm about to tell you something that I had sworn to my parents I would not reveal. They thought it would irrevocably damage the memory people had of Grace. But my father is dead and my mother is in a nursing home. As I told you, she has Alzheimer's disease and is totally unaware of what is going on."

Meredith lowered his voice as though afraid of being overheard. "At the time of her death, Grace was having an affair. She was very careful, in the sense that the baby absolutely was Peter's child. Grace wanted to give birth, then divorce Peter. The man she was involved with didn't have money, and Grace loved the lifestyle she had become accustomed to with the Carrington money behind her. I believe that the night of that party her first drink was spiked, with the goal being to get her drunk, because once she had one drink, it was all over. She couldn't stop."

"Grace was drunk when Carrington got home. Who would have spiked the drink?"

Philip Meredith looked directly at Greco.

"Vincent Slater, of course. He would do anything for the Carringtons, and I do mean *anything.* He's one of those sycophants who snuggles up to money and does the master's bidding."

"He spiked your sister's drink with the idea of getting her drunk and then drowning her? That's quite a stretch, Mr. Meredith."

"Grace was seven-and-a-half-months pregnant. If she had suddenly gone into labor, there was a very good chance the baby would have survived. She had already had some false labor pains. There wasn't any time to waste. Peter was not due home until the next evening. I believe that Slater spiked Grace's club soda with vodka, planning to get her drunk, then drop her in the pool after she passed out. When Peter got home, he grabbed the glass from my sister's hand and threw it on the carpet in the same kind of spontaneous reaction I had yesterday in court. I bet he's still kicking himself that he exploded at her. If he'd had time to think, he would have been the benevolent, understanding husband which was his usual role around her when Grace was drinking."

"You are telling me that you believe Slater spiked your sister's drink, and Peter then drowned her in the pool after she had passed out?"

"Either Peter or Slater threw her in the pool, I'm convinced of that. We only have Slater's word that he went home that night. I wouldn't be surprised if Slater helped Peter dispose of Susan Althorp's body, too. I wouldn't be surprised if he got rid of Peter's shirt for him after he killed her. He is that devoted. And that amoral."

"Why don't you go to the prosecutor's office with your theory, now that your mother will not be aware you are breaking your promise to her?"

"Because I don't want my sister's name dragged through the mud, and maybe to no avail. I can supply them with a motive and a theory, but inevitably there'd be a leak and some reporter would get hold of the story."

Nicholas Greco thought of his interview with Slater at his home. Slater was nervous that day, he thought. There's something he's concealing, something that he's afraid will come out. Could it be that he had a role in the death of either Susan Althorp or Grace Carrington, or *both?*

"I am interested in taking on the case, Mr. Meredith," Greco heard himself saying. "I have an idea of your current circumstances and am willing to adjust my fee accordingly.

We can include a provision that, if you receive a substantial civil award, then I will receive an additional sum."

34

Almost as if he had been pushed as far as it was possible to be pushed, I saw something change in Peter. We both slept well, out of exhaustion, but, also, I think, because we had a sense that we were in a war. The first battle had been won by the enemy, and now we had to gather our strength for what was to come.

When we went downstairs at 8:30 in the morning, Jane Barr had the table set for breakfast in the smaller dining room, with fresh juice and coffee on the sideboard.

"Why not?" we agreed when she suggested scrambled eggs with bacon, although I did make a firm promise to myself that I wouldn't keep up that menu.

The usual morning papers were not on the table. "Let's look at them later," Peter suggested. "We already know what's going to be in them."

Jane poured coffee for us and then went

back to the kitchen to cook breakfast. Peter waited until she left the room before he spoke again. "Kay," he began, "I don't have to tell you this is going to be a long siege. The Grand Jury is going to indict me, we both accept that. Then a trial date will be set which could be a year or more away. To use the word 'normal' is simply ludicrous, but I'm going to use it anyhow. I want our life to be as normal as is humanly possible until I go to trial and a jury renders a verdict."

He didn't give me time to comment before he continued, "I am allowed to leave these premises to confer with my lawyers. I'm going to confer with them a lot, and I'm doing it on Park Avenue. Vince has to be my eyes and ears at headquarters. He'll be spending a lot of time there as well."

Peter took another sip of coffee. In the brief time he stopped speaking, I realized that in less than two weeks I had become so accustomed to having Vincent Slater constantly present that it would seem odd if he weren't around.

"Gary can drive us back and forth to Manhattan," Peter was saying. "I intend to get the necessary permission to go to New York a minimum of three times a week."

There was purpose and direction in the way Peter spoke, and in his expression as well. Then he added, "Kay, I know I could never hurt another human being. Do you believe that?"

"I believe it and I know it," I told him.

We reached across the table to each other and our fingers entwined. "I think I fell in love with you the minute I saw you," I said. "You were so deep into your book, and you looked so comfortable in your big chair. Then, when you stood up, your glasses slipped off."

"And I fell in love with the beautiful girl whose hair was slipping around her shoulders. A line from 'The Highwayman' jumped into my mind: 'And Bess, the landlord's daughter, the landlord's black-eyed daughter, stood plaiting a bright red love-knot in her long, dark hair.' Remember that from grammar school?"

"Of course. The poem's rhythm had the cadence of horses' hooves. But think about it: I was the landscaper's daughter, not the landlord's," I reminded him. "And I don't have black eyes."

"Close enough."

It was odd, but that morning, my father was never far from my mind. I thought of how Maggie had told me only a few days ago that he loved working on the Carrington estate, and he especially loved the freedom of having the opportunity to design the magnificent gardens without regard to cost.

Over scrambled eggs and sinfully cholesterol-filled bacon, I asked Peter about that.

"My father was both a tightwad and burst-of-generosity guy," he said. "Which is what I intend to make our high-priced lawyers realize. If Maria Valdez was going back to the Philippines because her mother was very ill, it would have been like him to write a check to help her out with doctor bills. Yet on the same day he'd go nuts over the price of a set of china Elaine had ordered."

I thought of how Peter had told me to hire an interior designer and do whatever I wanted to redecorate the house. "It doesn't sound as though you're anything like him," I said. "At least not with what you've told me about making changes in the house."

"In some ways I am like him, I guess," Peter said. "For example, he hated it when Elaine hired the chef and the butler and the housekeeper and the maids. Like my father, I'd rather have a couple like the Barrs on a daily basis who go home to their own place at night. On the other hand, I never could see why my father would get upset about money spent on daily life here. I think he must have been a throwback to the Carrington who started out without a shirt on his back and made a fortune in oil wells — they say he was the all-time skinflint. I doubt if he'd have paid for grass seed, never mind acres of expensive plantings."

We finished breakfast and Peter started organizing the day as he had planned it. He called Conner Banks on his cell phone and told him to get permission for him to come into New York that afternoon for a meeting at a conference room in his law firm. Then he spent several hours on the phone with Vincent Slater and executives from his own company.

I realized I was looking forward to going with Peter into the city. At this time, it didn't make sense for me to sit in on Peter's meetings with his lawyers. I wanted to use what time I had to visit my little studio apartment. Some of my favorite winter clothes were still there, and I had some framed pictures of my mother and father that I wanted to have around me here.

Peter got the necessary permission to leave the premises, and we set out for New York in the early afternoon. "Kay, even though your apartment is on the way, I think I'll have Gary drive straight to Park and Fifty-fourth," he said. "If by any chance we're followed by the cops or media, and somebody takes a picture of the car stopped in front of your place, it might raise a question of violating bail. Maybe I'm paranoid, but I can't risk going back to jail."

I understood completely, and that was the way we did it. By the time we got to the front of the lawyers' building, the rain had at last begun to ease up. The weather forecast was for clearing skies, and it looked as though it was actually going to be accurate.

Peter was dressed in a dark business suit, shirt, and tie. His overcoat was a beautifully cut midnight blue cashmere, and he looked every inch the corporate executive that he was. When Gary opened the door for him, Peter gave me a quick kiss and said, "Pick me up at four thirty, Kay. We might as well try to beat some of the rush hour traffic." As I watched him walk rapidly across the sidewalk, I couldn't help thinking how absolutely incongruous it was that less than twenty-four hours ago, he had been standing in an orange jail jumpsuit, his hands manacled, hearing the charge of murder directed at him.

I had not been back to my apartment since the day Peter and I were married. Now on one hand it looked cozy and familiar, and on the other, with new eyes, I saw how small it really was. Peter had been here a few times in our whirlwind courtship. On our honey-moon, he had casually suggested that I just pay off the rest of the lease, and, except for personal items, get rid of everything in it.

I knew I wasn't ready to do that yet. Yes, I had a new life, but some part of me didn't want to completely cut off so much of my old life. I checked my phone messages. None of them was important, except one that had come in just that morning from Glenn Taylor, the guy I'd been dating before I met Peter. Of course, I had told him about Peter as soon as we started seeing each other regularly. "I was just about to take you shopping for a ring," he'd said, with a laugh, but I knew he was only half joking. Then he'd added, "Kay, be sure you know what you're doing. Carrington comes with a lot of baggage."

Glenn's message that morning was just what I would have expected of him — concerned and supportive: "Kay, I'm so sorry about what's happening to Peter. Some way to start a marriage. I know you can handle it, but remember, if I can be of help in any way, let me know."

It was nice to hear Glenn's voice, and I thought about how we had loved to go to the theatre together, and that perhaps one day he and Peter and I could go to dinner and a play. Then I realized that there weren't going to be any evenings out for Peter again unless he was acquitted at his trial. It's my confinement as well, I realized suddenly, because in that moment I knew that I would never leave Peter alone in the evenings.

I gathered some clothes from the closet and laid them on the bed. Almost all of them bore the labels of budget chain stores. Elaine wouldn't be caught dead in any of these, I thought. On our honeymoon, Peter had presented me with an American Express Platinum Card. "Shop till you drop, or whatever that expression is," he'd said with a smile.

I surprised myself by crying. I didn't want a lot of clothes. If it had been in my power, I would have traded all the Carrington money just to have Peter exonerated of the deaths of Susan and Grace. I even found myself wishing he could move into this apartment with me, and be struggling to pay off school loans, just as Glenn was doing. Anything to simplify our lives.

I dabbed my eyes and went over to collect the pictures on the dresser. There was one of my mother and father with me in the hospital right after I was born. They looked so happy together, beaming at the camera. I was wrapped in a blanket, a squished-faced infant, peering up at them. My mother looked so young and so pretty, her hair loose on the pillow. My father was thirty-two then, still boyishly handsome, and with a twinkle in his eyes. They had so much to live for, and yet she had only two weeks of life ahead of her, before that embolism took her from us.

When I learned the circumstances of her death, and that I was still at her breast when my father found her, I had been about twelve years old. I remember that I pursed my lips and tried to imagine what it must have felt like to be nursed by her.

I had showed the hospital picture to Peter the first time he was here, and he had said, "I hope someday we'll be taking pictures like that, Kay."

Then he picked up the picture of my father and me that had been taken shortly before Daddy drove his car to that remote spot and disappeared into the Hudson River. Peter had said, "I remember your father very well, Kay. I was very interested in why and how he chose the plantings. We had a couple of interesting conversations."

Still dabbing my eyes, I crossed to the mantel to get that picture to bring home, too.

That evening, with Peter's assent, I moved his favorite picture of his mother, and one of him as a child with his mother and father, and placed them on the mantel over the fireplace in the parlor of our suite. I added those of my parents that I had brought from the apartment. "The grandparents," Peter said. "Someday, we'll tell our children all about them."

"What should I tell them about him?" I asked, pointing to my father's picture. "Should I say that this is the grandparent who quit on life and on his child?"

"Try to forgive him, Kay," Peter said quietly.

"I do try," I whispered, "but I can't. I just can't."

I stared at the picture of my father and me, and although I know it seems fanciful, at that moment I felt as if he could hear what I was saying, and that he was reproaching me.

The next morning, just as the weatherman had promised, the sun was shining, and the temperature was up in the high forties. At nine o'clock, I heard the sound of barking outside, and realized that the cadaver dogs were back.

35

Nicholas Greco had made an appointment to see Barbara Krause in the prosecutor's office at 3:30 on Wednesday afternoon. "I did not anticipate paying a call on you so soon," he told her when he arrived.

"Nor, to be honest, did I expect to see you," she said, "but you are certainly always welcome."

"I am here because Philip Meredith has engaged me to look into the drowning death of his sister, Grace Meredith Carrington."

Krause had long ago learned to keep a poker face in court, but could not conceal the expression of surprise on her face at this news. "Mr. Greco, if you could come up with anything that could help us to tie that death to Peter Carrington, I'd be most grateful," she said.

"I'm not a magician, Ms. Krause. Mr. Meredith has confided to me a piece of information that I am not at liberty to discuss right now. What I can say is that it provides a compelling motive for Carrington to want to do away with his wife. However, despite that fact, I'm confident that in a court of law no sensible jury would find him guilty beyond a reasonable doubt based just on this information. That is why I would like to see the file you have on the case, and to be allowed to speak to the investigators who went to the scene."

"That's easy. Tom Moran headed up that investigation. He's sitting in on a trial right now, but should be free in an hour or so. If you want, you could wait in his office and read the file there."

"That would be fine."

As she pressed the intercom to send for an assistant to fetch the material, Barbara Krause said, "Mr. Greco, we've been over that file with a fine-tooth comb. We could not find anything that would stand up as evidence in court. From what you are saying, it's obvious that Philip Meredith has been withholding information that would help our case. Whether or not you find something in our file that seems relevant, I would encourage you to urge him to be forthcoming with us. You might remind him that an admittance of guilt from Carrington would open the door to a huge civil suit for the

Meredith family."

"I am very sure that Philip Meredith is quite aware of that. I also think that, in the end, even if I see nothing else in the file, he can be persuaded to reveal to you what he has already told me."

"Mr. Greco, you are making my day."

For the next hour and a half, Nicholas Greco sat in the one extra chair in Tom Moran's small office, making neat entries in the notebook that was ever present in his briefcase. Of special interest to him in Moran's notes was a reference to the fact that there had been a folded paper in the pocket of Grace Carrington's evening suit, a page from the August 25, 2002, issue of *People* magazine containing an interview with legendary Broadway star Marian Howley. "Howley had just opened in a one-woman show," the notes read. "Although the page was soaking wet, it was identifiable, and contained two words scrawled in Grace Carrington's handwriting: *'Order tickets.'* Page is now in evidence file."

Grace Carrington was planning to attend a Broadway show, Greco thought as he jotted down the date of the magazine. That is not the thinking of a woman contemplating suicide.

There had been another couple at the dinner the night Grace Carrington drowned, Jeffrey and Nancy Hammond, and as of four years ago, they were living in Englewood. Greco hoped they were still there. If so, he would try to talk with them in the next few days.

Gary Barr had served the cocktails and dinner that evening, he noted.

Interesting, that Mr. Barr, Greco thought. He had worked for the Althorps on and off, even as the occasional driver for Susan Althorp and her friends. He had been serving at the formal dinner at the Carrington estate the night Susan disappeared, and at the brunch the next day. He was also there and on the estate in the gatehouse the night Grace drowned.

The ubiquitous Mr. Barr. He may be worth another visit, Greco decided.

It was five o'clock, and Moran still had not returned to his office. He's been in court, Greco thought. He'll want to get home now. I'll phone him tomorrow and set up an appointment for a more convenient time.

He walked down the corridor to Barbara Krause's private office to return the Grace Carrington file. Moran was with her. Krause looked at Greco as though she had forgotten his existence. Then she said, "Mr. Greco,

I'm afraid we'll have to put off any further discussions now. Tom and I are on our way to the Carrington estate. It seems the cadaver dogs have dug up more human bones there."

36

Sometimes, when I held a storytelling hour for young children at the library, I would recite one of my favorite poems to them. It was "The Children's Hour" by Henry Wadsworth Longfellow, and begins like this: "Between the dark and the daylight, when the night is beginning to lower . . ."

The daylight was just fading away when I heard the cadaver dogs barking outside, the sound coming from the west side of the grounds. Peter had gone to the lawyers' office in Manhattan again, but I had elected to stay home. I felt overwhelmingly tired, and actually spent a good part of the day in bed, napping off and on.

It was four o'clock when I finally got up. Then I showered and dressed and went down to Peter's library and sat reading in his comfortable chair, waiting for him to get home.

At the sound of the barking, I hurried back

to the kitchen. Jane was coming in from the gatehouse to prepare dinner. "There are more police cars at the gate, Mrs. Carrington," she told me nervously. "Gary went over to see what's going on."

The dogs must have found something, I thought. Not bothering with a coat, I raced out into the cold twilight and followed the footpath that led to the yelping. Detectives were already taping off an area on the near side of the pond that in the summer was stocked with fish. Squad cars were racing across the frozen lawn, their lights flashing.

"One of the dogs dug up a leg bone," Gary Barr whispered to me.

"A leg bone! Do they think it's human?" I asked. Standing there in a light sweater, my teeth were chattering from the cold.

"I'm pretty sure they do."

I heard the sound of approaching sirens. More police are coming, I thought. The media will follow them. Who could be buried there? This whole area was once lived in by Indian tribes. Evidence of their graves has been found from time to time. Maybe it was the bone of one of those early natives they had found.

Then I overheard one of the dog handlers say, ". . . and it was wrapped in the same kind of plastic bags as the girl."

I felt my legs crumbling, and heard someone yelling, "Grab her." I didn't faint, but a detective held one arm and Gary Barr the other, as they led me back to the house. I asked them to take me to Peter's library. I was shivering when I sank down into his chair, so Jane got a blanket and wrapped it around me. I told Gary to stay outside and report on what was happening. Eventually he came back to tell me that he heard them saying they had found a complete human skeleton, and that there had been a chain with a locket around the victim's neck.

A locket! I had already suspected that the remains might be those of my father. When I heard about the locket, I knew that it had to be the one my father always wore, with my mother's picture inside. At that moment I knew with certainty that the remains the dogs had dug up had been flesh of my flesh, bone of my bone.

37

"I don't need any more proof that Carrington killed my sister," Philip Meredith told Nicholas Greco the morning after the skeletal remains of Jonathan Lansing were found on the Carrington property. "My wife and I have talked it over. I'm going to the prosecutor's office and tell them everything. That guy's a serial killer."

Greco was not surprised to get the phone call from Meredith. "I think that is a very wise idea," he said. "And it is possible that there may be no need to make public any information concerning your sister's relationship with another man. If Carrington is persuaded to admit to her death, the public assumption would be that he was trying to prevent the birth of a damaged child."

"But his lawyers would know about it, wouldn't they?"

"Of course. But as you can certainly understand, while they are trying to reach the best possible plea bargain for their client, they would not want the public to know that a man with Carrington's great fortune would commit murder to save money."

"And once he admits to killing Grace, I can file a civil suit?"

"Yes."

"I know it may sound as if my first interest is the money, but it's costing ten thousand dollars a month to keep my mother in her nursing home, and I need help. I don't want to have to move her."

"I understand."

"Thank you for being willing to help me, Mr. Greco. I guess the prosecutor will take over now."

This may be the shortest job I've ever had, Nicholas Greco thought as he amiably agreed with Philip Meredith. But after he replaced the receiver in its cradle, he leaned back in his chair. From the Internet he had obtained a copy of the page from *People* magazine that had been found on Grace Carrington's body the night she was drowned.

Grace was wearing a satin maternity evening suit when she was found in the pool. Why would she put that page in a pocket of the jacket instead of leaving the magazine open on the table? Greco wondered.

Sometimes, when Greco was visualizing a situation, he asked himself, What would Frances have done? In this case, he knew the answer. A fashion-conscious woman would not have taken the chance of creating an unnecessary bulge in the pocket of a satin evening suit. In her own home, if she saw an item in a magazine that she wanted to follow up on, Frances would have put some kind of marker in the magazine or turned it upside down on the table, open to that page.

There was no mention in the prosecutor's file of the magazine being with the evidence the investigators had collected. I must see what day that issue was on the stands or in the mail, Greco thought. And I am even more eager to have a meeting with the outsiders who were present at that dinner, the couple from Englewood, Nancy and Jeffrey Hammond.

I'm going to stick with this, even if I am breaking my cardinal rule, which is never to work pro bono, Nicholas Greco thought, smiling to himself. As Mother always reminded me, the laborer is worthy of his hire.

38

Five days after they found his remains, they gave me the locket they had found around my father's neck. They had photographed and analyzed it for any possible evidence, but then had agreed to let me have it. The lab had cleaned twenty-two years of grime off it, until the underlying sheen of silver appeared. The locket was closed, but the dampness had worked its way inside, and my mother's picture was darkened even though her features were still recognizable. I wore the chain and locket to my father's funeral.

Of course they blamed Daddy's death on Peter. Vincent Slater had driven Peter back and forth to Manhattan the afternoon the remains were found, and they arrived here minutes after the discovery was made. Slater immediately called Conner Banks, who contacted Prosecutor Krause. She told him that she had reached Judge Smith, and he had scheduled an emergency hearing for eight

P.M. that evening. She also said that, although she was not yet seeking a warrant for Peter's arrest in this newly discovered homicide, one might very well follow. Tonight she was planning to request that the judge raise Peter's bail and alter the terms of release so that he no longer would be allowed to leave the premises except for a dire medical emergency.

Banks told Vincent he'd meet him and Peter at the courthouse. I wanted to go with them, but Peter absolutely refused to allow it.

I tried to make him realize that after that first terrible shock, my second reaction was one of infinite regret that for so many years I had been angry at my father. I told him that all the anger I had felt at being abandoned had now evolved into pity for Daddy, accompanied by a raging desire to find who had killed him. Sitting on Peter's lap, the blanket still wrapped around me, the library door closed, I told Peter that I knew he was innocent, that I knew it with every bone in my body, with every fiber of my being.

Maggie phoned the minute she heard the story on the local news. When Peter realized she was calling, he told me to invite her to come over. Fortunately, she arrived after he and Vincent left for the courthouse. Then I sent home Jane Barr, who had been visibly upset at the discovery of Daddy's body.

"Your father was a lovely man, Mrs. Carrington," she said, weeping. "And to think of him lying out there all these years."

I was grateful that she clearly cared about my father, but I didn't want to listen. I told Gary to go home with her.

Maggie and I sat in the kitchen. She fixed tea and toast; neither one of us wanted anything more than that. While we sipped the tea and nibbled on a few bites of toast, we were both keenly aware that men were continuing to dig in the yard, and we could hear the dogs barking as they were taken back and forth over the grounds.

That night Maggie looked every day of her eighty-three years. I knew she was worried about me, and I completely understood. She thought I was crazy to believe in Peter's innocence, and she didn't want me to stay in the house alone with Peter. I knew that nothing I could say would reassure her.

Vincent called at nine o'clock to tell me that they had increased Peter's bail another ten million dollars, and that a messenger was on his way with a certified check in that amount from Manhattan.

"You'd better get going, Maggie," I said. "I don't like you driving alone at night, and I know you don't want to run into Peter."

"Kay, I don't want to leave you alone with him. My God, why are you so blind and so foolish?"

"Because there's another explanation for everything that has happened, and I am going to find it. Maggie, as soon as we know when Daddy's body will be released, we'll have a private funeral Mass. You must have the deed to the grave."

"Yes, it's in the safe-deposit box. I'll get it. Don't bring your husband to the funeral, Kay. You'd be thumbing your nose at your dad if Peter Carrington was there pretending to mourn him."

It took courage for Maggie to make that statement, knowing that it might cause me never to speak to her again. "Peter won't be allowed to attend Daddy's funeral," I said, "but if he were, he'd be there with me." As we walked to the front door, I said, "Maggie, listen to me. You thought Daddy was fired because of his drinking. That wasn't true. You thought he committed suicide because he was depressed. That wasn't true, either. I know that when Daddy disappeared, you were in charge of selling the house and getting rid of a lot of the stuff in it."

"I moved the living room and bedroom and dining room furniture over to my house," Maggie said. "You know that, Kay."

"And you stuck most of your own stuff in the attic. But what else did you move to your house? What happened to my father's business files?"

"There's just one. Your father was never a saver. I had the mover put the file cabinet in the attic, too. It was too tall, though, so he laid it down flat. My old couch is upside down on top of it."

No wonder I had never noticed it, I thought. "I want to go through that file soon," I said. We stopped at the guest closet and got her coat. I helped her put it on, buttoned it for her, and kissed her. "Now get home safe," I cautioned. "There still may be some black ice on the road. Be sure to lock the car. And mark my words, one of these days you and Peter are going to be the best of friends."

"Oh, Kay," she said, sighing deeply as she opened the door and let herself out. "There are none so blind as those who will not see."

39

For the last few days, Pat Jennings had not known what to make of her employer, Richard Walker. On Monday he had come in with the familiar look of relief which usually signaled that his mother had paid his gambling debts. That same day, his stepbrother, Peter Carrington, was arraigned on a charge of murder. The next day, on Tuesday, Walker had spoken freely about him: "We had dinner with Peter after he got home," he told Pat.

Pat asked him about the former maid, Maria Valdez.

"Naturally Peter's depressed by what has happened," Walker explained. "It is despicable that that woman changed her story, and now is tainting the memory of my stepfather. I hope they put me on the stand. I'd be able to tell them firsthand how the old man had bursts of spontaneous generosity. I remember one night I was having dinner at 21 with him and Mother. Somebody came to the table to talk about some worthy cause or another, and Carrington senior pulled out his checkbook and wrote a check for ten thousand dollars then and there. Then he stiffed the waiter with a cheap tip."

Walker also talked to Pat about Peter's wife, Kay. "Absolutely wonderful girl," he raved. "Just what Peter has needed for years. From what I've seen, even with all his money, he's never had much happiness."

On Wednesday morning, Walker came into the gallery with a pretty young artist, Gina Black, in tow. Like her predecessors, Gina was introduced to Pat as a brilliant talent, one whose career was going to flourish under Walker's guidance.

Uh-huh, was Pat's reaction.

She had heard about the skeletal remains found on the grounds of the estate on Wednesday night when she and her husband were watching the evening news. The fact that it was the body of Kay Carrington's father was revealed to her the next morning by Walker.

"They're not releasing any details yet," he confided, "but he was wearing a chain and locket with a picture of Kay's mother in it. My mother is freaking out. She was in her New York apartment and heard about it when she turned on the television. She said that when they were searching the grounds with the dogs before the rain started the other day, she asked the detectives if they thought the place was a cemetery."

"*Two* bodies found on the estate," Pat said. "You couldn't pay me to live there."

"Nor me," Walker agreed, as he passed her desk to go into his own office. "I'll be on the phone for a while. Hold any other calls."

Jennings watched as Walker closed the door firmly enough that she could hear a decisive click. He'll be on the phone with his bookie, she thought. He'll be head over heels in debt again in no time. I wonder when his mother will finally throw up her hands and tell him to figure it out for himself.

She reached for her copy of the *New York Post* which she'd tucked in the bottom file drawer in her desk. On the bus down to Fifty-seventh Street, she'd skimmed Page Six, but now she read it line by line. That poor Kay Carrington, she thought. What must it be like to be married to a man who's obviously a serial killer? She must worry that she'll wake up dead someday.

There was only one phone call in the next hour, that one from a woman who gave her name as Alexandra Lloyd. She had called last week and Walker had not called her back. Had he received her message? she asked.

"He definitely received the message," Jennings said firmly. "But I'll remind him."

"Please take my number again, and will you tell him that it's very important?"

"Of course." Thirty minutes later, when Walker opened the door of his office, Pat could see the flush of excitement on his face. There isn't a horse running anywhere today that he hasn't bet on, she thought. "Richard," she said, "I left a note on your desk last week that an Alexandra Lloyd phoned. She just called again and said that it's important you get in touch with her."

She held out the paper with the woman's number. Richard took it from her, tore it up, and went back into his office. This time he slammed the door shut.

40

"The force of the blow that killed Jonathan Lansing was so powerful that the back of his skull was caved in," Barbara Krause said, as she read the autopsy report. "I wonder what Kay Carrington is thinking when she looks at her husband now."

Tom Moran shrugged. "If she isn't getting nervous being alone in the house at night with that guy, I'd wonder if she's legally sane."

"This time we can be sure that Carrington had someone helping him," Krause said. "He didn't leave Lansing's car in that godforsaken spot and then hitchhike home. Somebody had to drive him home."

"I looked at our file from when Lansing disappeared and was reported as a possible suicide. The insurance company suspected it was a phony. They had their investigators all over the area where his car was found. A guy like Peter Carrington gets noticed. He has a look about him. I wouldn't care if he was wearing clothes from the Salvation Army, he would have been noticed. No one of Carrington's description got on a bus, or rented a car around there. At the very least, if he drove Lansing's car there, somebody was waiting to pick him up."

"Lansing was supposed to have been fired because of his drinking problem," Krause said, "but suppose there was another reason. Suppose someone was afraid that he was a threat. He was fired two weeks after Susan Althorp disappeared. He supposedly committed suicide two weeks later. By then the police had thoroughly searched the grounds with the cadaver dogs, and I include the property outside the fence."

Krause had the copy of Lansing's landscape design on her desk. "The question is, did he submit it after Susan's body was buried on the site. If so, he signed his own death warrant."

She looked at her watch. "You'd better be on your way. Lansing's funeral is at eleven o'clock. Keep your eyes open to see who's there."

41

I arranged to have my father's funeral Mass in the church nearest to MaryRest Cemetery where my mother is buried. It's in Mahwah, a town about twenty minutes northwest of Englewood. I had hoped to keep the time and place of the Mass and funeral private, but when we arrived at the church, the photographers were there in force.

Maggie and I had been picked up by the driver from the funeral home. On the way down the aisle, I saw familiar faces: Vincent Slater, Elaine, Richard Walker, the Barrs. I knew they were planning to be there, but I didn't want to arrive in a group with them. I was not part of their world when my father died. For these last hours I wanted to separate myself from them. I wanted to keep my father to myself.

In my grief I even felt isolated from Maggie. I knew she had loved my father, and had been very happy when he and my mother were married. I believe that after my mother's death, Maggie had encouraged Daddy to date other women, but knowing her, I am sure she was secretly pleased that he could not or would not do it.

On the other hand, Maggie had always bad-mouthed Daddy to me about his drinking, although I think she exaggerated those stories to help make sense of his disappearance.

The church was sparsely filled, mostly with Maggie's friends, so I knew she hadn't been able to keep her promise not to tell where the funeral would be held. But then I saw the tears in her eyes and my heart ached for her. She had told me once that she never attended a funeral without reliving the grief of my mother's death.

I sat in the front pew of the church, inches from the coffin, my fingers touching the pendant that until now had been on Daddy's body all these years. I kept thinking over and over again, I *should have known* he couldn't have killed himself. He never would have forsaken me.

Maggie began to cry when the soloist sang, "Ave Maria," just as it had been sung at my mother's Mass.

"Ave, Ave, Ave, Maria." How many times over the years had I heard that song? I wondered. I heard that song before. As the last beautiful notes faded into silence, for some reason, I began to think about that episode years ago in the chapel at the mansion. Could the scene between the man and woman possibly have had more significance than I had realized?

The thought passed through my mind, then was gone. The Mass ended. I followed Daddy's coffin down the aisle.

Once outside the church, the media closed around me. One of the reporters asked, "Mrs. Carrington, does it bother you that your husband can't be with you on this diffi- cult day in your life?"

I looked straight into the camera. I knew Peter would have the television on just in case the media did cover the funeral. "My husband, as you must be aware, is not per- mitted to leave our property. He is innocent of the death of Susan Althorp, innocent of the death of his first wife, innocent of the death of my father. I challenge Barbara Krause, the Prosecutor of Bergen County, to remember the legal and moral principle that in this country, a person is still pre- sumed innocent until found guilty. Ms. Krause, presume my husband is innocent of any crime, then take a fresh look at the facts of these three deaths. I assure you, *I* intend to do just that myself."

That night, when we went to bed, Peter wept as I held him in my arms. "I don't deserve you, Kay," he whispered. "I don't deserve you."

Three hours later, I woke up. Peter was no longer in bed. With a terrible sense of foreboding, I ran through the parlor into the other bedroom. He wasn't there, either. Then from the driveway I heard the sound of screeching tires. I rushed to the window in time to see Peter's Ferrari racing toward the gate.

Fifteen minutes later, squad cars, alerted by the Global Monitor System that tracked his electronic bracelet, converged on him as he knelt on the frozen lawn of the Althorp residence. When a cop tried to arrest him, Peter jumped up and punched him in the face.

"He was sleepwalking," I told Conner Banks later that morning at Peter's arraignment. "He never would have left the grounds otherwise."

Once more Peter was brought into court wearing an orange prison suit. This time, in addition to the handcuffs, there were shackles on his ankles. I listened numbly as the new charges were read: Bail jumping . . . assault on an officer . . . proven risk of flight."

The judge did not take long in coming to a decision. The twenty-million-dollar bail was forfeited. Peter would remain in custody.

"He's a sleepwalker," I insisted to Banks and Markinson. "He's a sleepwalker."

"Keep your voice down, Kay," Banks urged. "Sleepwalking in this country is no defense. As a matter of fact, there are two guys in this country who are currently serving life sentences because they killed someone while they were sleepwalking."

42

The shocking tape the police had made of Peter Carrington kneeling on the lawn of the Althorp home, and then attacking the police officer who reached him first, made Nicholas Greco wonder if there was any point in keeping his appointment with Nancy and Jeffrey Hammond, the couple who had been guests at dinner the night Grace Carrington drowned.

Explaining that they had been away, visiting relatives in California, Nancy Hammond called when she heard Greco's message on the answering machine and invited him to stop in.

The couple lived on a pleasant street in Englewood, where most of the houses were older and had wide porches and shutters, the kind of houses that had been built in the late nineteenth century. Greco climbed the five steps from the sidewalk and rang the doorbell.

Nancy Hammond answered the door, introduced herself, and invited him in. She was a small woman who appeared to be in her early forties, with silver hair that becomingly framed and softened her sharp-featured face.

"Jeff just got home a minute ago," she said. "He'll be right down. Oh, here he is," she added.

Jeffrey Hammond was on his way down from the second floor. "That's the way my wife introduces me?" he said with raised eyebrows. " 'Here he is'?"

Greco's immediate impression was of a tallish man in his late forties who reminded him of the astronaut John Glenn. Like Glenn, he had smile wrinkles at the corners of his eyes. He was balding, and made no attempt to disguise the fact. A particular peeve of Greco's was to see men not coming to grips with the inevitability of their DNA structure. He could spot a hairpiece a mile away, and even worse in his eyes was to see a man with a comb-over, long strands of hair combed over a shiny pate.

Greco had done a thorough profile on the couple ahead of time, and found the background to be about what he would expect of friends of Grace Carrington. Good solid family on either side: Her father had been a state senator; his great-grandfather, a presidential cabinet member. Both were well educated, and they had a sixteen-year-old son who was presently in boarding school. Jeffrey Hammond was employed as a fund-raiser for a foundation. Nancy Hammond worked part-time at the local congressman's office in some kind of administrative capacity.

He had explained in both the message he left and in his telephone conversation why he wanted to talk to them. As he followed them into the living room, he absorbed the details of their surroundings. One of them was obviously a musician. A grand piano with books of sheet music dominated the room. Family pictures covered the surface of the piano. The coffee table had copies of magazines, neatly stacked: *National Geographic, Time, Newsweek.* Greco could see that the magazines looked as though they'd been read. The couch and chairs were of good quality, but in need of reupholstering.

His overall impression was of a pleasant home with intelligent people. As soon as they were seated, he got to the point of his visit. "Four years ago, you gave statements to the police about Grace Carrington's demeanor at the dinner you shared with her the night of her death."

Jeffrey Hammond looked at his wife. "Nancy, I thought that Grace seemed perfectly sober when we got there. You didn't agree."

"She was restless, even agitated," Nancy Hammond said. "Grace was seven-and-a-half-months pregnant, and had had some false labor pains. She was making an effort to stay off the booze. She was torn. Most of her friends were in the city and were in and out of the apartment all the time. And Grace loved to party. But the doctor had told her to get plenty of rest and I think she felt safer at the mansion than in New York. Of course, then she was bored out here."

"Obviously you knew her very well," Greco commented.

"She was married to Peter for eight years. All that time we were members of the same gym in Englewood. Whenever she stayed at the mansion, she exercised at the gym. We got friendly."

"Did she confide in you?"

" 'Confide' is too strong a word. Just one time she let her guard slip and called Peter a rich genius and a stick-in-the-mud."

"Then you don't think she was depressed?"

"Grace was worried about her drinking. She knew she had a problem. She wanted this baby desperately, and she was always aware that she'd previously had three miscarriages. My guess is that she'd already had a drink by the time we got there, then, one way or another, was sneaking others."

For a number of reasons, she wanted her baby to live, Greco thought. Not the least of which, perhaps, was that the baby was her ticket to a lifetime income of twenty million dollars a year. He turned to Jeffrey Hammond. "What do *you* think, Mr. Hammond?"

Jeffrey Hammond looked thoughtful. "I keep going over that evening in my mind," he said. "I agree that Grace seemed restless when we got there, and then, sadly, in the course of the evening began to slur her words and became unsteady on her feet."

"Did anyone attempt to stop her from imbibing?"

"By the time I noticed, it was too late. She went to the bar and openly poured straight vodka into her glass. Before dinner, she was claiming to be drinking only club soda with a twist of lime."

"That was for our benefit," Nancy Hammond said dryly. "Like most problem drinkers, she must have had a bottle stashed somewhere. Maybe in the powder room."

"Did she expect her husband to be home

in time for the dinner?" Greco asked.

"Remember, this dinner wasn't a planned event," Jeffrey Hammond said. "Grace only called Nancy the day before to see if we were free. Early in the evening she told us that Richard Walker's birthday was coming up, so we'd call it a birthday celebration for him. There wasn't a place at the table set for Peter."

"Did Grace refer to an article she had read in *People* magazine about the actress Marian Howley?" Greco asked.

"Yes, she did," Nancy Hammond replied promptly. "In fact, she had it open to that page when we arrived, and she left it open. She commented on what a marvelous actress Marian Howley was, and said that she was going to get tickets to her new play, that she had met Howley at some benefits, and that she had marvelous taste. After dinner, when we were having coffee, she rambled on again about Howley, and repeated herself the way drunks do, going on about what great taste the actress had. Then Grace tore that page out of the magazine and stuck it in the pocket of her jacket, and dropped the magazine on the floor."

"I didn't see her do that," Jeffrey Hammond said.

"By then the rest of you were ignoring her.

That was just seconds before Peter walked in, and all hell broke loose. We left a few minutes later."

Greco realized he was disappointed. He had come hoping to glean something further, to learn if there was some significance in the crumbled page in Grace Carrington's pocket. He stood up to leave. "I won't take up any more of your time," he told them. "You have been very kind."

"Mr. Greco," Nancy Hammond said, "these past four years, I didn't believe for one minute that Grace's death was anything but an accident, but after seeing that tape of Peter Carrington slugging the cop in front of the Althorp home, I've changed my mind. The man is a psycho, and I can just picture him picking up Grace when she'd passed out on the sofa, and carrying her out to the pool and dropping her in. I wish I could tell you something that would pin her death on him."

"I do, too," Jeffrey Hammond agreed firmly. "It's just too bad that New Jersey is almost certainly going to eliminate the death penalty."

Greco was about to agree when he saw something that jolted him. It was a look of pure anguish in Hammond's eyes. With the instinct that seldom failed him, Greco calculated that he had stumbled upon the identity of the man who had been Grace Carrington's lover.

43

After the arraignment, the prosecutor allowed me to go back to the holding cell where Peter was being kept before he was transported back to the jail.

He was still handcuffed and shackled, and was standing in the middle of the cell. His head was down, his eyes were closed, and as I studied him, my heart was breaking. His whole body seemed so gaunt that he appeared to have lost twenty pounds overnight. His hair was untidy and his pallor was ghastly white against the stubble of beard on his face.

The cell had a grimy toilet in the corner and an unpleasant odor lingered in the closed area where the cell was located.

Peter must have sensed my presence because he lifted his head and opened his eyes. His voice composed, but his eyes pleading for understanding, he said, "Kay, I wasn't trying to escape last night. I was dreaming that I had to find something, and then I thought someone was attacking me. Kay, I did punch that cop last night. I hurt him. Maybe I am . . ."

I interrupted him. "I know you weren't trying to escape, Peter. We'll make them understand that."

Peter had taken a step back as if he was afraid I would reject him. But then he came forward to the bars, and raised his hands to entwine his fingers with mine. I noticed that the electronic bracelet was gone. It had served its purpose, I thought bitterly, alerting the police that Peter had left the grounds. Money well spent by the State of New Jersey.

"Kay, I want you to divorce me and get on with your life."

That was when I broke down completely, sobbing uncontrollably, angry at myself that I was only making it worse for him. "Oh, Peter, oh Peter, don't say that, don't even *think* that."

He shushed me. "Kay, they'll be here for me in a minute. Listen to me. I don't want you alone in the house. Get your grandmother to stay with you."

I shook my head. "No!"

That was when a sheriff's officer came in. "I'm sorry, Mrs. Carrington, you'll have to leave," he told me.

Still trying to stifle my sobs, I said to Peter, "I'll find out when I can visit you. I'll . . ."

"Kay, you must take care of this immediately," Peter said. "I want you to tell Vince to hire a security firm today. I want a twenty-four-hour guard around the house. *You are not to be alone there without it.*"

It was the statement of a protective husband. Peter was afraid for me.

I looked at him closely. The officer put his hand under my elbow to ease me out of the detention area. I didn't budge. I had something I had to say, and it was perfectly okay for the guard to hear me. "Peter, I'm going to throw one hell of a homecoming party for you when this nightmare is over."

I was rewarded by a sad smile. Then Peter said, "Oh, Kay, would to God I could believe that would happen."

The next morning, the full contingent of Peter's legal defense team gathered at the mansion. Walter Markinson and Conner Banks were there, of course. The other two chief counselors had flown in as well, Saul Abramson from Chicago and Arthur Robbins from Boston.

Vincent Slater took his usual place at the dining table. The Barrs had set out the usual coffee and pastries and bottles of water on the sideboard. Everything was the same, except that Peter was not sitting at the head of the table. I took his place instead.

If the atmosphere had been heavy the previous week, today it was positively grim. Conner Banks opened the discussion. "Kay, if there's any comfort in all of this for you, the police report from the other night indicated that Peter was disoriented and dazed, that he had a blank expression in his eyes, and was unresponsive to their orders to move after they cuffed him. When they were in the squad car he started to ask them what happened and why was he there. He even said, 'I'm not allowed to leave my property, I don't want to get in trouble.' They tested for drugs and there were none in his system, so at least I don't believe they think he was putting on an act."

"He wasn't."

"We've got to get his complete medical background," Markinson said. "Does he have a history of sleepwalking?"

Before I could answer, Vincent Slater said, "Yes, he does."

I could see beads of sweat on Slater's forehead and upper lip. "Horses sweat; men perspire; ladies glow." — Maggie would recite that old chestnut to me during my teenage

260

years if I ever came in after a game of tennis and said something about sweating. To remember it at this moment made me think that I was the one who was in some kind of fugue state.

"What do you know about Peter's sleepwalking?" Markinson was asking Slater.

"As you are aware, I've been working for the Carrington family since the day after I graduated from college. Peter's mother died when he was twelve. At the time I was twenty-four and Mr. Carrington senior appointed me as a kind of big brother to Peter. Rather than have him chauffeured back and forth to prep school, I would drive him and help him get settled. That sort of thing. When there were school breaks, his father would often be away, and if Peter wasn't invited to visit a friend, I would take him skiing or sailing."

I listened, my heart sick, to the story about the boy who had to have someone appointed to keep him occupied during the times when most kids came home to their families. I wondered whether Slater had enjoyed that job, or merely used it to ingratiate himself with Peter's father and then, eventually, with Peter.

"This is something I would never have discussed, except in the hope of helping Peter now," Vincent said. "I witnessed at least three episodes of sleepwalking."

"How old was Peter then?" Banks shot the question at him.

"He was thirteen the first time. It was here, at the house. He had gone to bed, and I was watching television in the room that I now use as an office. I heard a noise and went out to investigate. Peter was in the kitchen, sitting at the table with a glass of milk and some cookies in front of him. His father had warned me that he'd had a few episodes of sleepwalking, and I guessed immediately that I was witnessing one of those episodes. Peter drank the milk, ate the cookies, put the plate and glass in the sink, and left the kitchen. He passed inches away from me and never saw me. I followed him upstairs and watched him get back into bed."

"Was there ever an episode during which he exhibited violence?" Conner Banks demanded.

"When Peter was sixteen, he and I were in Snowbird, skiing during a school break. We had a two-bedroom suite in the lodge. We'd skied all day and went to bed around ten o'-clock. About an hour later, I heard him moving around and looked into his room. He was fully dressed in ski clothes. I realized I shouldn't wake him up, so I followed him to make sure he'd be okay. He went downstairs. There were still people at the bar, but he ignored them and went outside. I had thrown on a heavy jacket over my pajamas, so I followed him out — in bare feet. His skis were locked outside, but he had the key and unlocked them."

"He unlocked his skis when he was asleep?" Markinson asked, his tone incredulous.

"Yes. Then he started to walk toward the lift. I couldn't let him go. I was sure the lift was secured, but, on the other hand, I didn't know what he might do. Remember, I was in my bare feet. I ran behind him and called his name."

I was afraid to hear what Vincent was going to tell us.

"Peter spun around and, much as he attacked the cop last night, he attacked me. I managed to jump aside, but the tip of his ski caught me on the forehead over the eye." Slater pointed to his left eyebrow. "This scar is proof of what happened that night."

"Were there any other episodes of Peter sleepwalking after that?" This time the question came from Arthur Robbins, the defense attorney from Boston.

"None that I'm aware of. I'm only talking about this because maybe in some way it might show a pattern that would be helpful to Peter's defense."

"Was he treated by a doctor after that alarming incident at the ski resort?" Conner Banks asked.

"Yes, by an elderly doctor at Englewood Hospital. That was twenty-five or -six years ago, so I doubt he's still alive, but maybe his medical records are stored somewhere."

"From what I understand, boys are more likely to be sleepwalkers than girls, and I gather that it often starts in adolescence," Markinson said. "However, I'm not sure that making the prosecutor aware of Peter having experienced a violent sleepwalking incident twenty-six years ago would necessarily help him in any way."

"There was another incident last week" I told them. "It was right after Peter got home from the first arraignment." I explained how he had taken a nap, and when I went to check on him, I found him standing up with a suitcase open and partially packed on the bed.

I did not tell them about Peter's sleepwalking incident the night we came back from our honeymoon. I could not put into words the fact that his arm had been in the pool as though he was pushing or pulling an object. I reasoned that these lawyers were being paid handsomely to defend my husband, but also that my information might make them actually believe that he had been responsible for Grace's death.

I was afraid that, even as they worked to acquit him, in their minds they would be thinking, Guilty, as charged.

44

"The lawyers are staying for lunch," Jane Barr told her husband when he returned from the errands she had sent him to complete. "Wouldn't you think three straight hours would be enough? Mrs. Carrington looks absolutely terrible. I swear that girl is getting sick."

"It's been a lot of strain on her," Gary Barr agreed as he hung his coat in the closet by the kitchen door.

"I made chicken soup," Jane said unnecessarily. The aroma of simmering chicken and onions and celery was permeating the kitchen. "I'll bake some biscuits and have a salad and cheese. None of them are vegetarians."

Gary Barr knew his wife. For the last two weeks, since Susan Althorp's remains had been found, Jane had been unraveling. He watched as she went over to the sink and began washing lettuce. He came up behind

266

her. "Do you feel okay?" he asked timidly.

Jane swung around, her face contorted with guilt and rage. "There never was a finer human being in the world than Peter Carrington, and he's in jail right now be-cause —"

"Don't say it, Jane," Gary Barr ordered, his own face mottled with anger. "Don't say it, and don't *think* it. Because it isn't true. I swear on my immortal soul that it isn't true. You believed me twenty-two years ago. You'd better keep believing me now, or else we both may be living under the same roof as Peter Carrington again, and I don't mean on this estate."

45

"I did not find any mention in the file of the magazine Grace Carrington had been reading before her death," Nicholas Greco told Barbara Krause as he sat in her office.

"From what I understand, it had been thrown out," Krause told him. "Grace had torn one page from it because she wanted to remember to order tickets to a one-woman show that had just opened on Broadway."

"Yes, so I understand. I have met with the Hammonds, the couple who were at the dinner that night, and we talked about this."

"We questioned them at the time," Krause replied. "In their statements, they both confirmed that Grace had been drinking and that Peter arrived home and made a scene. The Hammonds left shortly after that. It's just unfortunate that Philip Meredith did not tell us four years ago that Grace was involved with another man, even though she never told him who it was."

To Greco it was obvious that Barbara Krause did not share his suspicion that Jeffrey Hammond had been the "other man" Grace had been planning to marry, and it was nothing that he intended to share with her. There was no need to drag Hammond into this. At least not now. His guess was that the man was in his own private hell if he believed that Peter Carrington had learned about the affair, and that knowledge might have contributed to his reason for killing his wife.

"Mrs. Hammond is absolutely positive that the magazine was on the coffee table when they left," Greco told Krause. "I took the liberty of calling Mrs. Barr, the housekeeper, this morning. She distinctly remembers that she did *not* dispose of the magazine, and she says she and her husband went to their residence in the gatehouse before the Hammonds went home. In the morning, she was the one who found the body in the pool. She dialed 911 even before she woke Peter Carrington."

"He would have had time to dispose of the magazine before the squad car got there, but what would be the point of doing that?" Krause asked. "It would be easy enough to get another copy of it. I don't get the significance."

Greco could see that the prosecutor was becoming irritated. He got to his feet immediately. "I must not detain you," he said. "I simply wanted to be sure I had the facts straight."

"Of course." Krause stood up and reached out her hand. "Mr. Greco, you've pulled one rabbit out of the hat. I don't mind telling you that we are following every possible lead to see if we can track down Grace Carrington's lover. Even if we find him, his testimony won't be enough to convict Carrington of her murder, but it certainly gives him a strong motive. The more we know about that situation, the better the chance we have of making Peter come clean, and negotiate a plea."

This isn't about who the lover was, Greco thought. It's about the magazine. He had come to this office today for one reason only — to confirm the fact that the magazine had disappeared either just before or just after Grace Carrington had drowned.

46

It's a time when Kay needs me most, yet she's distancing herself from me, Maggie thought as she aimlessly puttered around the house. If only she'd listened to me and not married Peter Carrington in the first place. Thank God he's in jail, where he can't hurt her. It just made me sick to see the tape the cops made of him when he was outside the Althorps' house, and especially the way he leaped up and attacked that police officer. I hope they put him away for the rest of his life.

It's nine o'clock, Maggie thought. Kay's an early-morning riser — I'll give her a call. Yesterday when I phoned, the lawyers were there, but then she didn't call me back later.

Heartsick at the distance growing between her and her granddaughter, Maggie dialed Kay's cell phone. There was no answer. Maybe she's with the lawyers again, she decided. I'll try the house. This time Jane Barr answered. "Mrs. Carrington stayed in bed this morning," she told Maggie. "I went upstairs to make sure she was all right, and she said she hadn't felt well during the night. The lawyers aren't going to be here today."

"Tell her whether she likes it or not, I'm coming over for dinner," Maggie said firmly.

The front doorbell began ringing as she replaced the receiver. Through the glass panel of the door she could see two men standing outside. When they saw her, both held up IDs identifying them as detectives from the prosecutor's office.

Reluctantly, Maggie opened the door and invited them in. "Mrs. O'Neil," the older detective began politely, "we understand that at the time Jonathan Lansing disappeared, the contents of his home were moved here. By any chance, were there any records or files from his office included in that move, and, if so, do you still have them?"

Maggie thought of her cluttered attic. "I gave away his clothes," she hedged. "The furniture I used. It was better than mine, and after all, his daughter, Kay, was living with me. It made it a nicer home for her." I wonder if they think I stole the furniture, she asked herself nervously. Maybe I should have paid taxes on it.

"Of course, we can understand that," the

younger detective said reassuringly. "Were there any business records or personal files belonging to Jonathan Lansing that you may have kept?"

"That's the same thing Kay asked me about. There is one of those old three-drawer steel cabinets that was in the room Jonathan used as an office. It's on the floor of the attic now with my old couch on top of it. Kay says she is going to come over and take a look through it, but I'll have to get someone strong to move things around so that there's room for the couch someplace else, and then he'll have to stand the file upright."

"If you'll give us your consent to examine the contents of that file, we'll be happy to place it where it's convenient for Mrs. Carrington to go through it. You don't have to consent, but we would like to see it."

"I don't see anything wrong with that," Maggie said.

She led the detectives upstairs, then apologized at the mess and the dust. "I always mean to get up here and get rid of things," she explained, as, with minimal effort, they cleared the space around the file and righted it, "but you know how it is. There are some things you never get around to doing. Kay says I'm a pack rat, and she's right."

The detectives did not respond. Each man

had taken a folder from the top drawer and was flipping through the contents.

With growing unease, Maggie watched them, wondering if she had done the right thing in letting them come up here. Maybe I should have checked with Kay, she thought. I don't want her to have another reason to be upset with me. On the other hand, if Peter Carrington was the one who killed her father, and they find some proof here, she'd be crazy to waste another minute of her life worrying about him.

"Look at this," the older detective said to his partner as he handed him a sheet of paper. It was a copy of a note and a landscaping sketch sent to Peter Carrington by Jonathan Lansing. The note read:

Dear Peter,

It seems a pity not to complete the project. As you probably know, your father and I discussed creating a simple plan for the grounds beyond the fence. Since I am no longer in his employ, and since I believe Mrs. Elaine Carrington does not care to have me in contact with your father, I wonder if you would be so kind as to pass on this design to him. I enclose the card of a landscaper I know who could execute this plan to your father's specifications.

I have enjoyed our conversations very much, and I wish you well.

Jonathan Lansing

As the younger detective read the note, the older one looked at Maggie. "Never apologize for being a pack rat, Mrs. O'Neil," he said.

47

Conner Banks sat across the table from his client in the small room reserved for lawyer-inmate conferences in the Bergen County Jail. He had been the member of the legal team chosen to review Peter Carrington's options with him.

"Peter, this is what we're facing," he said. "The good news is that while you've been a 'person of interest' in the death of your late wife, Grace, that is a separate issue. It will not be allowed to be mentioned at this trial since they can't connect it to the earlier deaths. However, the fact that the remains of both Susan Althorp and Jonathan Lansing were found on the grounds of your estate means that the prosecution will attempt to try the cases together. Even so, the bottom line is that we think they will not be able to prove guilt beyond a reasonable doubt."

"What constitutes 'reasonable doubt,' given everything that is piling up around me?" Peter asked, quietly. "I was the last person to see Susan alive. Maria Valdez is going to testify that the shirt I swear I put in the hamper was never there, and that my father paid her to keep her mouth shut. Now you tell me that Kay's father sent me a note with a landscaping design for the area beyond the fence, where Susan's body was found. If I had been guilty of killing Susan, I would have been terrified, because executing that design would have meant her body *would* be found. That would give me reason to get rid of Jonathan Lansing. There's no way out for me."

"Peter, I agree that it looks bad, but listen to me. Somebody else may have intercepted that letter. They have no proof that you received it."

"They have proof my father gave five thousand dollars to Maria Valdez."

"Peter, it's your word against hers that your dress shirt was in the hamper, and don't forget she's refuting her own previous sworn statement. Juries are skeptical of people who change their testimony. And yes, your father gave her a check, but we'll line up other instances of his spontaneous generosity to show that he might have been sympathetic and was helping her because Maria told him her mother was dying."

"The jury won't believe that," Peter said.

"Peter, just remember, we only need to make one juror uncertain of your guilt beyond a reasonable doubt to get a hung jury. If we can't get an outright acquittal, I absolutely believe we *will* get that for you."

"A hung jury — that's not much to hope for." Peter Carrington looked straight at his lawyer, glanced away, then, with an obvious effort, looked back at him. "I did not think I was capable of violence toward another human being," he said, carefully choosing each word as he spoke. "What I did to that police officer makes me understand that simply isn't true. Has Vince Slater told you that I assaulted him when I was about sixteen?"

"Yes, he has."

"What will happen if, despite your best efforts, I do not get a hung jury, and I am not acquitted?"

"Peter, the prosecution would ask for and probably get two consecutive life sentences. You would never get out."

"Suppose somehow they are able to tie me to Grace's death. What would I get in that case?"

"That would undoubtedly be another life sentence. But Peter, there's no way anyone is going to prove that you killed her."

"Conner, give me some credit. There's no such thing as 'no way.' Until now I have absolutely believed in my innocence. I'm not so sure anymore. I do know that I would never willingly harm another human being, but I did serious bodily harm to that cop the other night. I did the same thing years ago to Vince. Maybe I've done it in other instances, too."

Conner Banks felt his mouth go dry. "Peter, you don't have to answer this next question and think carefully before you do. Do you actually believe that, in an altered state of mind, you might have killed Susan Althorp and Jonathan Lansing?"

"I don't know. The other night I thought I was looking for Susan's body on the lawn of her parents' home. I had to make certain that she was dead. Was that a dream, or was I reliving what happened? I'm not sure."

Banks had seen Carrington's expression on the faces of other clients, people who knew they were almost certainly facing a lifetime in prison.

"There's more." Peter's voice lowered and became halting. "Did Kay tell you that the night we got home from our honeymoon, she saw me sleepwalking at the pool, and that I had my arm in the water, under the cover?"

"No, she did not."

"Again, maybe it was just a nightmare, or maybe I was reenacting something that actually took place. I don't know."

"Peter, none of this will come out in court. We'll make a case for reasonable doubt."

"You can keep your reasonable doubt. I want my defense to be that if I committed those crimes, I was sleepwalking and unaware of what I was doing."

Banks stared at him. "No! Absolutely not! There isn't a prayer in hell that you wouldn't be convicted with that defense. You'd be handing the prosecutor your head on a platter."

"And I say there isn't a prayer in hell that I won't be convicted with the defense you're planning. And even if there is, see it my way. My trial will get plenty of publicity. This is a chance to let the world understand that if you are cursed with sleepwalking, and unknowingly commit a crime, you may not be responsible."

"You can't be serious!"

"I have never been more serious in my life. I've had Vince look up the statistics for me. Under British and Canadian law, a crime committed during sleepwalking is called a 'noninsane automatism.' According to the laws in those countries, the deed does not make a man guilty unless his mind is guilty. If at the time of the offense there is an absence of mental control so that any action carried out was automatic, then in law the defense of automatism is possible."

"Peter, listen to me. That may be true in British and Canadian law, but it doesn't work here. I'd be a fool on a fool's errand if I went to court with that defense. We have two cases in this country in which men were convicted of killing people they loved very much while sleepwalking. One man bludgeoned his wife to death, then threw her body in the pool. Another drove miles to his in-laws' home. He was devoted to them, but he was also under great stress. He brutally beat his father-in-law and stabbed his mother-in-law to death. He woke up as he was driving home, went straight to the nearest police station, and told them that something terrible must have happened because he was covered in blood and had a vague memory of seeing a woman's face."

"Vince told me about those cases, Conner. Don't forget, I have lived as a 'person of interest' since I was twenty years old. Even if I'm acquitted, I'll be treated as a pariah who beat the system and got away with murder. I'm not prepared to live like that any longer. If you won't defend me on those grounds,

I'll find someone who will."

There was a long silence, then Banks asked. "Have you talked to Kay about this?"

"Yes, I have."

"Then she agrees to it, I gather?"

"Reluctantly, but yes. And she's also agreed to another condition."

"Which is?"

"I'll let her stand by me during the trial. But after I'm convicted, and I understand that I probably will be, she has agreed to divorce me and begin a new life for herself. If she had not agreed to that, I would have refused to allow her to visit me anymore."

48

Maybe it sounds crazy, but after the first day or two, I began to welcome solitude at night. If Peter couldn't be with me, then I wanted to be alone. There was something about Jane and Gary Barr that was making me uneasy. Jane was always fussing over me. I knew she was concerned because I was feeling so rotten, but I still didn't want to feel as though they were observing me like an insect under a microscope.

After the visit from the detectives, Maggie came rushing over in tears, trying to explain that she never would have let the detectives up to the attic if she thought I'd be upset.

I owe her far too much, and love her far too much, to have made her feel any worse than she did. As the lawyers explained to me, even though that letter from my father had been addressed to Peter, there was no proof that it had not been opened by someone else. During the search of the house, another copy of that design had been found in his father's files.

I managed to reassure Maggie that I wasn't avoiding her, and made her realize why I couldn't let her live with me. She finally agreed that she was comfortable in her own home, in her own easy chair, in her own bed. As I pointed out to her, it was safe here — security guards were ever present at the gate, and on foot on the grounds. Unspoken was the fact that because Peter was in jail, she did not have to fear for my personal safety.

My visits with Peter were heartbreaking. He was allowing himself to become so convinced that he was guilty of the deaths of Susan and my father that his interest in his defense began to take on a curious detachment. The grand jury had voted to indict him on both murders, and the trial had been set for October.

The lawyers, chiefly Conner Banks, were conferring with him in jail, so I now saw less of them. I did begin to hear from people I worked with at the library, and other friends, both from around here and from Manhattan. They were all so careful in the way they spoke to me, solicitous but embarrassed, not knowing what to say.

"I'm so sorry about your father. I would have

gone to the service if I had known where it was . . ."

"Kay, if there's anything I can do, I mean maybe you feel like having dinner, or going to a movie . . ."

I knew what was going through the heads of these good people: it's tough to deal with this kind of thing in any rational way. I was Mrs. Peter Carrington, wife of one of the wealthiest men in the country, and I was also Mrs. Peter Carrington, wife of a double — or maybe even triple — killer.

I put off any get-together dates. I knew even the simplest lunch would be uncomfortable for all of us. The one person I regretted not seeing, however, was Glenn. He sounded so normal when he called me: "Kay, you must be going through hell," he said.

Once again, it was good to hear his voice. I didn't try to pretend. "Yes, I am."

"Kay, this may sound dopey, but I've been trying to figure what I'd want if I were in your boots. And I have the answer."

"And it is?"

"Dinner with an old pal like me. Look, I know that's all I've ever been to you, and it's okay. You lead the conversation."

He meant it. Glenn knew it was never "there" between us for me. Actually, I never thought it was "there" for him, either. I still didn't. I'd love to have taken him up on his dinner offer, but, on the other hand, I couldn't even imagine how I would feel if I could reverse positions with Peter, then read that he'd been seen having dinner with a former girlfriend. "Glenn, it sounds so tempting, but it's not a good idea," I told him, and then was surprised to hear myself say, "at least, not yet."

At what point did I begin to believe that Peter was right, that in an altered state, he had committed the crimes he'd been accused of committing? I began to reason that if he believed it himself, how could *I* not accept it? And, of course, that consideration tore me in half.

I began to picture my father in the last few weeks of his life. Always the perfectionist, he'd been eager to see the last part of his overall design for the estate completed, even though he could not do the job himself.

According to the police report, the blow on his head had been so hard that his skull had been caved in. Had Peter been the one to raise some heavy object and inflict that blow?

Then good memories of my father flooded my mind, memories I had always tried to suppress because I had believed myself abandoned by him.

Memories like: Sunday mornings, when, after church, he would take me to Van Saun Park for a pony ride.

. . . The two of us cooking together in our kitchen. His telling me that Maggie was no cook, that for sheer survival my mother was forced to learn how to follow recipes. Maggie still isn't a cook, Dad, I thought.

. . . The note he had written to Peter: "I have enjoyed our conversations very much, and I wish you well."

. . . The day I had sneaked in this house and gone up to the chapel.

During this time alone, I began to go up to the chapel almost every day. It hasn't changed in all these years. The same nicked statue of the Virgin Mary is there, as are the table that must have served as an altar, and the two rows of pews. I brought a new electric votive candle to put in front of the statue. I would sit there for ten or fifteen minutes, half praying, half remembering that brief quarrel I had overheard that day, twenty-two-and-a-half years ago.

It was there that a possibility began to take root in my mind. It had never occurred to me that perhaps Susan Althorp was the woman I had heard begging for money. Her family was wealthy. I had always read that she had a big trust fund in her own name.

But suppose it *was* Susan? Then who was the man who had snarled at her, "I heard that song before"? After she left the chapel, the man had whistled the last line of the song. Even as a child, I had recognized how angry he was.

It was in the chapel that my desperate hope took root, a hope that maybe I could find another solution, one that would solve the crimes Peter was accused of committing.

I was afraid to give Peter even a hint of what I was thinking. If he began to believe me, and decided that he was completely innocent, then his next thought would be that whoever was guilty might still be nearby. And then he would start worrying about me.

As it was, although he was actively cooperating in preparing his own defense, I could see that the lawyers had convinced him it was hopeless to expect anything but a "guilty" verdict. On my visits to him, he began urging me to move away, to divorce him quietly. "Kay, in your own way, you're as imprisoned as I am," he would say. "I know perfectly well that you can't go anywhere without people looking at you and talking about you."

I loved him so dearly. He was in a cramped jail cell, and worrying that I was holed up in a mansion. I reminded him we had a deal. I could visit him in jail and be with him at the trial. "So don't let's ruin our little time together by talking about my leaving you," I told him. Of course, I had no intention of keeping my part of our so-called deal. If Peter was convicted, I knew I would never divorce or abandon him, or stop believing in his innocence.

But he didn't stop bringing up that subject. "Please, Kay, I beg of you, get on with your life," he said to me during a visit in late February.

I had something to tell him, something I had known with certainty for a few days now, but hadn't yet decided the best time to tell him. Then I recognized that there would never be a *best* time, but that this was the *right* time. "I *am* getting on with my life, Peter," I said. "I'm having our baby."

49

The part-time job that Pat Jennings had taken at the Walker Art Gallery had begun to make her something of a celebrity. Now that Peter Carrington had not only been charged with murder, but had been caught on tape bail-jumping and assaulting a cop, all her friends were anxious to have any tidbits of gossip that she could pass on about anyone in the Carrington family.

Pat was closemouthed with everyone except Trish, her best friend for the last twenty years. They had been assigned to the same dorm as freshmen in college, and had thought it a riot that each had chosen to be known by a different variation of their shared name, Patricia.

Now Trish worked in the business office of the tony department store Bergdorf Goodman, located at Fifth Avenue and Fifty-seventh Street, only a block away from the gallery. Once a week, the two women grabbed a quick lunch together, and, in deepest confidence, Pat caught her up on the gossip as she heard it.

She confided that she thought Richard Walker was having an affair with a young new artist, Gina Black. "He had a cocktail party for her and it didn't draw flies. When she stops in at the gallery, I can tell she's crazy about him. I feel sorry for her because my bet is that she won't last. From the way he talks, he's had plenty of girlfriends over the years. Think about it — he has two ex-wives, and both those marriages didn't last long enough to have the tea towels washed. I bet both wives got sick of his womanizing and gambling."

The next week, Pat discussed Elaine Carrington: "Richard told me that his mother has been staying in her New York apartment most of the time. Her feelings are hurt because she thinks that Peter Carrington's new wife, Kay, really doesn't want her stopping in the mansion unless she's specifically invited to be there.

"I don't think Richard has gone to New Jersey much, either," she continued. "He told me that he understands how difficult it must be for Kay, knowing that in all likelihood her husband killed her father, even though he may not remember it. Richard said that he believes it must have been like the way Peter attacked that cop. Well, we both saw the tape on television. You could tell Peter Carrington was absolutely out of it. He looked scary."

"He sure did," Trish agreed. "What a shame to marry a guy with all that money and then find out he's insane. Other than that young artist, are there hints of anything new in Richard's love life?"

"Well, there are hints, but I'm not sure it's anything new. There's a woman who's been calling him who must be an old flame. Her name is Alexandra Lloyd."

"Alexandra Lloyd. That's a fancy name," Trish commented. "Unless it's one she made up. Maybe she's in show business. Did you ever meet her?"

"No. My bet is that she's an artist. Anyhow, he's ignoring her calls."

Three days later, Pat Jennings couldn't wait until their next lunch to talk to Trish, so she called her. "Richard is an absolute wreck," she whispered into the phone. "I know he's had a couple of big losses on the ponies. This morning his mother stopped in to see him. When I got here they were in his office with the door closed, and boy, were they going at it! He was telling her that he absolutely had to have money, and she was screaming she didn't have it. Then he yelled something about how she knew perfectly well where she could get it, and she screamed, *'Richard, don't make me play that card.'* "

"What did she mean?" Trish asked breathlessly.

"I have *no* idea," Pat admitted, "but I'd sure love to know. If I find out, I'll call you first thing."

50

The nurse who met him at the door of Gladys Althorp's bedroom cautioned Nicholas Greco not to stay too long. "She's very weak," the nurse told him. "Talking tires her."

His former client was lying in a hospital bed that had been set up next to her regular queen-sized bed. Her hands were resting on the coverlet, and Greco noticed that the wedding ring she had always worn was missing.

Is her finger too thin now to keep the ring from sliding off, or is this one final rejection of her husband? he wondered.

Gladys Althorp's eyes were closed, but she opened them a moment after Greco reached the side of the bed. Her lips moved and her voice was very low when she greeted him.

Greco got right to the point. "Mrs. Althorp, I didn't want to disturb you, but there is something I'd like to follow up on. It might even have to do with someone who may have helped Peter Carrington hide Susan's body."

"I heard the police sirens the night he came here. I made the nurse take me to the window. I saw them drag him into the car . . . and . . ." Gladys Althorp's chest began to heave as she gasped for air.

The nurse rushed to her side. "Mrs. Althorp, please don't try to talk. Just breathe slowly."

I should not be here, Greco thought. He laid his own hand over the woman's emaciated hand. "I am so sorry. I should never have troubled you, Mrs. Althorp."

"Don't go. You came for a reason. Tell me."

Greco knew that it was best to be blunt. "I would very much like to know the names of your daughter's best friends, the ones who used to go with her to parties when Ambassador Althorp had them chauffeured."

If Gladys Althorp was surprised at the request, she did not show it. "There were three other girls. They went to Elisabeth Morrow School with Susan."

Mrs. Althorp was speaking more slowly, giving herself time to take a long breath between every word. "Susan's closest friend was Sarah Kennedy. She married Stuart North. Vernie Bauer and Lenore Salem were the others. I'm afraid I can't . . ." She sighed and closed her eyes.

"Mr. Greco, I really think you must not ask any more questions right now," the nurse said firmly.

Susan would be only forty now, Greco thought. The others would be the same age, within a year or two. He would expect their parents to be in the midsixties to midseventies age range. He wanted to ask Susan's mother if the families of those women still lived locally, but instead he nodded to the nurse and turned to go. Then he saw Gladys Althorp open her eyes again.

"The girls were all at Susan's funeral," Gladys Althorp said. A hint of a smile played at the corners of her lips. "They used to call themselves the four musketeers . . ."

"Then they still live here?" Greco asked quickly.

"Sarah does. When she married Stuart, they bought the house next door. They're living there now."

When Greco left the Althorp home, he doubted that he would ever see Gladys Althorp again. On one hand, he chided himself for disturbing her even for those few minutes. On the other hand, however, he recognized that he felt a growing sense of uneasiness about how neatly everything had fallen into place, which made him believe that there were important pieces of the puzzle that still had not been put in place.

Some of the facts that did not add up were beginning to command all his attention. He had come to the conclusion that Peter Carrington must have had help in hiding Susan's body until after the cadaver dogs had completed their search.

And if Peter *did* kill Jonathan Lansing, he must have had someone follow him to the place miles up the Hudson where he left Lansing's car, Greco mused.

And there was significance to the missing copy of *People* magazine that had been on the table the night Grace Carrington died. He thought he knew what that might have been about. Nancy Hammond saw Grace tear that page out of the magazine. Her husband, Jeffrey, claimed he hadn't noticed her do that. Nancy Hammond said that the attention of the other guests was diverted by Peter's sudden arrival home. She thinks that she is the only one who saw Grace tear out the page and jam it in her pocket.

Did someone who later took that magazine believe that page was still in the magazine?

If so, that would answer a lot of questions.

It would also raise another question, however. Peter Carrington did not know about the magazine. According to all of them —

Elaine, her son Richard, Vincent Slater, and the Hammonds, Peter went straight upstairs after he took the glass out of Grace's hand and berated her for drinking.

Greco looked at his watch; it was five o'clock. He picked up his cell phone and dialed information. He had been afraid that the phone number for Stuart and Sarah North would be unlisted, but it was not. He heard a computerized voice saying, "We are dialing 201-555-1570 for you. If you wish to send a text message . . ."

The phone in the North home was answered on the second ring. The woman's tone of voice was warm. Greco hurriedly introduced himself and explained that he had just left Gladys Althorp. "I was hired to reopen the investigation into Susan's death. Are you Sarah Kennedy North?" he asked.

"Yes, I am. And you must be the investigator who located the maid. The ambassador told us about you."

"Perhaps this is an impossible request, but I am in my car outside the Althorp home. I know you live next door. May I stop in now, for just a few minutes? Mrs. Althorp said that you were Susan's best friend. I would very much like to ask you a few questions about Susan."

"I *was* Susan's best friend. Of course you

can stop in now. We're the first house to the right of the Althorps."

Three minutes later, Nicholas Greco was walking along the path from the street to the North home. Sarah North was waiting for him, holding the door partially open.

She was a tall woman with wide-set eyes, dark-red hair, and had the look of an athlete about her. She was dressed casually in a sweater and jeans. Her warm smile seemed genuine as she invited him into the study off the foyer. Greco's immediate impression of the interior of the home was that it had been furnished with taste and money.

"My husband doesn't get home until six thirty," North explained as she sat down on the couch and indicated the chair next to it for Greco. "His office is way downtown in Manhattan, and he insists on driving back and forth. During rush hours, as I'm sure you know, it can take forever."

"I understand that in the early twentieth century, Englewood was referred to as 'the Bedroom of Wall Street.' "

"It was, and to a certain extent that's still true. How is Mrs. Althorp doing?"

"Not well, I'm afraid. Mrs. North, I have located the maid whose testimony may help convict Peter Carrington, but I am not satisfied. Some things don't add up, and I now feel he must have had an accomplice. I am interested in that year before Susan died. I understand that, at times, her father hired a chauffeur to drive her and her friends around. Weren't you all old enough to drive yourselves?"

"Sure we were, but if we were going to a party that was any distance away, the ambassador insisted that Susan be driven. My parents loved that idea, of course. They didn't want us riding with teenage guys who might have had a couple of drinks, and would then speed on the way home. Of course, a lot of the time we all were at college, and the ambassador couldn't control what we did there. But at home that was the way it was."

"Yet the night of the party at the Carrington estate, he allowed Susan to be driven home by Peter Carrington."

"He loved Peter. He trusted him. He felt Peter was different. In the summer, when the rest of us were at the club playing tennis or golf, Peter had a shirt and tie on and was at the office with his father."

"So when you were chauffeured, it was Susan and you and two other girls in the car?"

"Yes. Susan sat in front with Gary, and Vernie and Lenore and I sat in the back."

"Gary?" Greco did not want Sarah North

to suspect that this was the very person he had come to learn more about.

"Gary Barr. He and his wife would help with dinners when the Althorps had guests. He was also the chauffeur whenever we were driven somewhere."

"What was his manner? Did he become friendly?"

"Oh, yes. Susan referred to him as her pal."

"Was there any chance that there was a . . ." Greco hesitated, "a *romantic* interest there? Did Susan have what in my day we called a 'crush' on him?"

"On *Gary!* Oh, no, *nothing* like that. She said he made her feel good, but by that she meant safe, secure."

"Mrs. North, I hope you understand that I don't wish to pry when I ask questions that you, as Susan's friend, may not want to answer. But I am just not satisfied. I believe that Peter Carrington must have had help in disposing of Susan's body. Is there anything you can tell me about Susan that may help me to understand why she would have left her home that night after telling her parents she was in?"

"I've spent twenty-two years trying to figure that out," Sarah North said frankly. "It didn't ring true that Peter would be a party to her deceiving her parents. In fact, until I heard the police sirens the night he showed up in the Althorps' yard, I had doubted his guilt. But that night we grabbed our robes and ran outside to see what was going on. I saw the cop he punched. He was badly hurt. It makes sense that the same sort of thing may have happened if he hurt Susan while he was sleepwalking."

"Were you at the party at the Carrington home that night?"

"We all were."

"How late did you stay?"

"Till 12:30 or quarter of one. I had to be home by one o'clock."

"But Susan was Cinderella that night. She was told to be home at midnight."

"I could tell at the dinner that night that her father was furious at her. I think he was just being mean."

"Why was he being mean?"

"I don't know."

"Was Susan upset by her father's attitude?"

"Yes. In fact, Susan was not herself all night. Although, you had to know her well to realize that."

"The ambassador has a reputation for having a very quick temper, doesn't he, Mrs. North?"

"When we were kids, we called him the diplo-NOT. We could always hear him yelling at Susan and her brothers. He's a pill."

"Have you ever wondered what he might have done if he had seen Susan sneaking out of the house?"

"I think he'd have killed her." Sarah North looked startled at her own words. "Of course, I didn't mean that literally."

"Of course you didn't," Greco assured her. He got up to leave. "You have been very kind. May I call you again if I feel it necessary?"

"Certainly. I don't think any of us will be happy until the entire truth comes out about both Susan's death and her father's death."

"Her father's! You mean Mrs. Carrington's father?"

"Yes." An expression of distress came over Sarah North's face. "Mr. Greco, Kay Carrington came to see me. She asked the same kinds of questions you've been asking. I promised her that I would not tell anyone she was here."

"You have my word that I will not reveal it to anyone, Mrs. North."

As Nicholas Greco walked back to his car, he realized he was deeply troubled. He found himself asking the two questions that he always asked himself in the process of solving a case: "Suppose?" "What if?"

Suppose Peter Carrington is completely innocent of any involvement in all three deaths?

What if there is someone else out there, someone connected to the Carringtons, who is the real killer? What would that person do if he learned that Peter Carrington's young wife was asking questions that might lead to the truth being uncovered?

Kay Carrington may not want to speak to me, but I *am* going to meet with her, Greco decided as he got in his car. She *must* be warned.

51

The fact that I was expecting a baby both thrilled and saddened Peter: "It's wonderful, Kay, but you must get plenty of rest. This terrible stress you're under could hurt both you *and* the baby. Oh, God, why did all this happen? Why can't I be home with you, taking care of you?"

He also had decided that the defense he had chosen would help explain him to our child: "Kay, when our child is growing up, I want him or her to understand that the crimes I probably committed happened when I had absolutely no control of myself."

He pressed the lawyers to make a motion to the court to have him tested at a sleep disorder center. He wanted to have it on record that he was, indeed, prone to sleepwalking, and that, while he was in that state, was unaware of his actions.

The issue became a battle between him and his legal staff. "To have it out in open court that sleepwalking is or may be your defense is the same as saying, 'Not guilty by reason of insanity,'" Conner Banks told Peter. "It's skywriting so everyone can see it. 'Guilty. I did it, but I can explain it.'"

"Make the motion," Peter told him.

It meant another day in court before Judge Smith. I pressed my hand against my abdomen, seeking comfort in that tiny being growing inside me, as I saw my child's father led into court once again, manacled and shackled, wearing his orange jail jumpsuit.

It was Conner Banks who made the argument. "Your Honor," he addressed the court, "I know these are extraordinary circumstances, and I am not denying that Mr. Carrington left his premises, which, on the surface, is a violation of the conditions of his bail."

Vincent Slater was sitting with me; I knew he did not approve of having the lawyers make this motion.

"However, Your Honor," Banks continued, "I believe that even the police reports explicitly detailed Peter Carrington's dazed condition at the time of his arrest. Subsequent tests have shown that there was no evidence of either alcohol or drugs in his system. It is imperative to our defense to have Mr. Carrington properly evaluated at a sleep disorder clinic at Pascack Valley Hospital. That would require an overnight stay in which his sleep patterns would be monitored."

"Imperative to our defense," Vincent whispered to me. "Those are the words that the media is going to leap on."

"We implore Your Honor to allow this test. We would be willing to post twenty-five million dollars in bail if this test is allowed. We recognize that it is not the Sheriff's responsibility to escort the defendant while he investigates possible defenses in his case, and so we would compensate the state for the salaries of the sheriff's officers assigned to guard him. We are also willing to retain a private security firm which will hire several retired police officers who will restrain Mr. Carrington if there should be any attempts to escape, which I assure you there will not be.

"Your Honor, one in two hundred people is a sleepwalker. The potential danger of a sleepwalker to himself and to others has not been recognized or understood by the general population. I doubt that many in this courtroom realize that sleepwalkers are not allowed to serve in the armed forces of the United States. The fear is that they may be a risk both to themselves and to others because they may have access to weapons or vehicles and are unaware of what they are doing when they move about while asleep."

Conner Banks's voice became stronger and firmer as he punched those last words home. Then, when he spoke again after a brief pause, his voice was quieter. "Allow Peter Carrington to establish once and for all that his brain waves indicate that he is the victim of sleepwalking disturbance. Give him this chance."

Judge Smith's face was impassive. I didn't know what to expect. But I knew what Peter was feeling, and it was satisfaction. He was getting his message out. He was beginning to try his own case in the media.

Banks and Markinson were worried; I could see it. During the recess following the request, they came over to talk to me. "The judge is not going to grant this request, and we've tipped our hand. There isn't a person in this room who doesn't think that this is just an insanity defense with a new twist."

The judge returned. He began by saying that in nearly twenty years as a criminal judge, he'd never had an application that included these kinds of circumstances. He said that while the state was concerned about the risk of flight, the prosecutor did not dispute the police report that indicated Mr. Carrington was in a dazed condition when apprehended on the Althorp lawn. He said that on the condition that a member of the defense counsel would always be present, and private security ready to restrain Peter if he attempted to leave, a twenty-four-hour stay at a sleep disorder center was approved.

Peter considered the judge's ruling a victory. His lawyers did not. I knew that even if the medical cause for his sleepwalking was confirmed by experts, it would not make a difference in the verdict at trial. So in that sense, it was a no-win.

After court recessed, I wanted to talk to Banks and Markinson, and asked them to meet me back at the house. Once again I received permission to visit Peter in the holding cell before leaving.

"I know you consider this a Pyrrhic victory, Kay," he said.

"There's only one victory, Peter," I told him fiercely. "We want you home with us. And it's going to happen."

"Oh, love, you look like Joan of Arc. Everything but the sword." For just a moment Peter's smile was genuine, a reminder of the look I saw when we were on our honeymoon.

I wanted so much to tell him that I was digging into every aspect of the evidence surrounding the deaths of Susan and my father, and that I was beginning with the premise that perhaps it had been Susan I overheard in the chapel that day. But I knew that to put those thoughts into words would have a negative effect — he'd only start worrying about me.

Instead, I told him that I was spending time going through the third floor of the mansion. "Peter, those rooms are a refined version of Maggie's attic," I said. "Who was the art collector?"

"My grandmother, I think, although my great-grandmother was responsible for some of it, too. Anything that's any good is on the walls downstairs. My father had everything appraised way back."

"Who collected the china? There's a ton of it up there."

"My great-grandmother collected most of it."

"There's a set of Limoges that's really gorgeous. It's still in the crate. I unpacked a few pieces. I absolutely love the pattern. That's the china I want to use at our dinner parties."

The guard was standing in the doorway. "Mrs. Carrington."

"I know." I looked at Peter. "Of course, if you don't like that pattern, we'll look at the others. Plenty to choose from."

I could see the expression of sympathy in the guard's eyes as I passed him. He might as well have been shouting, "Lady, he's no more going to eat off that china than I am." I wish he *had* said it aloud. I would have told him that when Peter comes home, I'll invite him for dinner.

Conner Banks and Walter Markinson were already at the mansion when Vincent dropped me off. There was a meeting later that day of the board of directors of Carrington Enterprises, and he was sitting in as Peter's representative. Peter now referred to Vincent Slater as "my eyes and ears." He had no voting power, of course, but he did keep Peter apprised of everything that was going on in the multifaceted corporation.

As usual, Jane Barr had brought the lawyers to the dining room, where I joined them. I decided to share with them my growing belief that it was possible that Susan Althorp had been the woman I overheard in the chapel twenty-two years ago.

They had not known about my escapade as a six-year-old, but when they did, their response stunned me. They looked horrified. "Kay, do you know what you are saying?" Banks asked.

"I am saying that it may have been Susan in the chapel that day, and that she may have

311

been blackmailing someone."

"Maybe she was blackmailing your husband," Markinson snapped. "Have you any *idea* what the prosecutor could do with that information?"

"What are you talking about?" I asked, genuinely baffled.

"What we're talking about," Conner Banks said gravely, "is that, if your supposition is true, you have just provided a motive for Peter to kill Susan."

"Did you ever tell Peter about being in the chapel and overhearing that conversation?" Markinson asked.

"Yes, I did. Why?"

"When did you tell him, Kay?" Banks demanded.

I was beginning to feel as if I were being cross-examined by two hostile prosecutors. "I told him the night of the literacy benefit reception in this house. My grandmother fell. Peter went with me to the hospital and waited until she was all right, then brought me home. He came in for a while and we talked."

"That reception was held on December sixth, as I recall," Markinson said, flicking through his notes.

"That's right." I was beginning to feel defensive.

"And you and Peter Carrington were married on January eighth, less than five weeks later?"

"Yes." I realized I was becoming both frustrated and angry. "Will you please tell me what you're driving at?" I demanded.

"What we're driving at, Kay," Conner Banks said — and now his tone was both serious and regretful — "is that we've all wondered about your whirlwind romance. Now you've just given the reason for it. If that was Susan Althorp in the chapel that day, and she was blackmailing Peter, the minute you told him you had overheard the quarrel, you became a threat.

"He couldn't take the chance that you might talk about that encounter to someone else who would put two and two together. Remember, that reception was right after *Celeb* magazine did that big story on him. By rushing you into marriage, he made you unavailable as a witness in case he was ever brought to trial. He could invoke the marital privilege in court, and besides that, he probably worked to make you fall in love with him so that emotionally you'd never give him up."

As I listened, I become so enraged that if I had had something to throw at both of them, I would have done it. Instead I shouted at them. "Get out! Get out and don't come back. I'd rather have the *prosecutor* defending my husband than either one of you. You don't believe that even if he *did* kill Susan and my father, he did it while he was unaware of what he was doing. Now you're saying that his marrying me was pure calculation, just a way to shut me up. Go to hell, both of you!"

They got up to leave. "Kay," Banks said quietly, "if you go to a doctor, and he finds a cancer, but tells you that you're doing just fine, he's a liar. The only way we can defend Peter is to know every possible factor that could influence a jury. You've just delivered a blockbuster that fortunately we are not obliged to share with the prosecutor because it's something that *we* uncovered. We only have to tell the prosecutor if we plan to use it as defense evidence at the trial. Obviously, we won't do that. But for the love of God, please don't tell anyone else what you've just told us."

The fight went out of me. "I already have," I said. "The night Peter came home after he was arraigned."

"You told someone you thought that it might have been Susan in the chapel? Who heard you say that?"

"Elaine and Richard and Vincent Slater

were here. I didn't say I thought it might have been Susan. In fact, I told them I didn't know who it was. Elaine even joked that it might have been her and Peter's father because they had been fighting all day about the money she was spending on the party."

"That's a relief. But never mention your visit to the chapel again to anyone. If one of them brings it up, stress the fact that you have no idea who was there because in truth you *don't* know."

I saw the two lawyers exchange glances. "We'll have to talk to Peter about this," Banks said. "I'd like to persuade him to cancel that sleep center business. His only prayer of ever getting home is 'reasonable doubt.'"

I had confided to the lawyers that I was expecting a baby. As they left, Markinson said "Maybe now that he knows he's going to become a father, he'll let us take control of his defense and have a shot at getting him acquitted."

52

Nicholas Greco sat in the reception room of the Joined-Hands Fund, a charity created to benefit the victims of disasters. Jeffrey Hammond was vice president of the organization, and according to Greco's research, his chief responsibility was not to give away money, but to raise it.

The offices of the charity were in the new Time Warner Center on Columbus Circle in Manhattan, an expensive address that certainly added to the overhead, Greco thought. Hammond made one hundred and fifty thousand dollars a year, a princely salary to average Americans, but not so for those who had a child in a prep school that cost forty thousand dollars a year.

Jeffrey's wife, Nancy, worked part-time in the local congressman's office in New Jersey. Without knowing her actual salary, Greco knew that the amount had to be minimal.

He knew also that the congressman's own salary was far too low to allow him to be generous to his staff. It was no wonder that, without personal wealth, many members of congress shared apartments in Washington.

All these thoughts were going through Greco's mind as he sat waiting until the perky young receptionist invited him into Hammond's office. Ninety-nine percent of receptionists were born cheerful, he thought, as he walked down the corridor.

The smile wrinkles at the corners of Jeffrey Hammond's eyes were not in evidence today. His greeting had a forced heartiness to it, and his palm was slightly damp when he shook Greco's hand and invited him to sit down. Then he made sure the door to his office was tightly closed before he went back behind his desk and settled in his swivel chair.

"Mr. Hammond, I asked to see you in your office because I thought it better not to discuss the subject I want to raise in front of your wife," he began.

Hammond nodded without replying.

"I have done a little homework, shall we call it, and find that Grace Carrington had been a great supporter of your charitable fund."

"Mrs. Carrington was very generous to

many charities." His voice was carefully neutral.

"Of course. However, she was chairman of your fund for two years, and helped to raise a considerable amount of money, all of which was very beneficial for your position here. To be frank, your job depends on your success in bringing in donations, does it not?"

"I'd like to think that my job is to raise money because that money benefits so many needy people, Mr. Greco."

Perhaps, Greco thought. "Peter Carrington did not attend the many formal dinners that his wife enjoyed, did he?" he asked.

"Peter hated them. He didn't mind what Grace donated to those events as long as he didn't have to attend."

"Then, for several years, you were her escort of choice at a number of these affairs?"

"Yes."

"What did Mrs. Hammond think of that?"

"She thought of it as part of my job. She understood."

Greco sighed. "I think we are beating around the bush. I'm afraid you would not make a very good spy, Mr. Hammond. The inscrutable expression is not in your makeup. When I visited you at your home and we talked about Grace Carrington's death, I looked into your eyes and saw an expression that was nothing short of anguish."

Hammond looked past him. His voice a monotone, he said, "It's true. Grace and I were very much in love. In so many ways we were alike — good family background, good schools, and no money. She never loved Peter. She liked him well enough, and God knows she enjoyed his wealth. She was coming to terms with her drinking problem and wanted to overcome it. In fact, she had joined AA.

"If she had divorced Peter, she would have received a twenty-million-dollar settlement, wonderful money to you and me, but certainly the income on that sum would not have maintained the lifestyle she had come to love: the private jet, the palazzo in Tuscany, the apartment in Paris, all the trappings that Peter Carrington doesn't even bother with, except for the jet, which he uses for business."

"So you intended to have a long-term affair?"

"No. I decided I had to break it off. I know how my behavior must look to you, but believe it or not, I never wanted to be a gigolo. I loved Grace with all my heart, but I also recognized how unfair we were being to both Peter and Nancy."

Jeffrey Hammond bit his lip, got up, and walked to the window, turning his back on Greco. After a moment, he went on: "I called Grace and told her that it had to be ended. She hung up on me, but then called the next morning. She said that she was going to ask Peter for a divorce, that all his money wasn't, after all, what she wanted for the rest of her life. She joked that she was giving up a guy who has money for one who raises money. Peter was away on one of his long trips at the time. My son was graduating from grammar school. We agreed to wait a month before we told Peter and Nancy what we had decided. Before that happened, Grace realized she was pregnant."

"She was planning to divorce Peter before she knew she was pregnant?" Greco asked. "That was quite a change of heart."

"It was Grace's decision. She had been unhappy, and I guess decided that fantastic luxury wasn't compensation for feeling lonely and unfulfilled. But of course, learning that she was pregnant changed everything. She had had three miscarriages in the past and had given up hope of having a baby. But she realized that now, when she gave birth to Peter Carrington's child, she would have not only the baby she had wanted, but would be able to divorce Peter and still have the lifestyle she wanted. So prior to all that, I had been about to tell Nancy that I wanted my freedom, and Grace had been about to tell Peter the same thing. But then we decided to wait."

"Was there any chance that the baby Grace was carrying was yours?"

"Absolutely none. We took every possible precaution to make sure that didn't happen."

"Do you think your wife suspected your relationship with Grace?"

"Toward the end, yes, I think she did," Hammond admitted.

"I would believe that is true. Your wife seems to me to be a very astute woman. Yet she never challenged you about it, either before or after Grace Carrington's death?"

"Never. Early in our marriage, Nancy told me that her father had had a couple of affairs. She believed that her mother was right to pretend she wasn't aware of them. When he was in his fifties he settled down, and he and his wife had a good life together. I think after Grace died, Nancy was hoping that she and I would get closer again."

"Had Grace been drinking much during her pregnancy?"

"In the beginning, yes, but she was trying to stop. She had not had a single drink for the month before she died."

"And then, in the presence of other people, the night of the dinner party, she fell off the wagon. Mr. Hammond, if, as you have just suggested, your wife was aware of your affair, is it possible that she spiked Grace's club soda that night?"

"Unlikely, but I guess it's possible. Somebody did, that's for sure. Grace would never have risked drinking in front of Elaine and Vincent Slater. Either one of them would have told Peter — she knew that."

"You have told me that you went home minutes after Peter went up to bed. Were the gates in the driveway open?"

"Yes. Of course, they can be closed, but they seldom were, even at night. I doubt if Peter and Grace even remembered to turn on the alarm system half the time."

Greco wondered if that was really true, or if Hammond was indicating, for some reason of his own, that both the grounds and the house were easily accessible. "You would have gone home about what time?" he asked.

"A little after eleven. As you have seen, we live quite close to the Carringtons, even though we're not in the estate section of town."

"What did you do after you got home?"

"I went up to bed. Nancy wasn't tired and

stayed downstairs to read."

"Do you remember what time she came to bed?"

Jeffrey Hammond's face turned red. "I wouldn't know," he said. "We had had a pretty big row, and I was sleeping in my son's room. He was away at a sleepover with a friend."

"You have been more than candid with me, Mr. Hammond," Greco said. "Frankly, I wonder why."

"I'll tell you why." Suddenly Jeffrey Hammond's voice was filled with the controlled fury Greco had heard earlier when he expressed the wish that the death penalty would be kept in New Jersey. "I *loved* Grace. We could have had a lifetime of happiness together. I want her killer found. If there's one thing I *don't* have it's a motive for killing her. I think you can see that, so I don't have to worry about being a suspect in her death. Maybe she got up, went outside, and lost her balance at the edge of the pool. I know that's possible. But if someone *did* take her life, I want that person found and convicted, even if it means publicly acknowledging our relationship, with all that implies. I love my son, but not enough to let a beautiful woman's life be snuffed out by someone who gets away with it."

"Do *you* think Peter Carrington killed Grace?"

"I do and I don't. Not over the issue of the money — that wouldn't have mattered to him. Peter is not his father's son in that respect. I don't think he'd kill her out of pride, either, the cuckolded-husband outrage. I just don't see Peter doing that. He was frustrated rather than furious when he grabbed the glass out of her hand. From what I know now, I do think it's possible he might have killed her in a sleepwalking state. After seeing that tape of him attacking that policeman, I think that's entirely possible."

"Do you also think it's possible that your wife went back to the mansion, perhaps woke up Grace, and suggested they go outside for a breath of air, and then pushed her into the pool?"

"Nancy never would have done that," Hammond said vehemently. "She's far too clearheaded to lose control that way. She'd never risk going to prison, because then she'd surely be separated from me and our son for good. The ultimate irony has been that she feels about me the way that I felt about Grace. She still hopes that in time I'll fall in love with her again."

"Will you, Mr. Hammond?"

"I only wish I could."

53

After Banks and Markinson left, I went upstairs and lay down to rest. It was almost five o'clock. I knew that a security guard was at the gate and another on the grounds. I had sent Jane home, telling her that I wasn't feeling well, and that I would heat some of her homemade soup later on. Thank God, she didn't protest. I think it must have been evident from my manner that I absolutely wanted to be alone.

Alone in this great, sprawling house from which, hundreds of years ago, in another country, a priest had been dragged out and hacked to death on the lawn. As I lay on the bed in our suite, I, too, felt like I had been hacked to pieces.

Was it possible, I asked myself, that my husband, Peter Carrington, had rushed me to the altar because he needed to make sure I could never testify against him?

Was it possible that all his declarations of

love were merely the calculations of a cold-blooded killer who, rather than take the chance of murdering me, married me instead?"

I thought of Peter standing in that holding cell, looking at me, with eyes that were alive with his love for me. Behind that expression, had he been mocking me, Kay Lansing, daughter of the landscaper, who had the colossal stupidity to think that he had fallen in love with her at first sight?

There are none so blind as those who will not see, I reminded myself.

I put my hand on my abdomen, a gesture that was becoming almost a reflex reaction to thoughts or situations I did not want to deal with. I was sure the baby was a boy, not because I preferred to have a boy rather than a girl, but because I just knew it was a boy. I was sure I was carrying Peter's son.

Peter *does* love me, I told myself fiercely. There is no other answer.

Am I deluding myself? No. No. No.

Hold fast to what you have, for it is happiness. Who said that? I forget. But I shall and will hold fast to my love for Peter, and to his belief in me. I must, because every instinct tells me that this is truth. This is what is real.

I eventually felt myself calming down. I guess I even dozed a little, because the ring of the phone on the bedside table startled me awake. It was Elaine.

"Kay," she said, I could hear a quivering in her voice.

"Yes, Elaine." I was hoping that if she was in her house, she didn't want to drop in on me.

"Kay, I must talk with you. It's desperately important. May I come over in five minutes?"

I clearly had no choice but to tell her to come. I got up and dashed some cold water on my face, then touched my lashes with mascara and my lips with a light touch of color, and went downstairs. It may sound silly that I bothered to go to that trouble for Peter's stepmother, but I had a growing sense of a looming turf battle between me and Elaine. With Peter in jail and me so new on the scene, she had been getting in the habit of walking in and out of the house as if it were once again her home.

When she came in this evening, however, there was nothing of the lady of the manor reestablishing her position about her. Elaine was ghastly pale, and her hands were trembling. There was no question that she was nervous and terribly upset. I noticed that she was carrying a plastic bag under one arm.

She didn't even give me a chance to greet

her before she said, "Kay, Richard is in terrible trouble. He's been gambling again. I must have a million dollars right away."

A million dollars! That was more money than I would have made if I had worked my entire life at the library. "Elaine," I protested, "first of all, I don't have anything like that kind of money, and it's useless to ask Peter for it. He has told me he thinks you're very foolish to keep bailing Richard out. He said that the day you refuse to pay his gambling debt is the day Richard is finally going to have to do something about his addiction to gambling."

"If Richard doesn't pay this debt, he won't be alive long enough to do anything about his addiction." Elaine said. She was clearly on the verge of hysteria. "Listen to me, Kay. I've been protecting Peter for nearly twenty-three years. I saw him come home the night he killed Susan. He was sleepwalking, and there was blood on his shirt. I didn't know what kind of trouble he was in, but I knew I had to protect him. I took that shirt out of the hamper so that the maid wouldn't see it. If you think I'm lying, look at this."

She dropped the plastic bag she was carrying on the coffee table and pulled something out of it. It was a man's white dress shirt. She held it up for me to see. There were dark smudges on the collar and around the top three buttons. "Do you understand what this is?" she asked.

A wave of dizziness made me sink down onto the couch. Yes, I understood what she was holding. I did not doubt for a single instance that it was Peter's shirt, or that the dark stains were Susan Althorp's blood.

"Have the money for me tomorrow morning, Kay," Elaine said.

My mind was suddenly filled with the image of Peter hurting Susan. The autopsy report showed that she had suffered a severe blow to her mouth. That was the way he had flailed out at the cop. My God, I thought, my God. There is no hope for him.

"Did you see Peter come home that night?" I asked.

"Yes, I did."

"You're *sure* he was sleepwalking?"

"I am positive. He walked past me in the corridor and never even saw me."

"What time did he come in?"

"At two o'clock."

"Why were you in the corridor at that time?"

"Peter's father was still ranting about the cost of the party, so I decided to go to one of the other bedrooms. That's when I saw Peter coming up the stairs."

"And then you went into Peter's bathroom to get the shirt. Suppose he had seen you, Elaine. What then?"

"I would have told him that I knew he'd been sleepwalking, and was concerned that he went safely back to bed. But he didn't wake up. Thank God I took the shirt with me. If it had been found in the hamper the next morning, he'd have been arrested and convicted. He'd probably still be in prison."

Elaine started to look relieved. I guess she realized that I would get the money for her. She folded the shirt neatly and put it back in the plastic bag, as though she were a clerk in a department store, completing a sale.

"If you were really trying to help Peter, wouldn't it have been a good idea to get rid of the shirt?" I challenged her.

"No, because it was proof that I did see Peter that night."

A kind of insurance policy, I thought. Something tucked away against a rainy day. "I'll get you the money, Elaine," I promised, "but only if you give that shirt to me."

"I will. Kay, I'm sorry to do this. I've protected Peter because I love him. Now I have to protect my son. That's why I'm here bargaining with you. When you have a child of your own, you'll understand."

Maybe I do already, I thought. I had not

told anyone except the lawyers that I was pregnant. It was too soon, and besides, I didn't want it leaked to the press. I certainly was not going to tell Elaine about the baby now, I thought bitterly, not when I was bargaining to buy the bloody shirt that proved its father was a killer.

54

Vincent Slater had attended a business dinner in Manhattan and was not home in time to respond to Kay's urgent request to call him. "If you don't get back to me this evening, be sure to call first thing in the morning," she told his answering machine.

It was 11:30 P.M. when he got the message. He knew Kay went to bed fairly early, so he wouldn't try to call her now. But what could be so urgent? he wondered. That night, even though he was usually a sound sleeper, he found himself waking up several times.

His phone rang at seven A.M. It was Kay. "I don't want to talk over the phone," she said. "Be sure to stop by here on your way to the city."

"I'm up and dressed already," he said. "I'll be right there."

When he got to the mansion, Kay brought him back to the kitchen, where she had been having a cup of coffee. "I wanted to see you before Jane gets here at eight o'clock," she said. "Last month, that first morning after we got back from our honeymoon, Peter and I went jogging early. I made coffee for us before we went out. It was fun being just the two of us, Mr. and Mrs. Newlywed living in suburbia. It seems a lifetime ago."

In the harsh morning light, Slater could see that it looked as if Kay was losing weight. Her cheekbones seemed more prominent, her eyes enormous. Afraid of what he might hear, he asked what had happened to upset her so much.

"What happened? Nothing very much. It's just that it seems Peter's loving stepmother claims she has been protecting him for years, and now she needs a little help in return."

"What do you mean, Kay?"

"She is willing to sell me an object that could hurt Peter very much if it fell into the hands of the wrong person — meaning the prosecutor. The price is one million dollars, and she must have it today."

"What object?" Slater snapped. "Kay, what are you talking about?"

Kay bit her lip. "I can't tell you what it is, so don't ask me any questions about it. She needs that money today because her wonderful son Richard is deeply in debt after making losing bets. I know Peter opened a joint account for us. How much is in it? Is there enough for me to write a check to her?"

"Kay, you're not using your head. A check takes time to clear. The only way I can get money that fast is to wire it directly into her account. Are you *sure* you want to do this? You know how Peter feels about Richard's gambling. He'd want no part of subsidizing it. Maybe Elaine's bluffing."

"She — is — not — bluffing! She — is — not — bluffing!" Kay shouted, then clasped her hands to her face as a flood of tears rushed down her cheeks.

Startled, Slater watched as she impatiently brushed the tears away in an effort to control her emotions. "I'm sorry. It's just —"

"All right, Kay," he said soothingly. "All right. Don't do this to yourself. I'll wire the money to her."

"I don't want Peter to know," Kay said, her voice low but controlled. "At least not yet. He goes to that sleep disorder center tonight. He's got enough to deal with without having to worry about this, too."

"He doesn't have to know yet. I have power of attorney to transfer money. But realize something: Once that money is transferred, you can't get it back. Will she turn this object over to you before the transfer?"

"I doubt it very much. Let me finish this cup of coffee, then I'll call her. I don't want to sound upset when I'm talking to her."

Slater watched as Kay folded her hands around the cup as if to warm them. They sat at the table for a few minutes, not speaking, both sipping their coffee. Then Kay shrugged. "I'm all right now." She dialed Elaine's number and waited as the telephone rang repeatedly. "There's some satisfaction in knowing that I'm waking her," she said bitterly. "She was falling apart when she first came in here last night, but when I promised to get the money to her today, she managed to cheer up really fast. Oh, here she is."

Slater watched Kay's expression harden as she and Elaine talked. It was obvious, as he listened to one side of the conversation, that Elaine was not parting with whatever it was that she was holding until the money transaction was complete.

What could it be? he wondered.

Elaine was still living in the mansion the night Susan disappeared, Slater thought. The master suite is just around the corridor from Peter's old room.

Was it possible that she saw Peter come

home that night wearing a bloodstained shirt?

It was possible, he concluded, nodding slightly.

Slater remembered the sleepwalking episodes he had witnessed years before, when he accompanied Peter on vacation trips. There had been the one incident outside the ski lodge when he woke Peter too quickly and Peter had lashed out at him. The three or four other times he'd witnessed him sleepwalking, when Peter returned to his bed he immediately fell into a deep sleep. Elaine could have gone into his room and retrieved the shirt from the hamper without his even being aware of her presence, he decided.

Kay hung up the phone. "She doesn't trust me. She says her banker will call her the minute the money is in the account, and only then will she come over here with the package I'm talking about."

"Is it the formal shirt he was wearing that night, Kay?" Slater asked.

"I won't answer that. I can't."

"I understand. All right. I'm on my way to New York now. I have to sign some papers to transfer the money."

"Money! That's the cause of most crimes, isn't it? Love or money. Susan needed money, didn't she?"

Slater stared at her. "How could you possibly know that?"

"Oh, of course I *don't* know it." She avoided his eyes by turning her head. Then, in a surprised tone, she said, "Oh, Gary, I didn't hear you come in!"

"I stopped to speak to the guard outside the front door, Mrs. Carrington. I offered him a cup of coffee, then came into the house right there."

Meaning he used the front door, Slater thought. He should know better. Had he been standing in the hall, and if so, how much did he hear? He knew the same thought was occurring to Kay.

Kay stood up. "I'll walk you to the door, Vince."

She did not speak again until they were in the reception area, then in a whisper asked, "Do you think he overheard what we were saying?"

"I don't know, but he had no business coming in the front entrance. I think he saw my car, spotted us through the kitchen window, then backtracked and used that as an excuse to try to eavesdrop."

"That's what I think, too. Call me when the transfer is done and I'll —" Kay hesitated, "and I'll complete the transaction."

At noon Slater called Kay to tell her that

337

the million dollars was in Elaine's bank account.

At twelve thirty, Kay called him back, her voice angry and upset. "She won't give it to me. She said she sold it too cheap. She said her pre-nup was much too small. She wants to discuss an amount that would be appropriate for her future needs."

55

"This is one way of getting out of the Bergen County Jail," Peter Carrington observed to Conner Banks as, shackled and manacled, escorted by two sheriff's officers and four private security guards, he was led through the lobby of Pascack Valley Hospital and up to the Sleep Disorders Center on the second floor.

"Not the way I'd necessarily choose myself," Conner told him.

"It's obvious you think this is nonsense," Peter said.

"I didn't mean that. What I meant was that I wish you were going home instead of coming here."

"Well, it seems as if I'm here for the night. Sorry to inconvenience you."

It was eight P.M. Banks had read up on what to expect from this experiment. Peter would be interviewed by a sleep specialist, answer a series of questions, then be put into a bedroom in the testing suite. A polysomno-gram recording would be made of his heart rate, brain waves, breathing, eye muscles, leg movement, and all five stages of sleep. A television camera in the bedroom would also monitor him all night. In the morning he would be transported back to jail.

A special bolt and chain had been put on the outside of the door of Peter's bedroom. Banks and three of the guards would sit on chairs in the corridor, while the fourth one, accompanied by a hospital technician, would watch the video monitor that showed the interior of the room with Peter in bed. The sheriff's officers stood outside his door.

At one A.M. the knob on the bedroom door turned. The guards sprang up, but the chain they had installed on the outside prevented the door from opening more than an inch. The tugging from the other side lasted for more than a minute, then the door closed again.

Banks hurried to the monitor; he could see Peter sitting on the bed. He was looking directly in the camera, his face expressionless, his eyes staring. As Banks watched, Peter attempted to reconnect himself to the breathing tube, then lay down and closed his eyes.

"He was sleepwalking, wasn't he?" Banks asked the technician.

"You've just witnessed a classic example of it," the technician replied.

56

For the second morning in a row, Vincent Slater received a seven A.M. phone call; this time it was from Conner Banks. "We've got a problem," Banks said without introduction. "Peter was sleepwalking last night, during his stay at the sleep clinic, and tried to open the door of his bedroom. It could be viewed as a violation of the terms of his release. As soon as the prosecutor hears about it, there'll be another bail hearing. Krause will move to have the bail forfeited."

Slater swung his legs over the bed and sat up. "What do you want me to do?"

"I don't want you to do anything except pray that the judge sees it our way — that Peter didn't know what he was doing. Otherwise you can kiss another twenty-five million dollars good-bye."

"You absolutely *cannot* let that happen!"

"Do you think I won't give it my best shot? Vince, I've been telling you all along that this sleepwalking defense is madness. There is no way that the judge is going to buy it. He certainly wasn't happy with allowing Peter to go to the sleep disorder center, even with the guards. My big worry is that it might look as if this is a stunt to boost Peter's sleepwalking defense at trial. If the judge views it that way, your money is going to help the State of New Jersey reduce its budget shortfall."

"Have you told Kay about this?" Slater asked.

"I didn't want to disturb her yet. The last time I saw her was Monday, and she was pretty upset then."

"I saw her yesterday and she was still very upset. Let me be the one to talk to her."

"I'm sure the prosecutor will ask for an emergent hearing regarding Peter's bail," Banks told him. "You'd better warn Kay. She'll want to be there. I'll let you know what time it's set for."

Warn Kay, Slater thought as he showered and dressed. Yesterday she had me send one million dollars to Elaine's account because she believes Elaine has something that could hurt Peter. Then Elaine upped the ante. Blackmail on top of blackmail.

It's got to be the shirt, he thought.

Or could it be something else?

There was no use going into the Manhattan office today, he decided. If there was going to be an emergent bail hearing, he intended to be there. Rather than going into the city, he would work out of his office at the mansion, then drive Kay to the hearing.

It wasn't easy to phone Kay and tell her what had happened at the sleep center, but he got the job out of the way. An hour later he drove through the gate of the Carrington estate. The security guard gave him a friendly wave. The guard stationed at the house nodded to him as he drove around the mansion and parked his car in the back. He used the key to his private office to enter the house. He was barely inside before his cell phone rang.

It was Nicholas Greco, requesting a brief meeting at his convenience.

"Mr. Greco," Vincent said, "I can see no reason for our meeting, today or any other time. Peter Carrington has been indicted for murder because you located that maid who, for her own reasons, now claims that the sworn statement she made twenty-two years ago was a lie. Why would I be interested in exchanging a single word with you?"

"Mr. Slater, I am not in anyone's employ at this time. For my own sake, I do not like to leave loose ends dangling when I work on a case. I understand that Peter Carrington may admit in court that it is possible he committed those crimes while he was unaware of his actions. But is it not also possible that there is, in fact, another answer? As his close friend and assistant, please give me half an hour. Hear me out."

Without answering, Vincent Slater slammed the phone shut.

"Who was that, Vince?"

He turned around. Kay was standing in the doorway.

"Nobody important, Kay," he told her. "One of those crank callers who somehow manage to get private numbers."

57

When the sheriff's officers reported to Prosecutor Barbara Krause that Peter Carrington had attempted to leave his hospital room by forcibly pulling on the locked door, she immediately requested, and was granted, another emergent bail hearing just as Conner Banks had expected.

At 2:30 that afternoon, she and the defense attorneys and Peter Carrington once more stood before Judge Smith. And as before, the courtroom was filled with the media and dozens of spectators.

I sat with Vincent Slater in the row behind Markinson and Banks. It's difficult to express how I felt. I guess the best way to put it is to say that I felt numb. In the space of a few days — by opening the possibility that Susan had been the woman I overheard in the chapel all those years ago — I had, according to Peter's attorneys, established a motive for him to have murdered her. I had seen the stained shirt he was wearing the night Susan disappeared, and I had paid one million dollars to his stepmother to get it from her. It was blackmail, but I felt I had no choice. And then after paying that money, I'd been held up for more blackmail. I had also visited Susan Althorp's closest friend and learned that Susan had referred to Gary Barr as "her pal." So much was happening, and I was still trying to make sense of it.

I watched as Peter, my husband, my love, was led into the court, emotionally wounded and degraded, wearing shackles and manacles, paraded around for all the world to see on the evening news.

The prosecutor had a triumphant yet outraged air about her as she got up to speak. With every word she uttered, I hated her more.

"Your Honor, this is the second time that this man, who is indicted for two murders, and is a suspect in one other death, has violated the conditions of his bail. The first time, he left his home and went on the property of Susan Althorp's family, which caused them enormous distress. One of the police officers who attempted to arrest him was seriously assaulted. Last night, Peter Carrington attempted to force open the door of his hospital room in yet another attempt to escape. The sheriff's officers reported to me that he desperately pulled on the door for at least a minute. Fortunately, he was not successful."

Peter, I thought, Peter. What are you thinking? Why is this nightmare happening to us?

"Your Honor," the prosecutor was saying, "the state moves that the twenty-five-million-dollar bail posted by Peter Carrington for the purpose of allowing him to go to the Sleep Disorders Center overnight be forfeited. We ask that he now remain in the Bergen County Jail while he awaits trial. It is hard to imagine a person who would constitute a greater risk of flight than he does."

Conner Banks had been waiting impatiently for the prosecutor to finish. Now it was his turn. I watched as he arose from his chair at the defense table and prepared to address the judge. He had a confident air about him that gave me a measure of hope. He glanced at the prosecutor as if he couldn't believe what he had just heard; then he began his argument.

"Your Honor, let's talk about the risk of flight. If Peter Carrington wanted to leave the country, he could have done it over twenty years ago. Instead he has lived in his own home, tried to ignore the scurrilous rumors, cooperated with all the investigations, and now, knowing he would never willingly harm another human being, he has tried to find an explanation for the crimes he may have committed. Or that he may *not* have committed."

It was far too soon for me to have any response from the child I was carrying, but I swear I felt a phantom kick of approval.

Conner continued with his argument: "The entire purpose of the neurological testing at the sleep disorder clinic was to determine whether Peter Carrington is a sleepwalker, and, if he is, to determine the severity and frequency of this problem. I have been informed by my client's doctors that his neurological readings, when he is asleep, are highly irregular, and clearly indicative of a person with a serious sleepwalking disorder called parasomnia. The doctors who have viewed the tape of this incident have told me that, in their judgment, it was clearly a sleepwalking episode, and that he was totally unaware of his actions."

He's doing a good job, I thought. Please God, let the judge believe him.

"Your Honor," Banks said, his voice rising, "we do not dispute that Peter Carrington got up and attempted to leave the room. However, given the substantial security measures that were in place, of which Peter Carrington was not only aware, but was paying for, it is abundantly clear that this episode was the result of his being afflicted with this terrible disorder. Your Honor, as per your previous order, he spent the night at the center, and now has been returned to jail. It would be a terrible injustice to forfeit the twenty-five-million-dollar bail as a result of actions over which he had no control."

Judge Smith had listened intently to both sides. He looked up, and our eyes locked for just a second before he addressed the courtroom. What did he see when he looked at me? I wondered. Did he see the way I am pleading with him to understand? I felt my heart pounding as he began to speak.

"I can candidly state that this is the most unusual set of circumstances that I have ever encountered with respect to a bail hearing," he said. "I am fully aware that sleepwalking may be an issue in Mr. Carrington's upcoming trial. I, of course, am taking no position at this time regarding the merits of the state's case, or the validity of any sleepwalking defense. The sole issue today is whether Mr. Carrington deliberately attempted to violate the conditions of his bail, and whether he should forfeit the twenty-five million dollars he posted. Defense counsel does not dispute that Mr. Carrington attempted to leave the hospital room in which he was confined."

I looked at the prosecutor. An angry frown was forming on her face. Dear God, let that mean that the judge isn't going to make Peter forfeit that bail. Because if he *does* make him forfeit it, it will mean he believes Peter was putting on an act.

The judge continued: "The defense counsel has proffered substantial indication that the medical testing has revealed a serious sleepwalking disorder. It is also a fair argument that Peter Carrington was fully aware of the intense security surrounding him, which would have made any attempt to escape a virtual impossibility. It is also true, as defense counsel notes, that Mr. Carrington had both agreed to and paid for this intense security. Under all of these circumstances, and again recognizing that the entire purpose of the hospital's evaluation was focused on whether there was or was not a sleepwalking disorder, this court is not convinced that Mr. Carrington consciously tried to escape, or otherwise deliberately violated conditions of his bail. The state's concern about flight is legitimate, and the defendant will remain in jail pending his trial. But given the information before me, I will not order the forfeiture of the twenty-five million dollars bail."

At last we had a sort of victory. I felt myself slump in my seat. Vincent Slater patted my shoulder, an unusual gesture for him to make. "Kay, this is *really* important," he said, his voice full of relief and concern.

Slater so seldom showed any emotion that I was both surprised and touched. I had always thought of him as someone who was efficient and devoted to Peter's interests, but otherwise was basically cold and unresponsive. His reaction offered an unexpected glimpse into the interior Vincent Slater. Of course, I reminded myself, he was undoubtedly thrilled about the return of the twenty-five-million-dollar bail.

I was allowed a few minutes with Peter while he was in the holding cell. "Kay," he said, "last night I was dreaming of kneeling on the Althorps' lawn, the way I was when the cops arrested me. When I was trying to open the door, it was because, in my dream, I had to go there again." His voice dropped to a whisper so that the guard standing nearby could not hear him. "But last night was different." He paused. "I thought that Gary Barr was sitting in the room watching me."

58

Nicholas Greco heard on his car radio that Peter Carrington might have tried to break out of the sleep center. Knowing there would be a bail hearing, he called Barbara Krause's office and learned what time it would be held.

That was why he was in the courtroom during the hearing, and why he waited outside in the hall after it was over, hoping to speak to Carrington's wife, Kay.

When she came out, she was accompanied by Vincent Slater. When Slater saw Greco, he tried to rush Kay Carrington past him, but Greco blocked his way. "Mrs. Carrington," he said, "I would very much like to speak with you. There is a possibility I might be of assistance to you."

"Assistance!" Slater snapped. "Kay, this is the investigator who located the maid and got her to change her testimony."

"Mrs. Carrington, I am seeking the truth."

Greco handed her his card. "Please take this. Please call me." Satisfied that she had slipped it in her pocket, he turned and walked in the opposite direction from the elevators.

He knew by now that he had become something of a familiar figure in the prosecutor's office. Barbara Krause's door was closed, but Tom Moran was standing in the hall outside, talking to a police officer. Greco managed to catch Moran's eye, then waited until Moran came over to speak to him.

Moran waved aside Greco's apologies for dropping in without an appointment. "Come in my office," he suggested. "The boss is not a happy camper after losing the motion for bail forfeiture."

"I understand," Greco said, with a silent prayer of thanks that he had not intruded on Barbara Krause. He knew there was a thin line between her considering him helpful and deciding he was a pest. He also knew that he should not take up much of Moran's time.

Once inside Moran's office, Greco got to the point. "I have been speaking with Susan Althorp's closest friend, Sarah Kennedy North. As you know, Gary Barr used to chauffeur Susan and her friends to parties. But according to Sarah North, it seems he had an unusually close relationship with Susan."

Moran raised an eyebrow. "I'm listening."

"Susan apparently referred to Barr as 'her pal.' Rather unusual, don't you think, for an eighteen-year-old and a servant who was then in his early forties? Also, the atmosphere in the Althorp home does not suggest familiarity ever existed between the family and the employees. If anything, I would say quite the opposite."

"Mr. Greco, we have always suspected that Peter Carrington had help in both hiding and later in burying Susan Althorp's body. We knew, of course, about the chauffeuring Gary Barr did. The police also spoke to Susan's friends at the time of her disappearance. None of them mentioned Barr as having an unusual relationship with Susan. Perhaps it's time for us to talk to him again. Maybe *his* memory has improved over the years as well."

Greco got up. "I won't take any more of your time. May I also suggest that you thoroughly investigate Gary Barr's background to see if there may have ever been any problem with the law. A possibility has occurred to me which I am not yet ready to share. Good day, Mr. Moran. It is always a pleasure to see you."

59

I despised Elaine for her trickery, but in an odd way, it was also a relief that I was not in possession of the infamous shirt. Even though she was blackmailing us, she also was postponing a moral dilemma for me. As Peter's wife, by law, I did not have to testify against him. To actively withhold or destroy evidence was, however, something else again. But now, I told myself, I was not withholding evidence because I did not possess it.

The media had a field day after the bail hearing. The cover of one of the tabloids had a picture of Peter standing before the judge, his back to the camera. The judge was looking down. The headline was, ZZZZZZZZZZZZZ. IS THE JUDGE ASLEEP, TOO? A cartoon in another newspaper depicted Peter with electrodes hanging from his forehead, a breathing tube over his shoulder, and a hatchet in his hand that he was aiming at a door.

I didn't know what access Peter had to the newspapers and didn't ask him. On my next visit, I did question him about the dream he had at the sleep center, when he tried to open the door because he wanted to go to the Althorp home again. "Do you think there was a possibility that you actually *saw* Gary hanging around Susan's house the night she disappeared?" I asked him.

"Absolutely not, Kay! If I had, I wouldn't have let him come within a mile of you!"

Of course he wouldn't. He was convinced it was just a confusing twist to his dream — but I was not.

Our visits were so painful: We looked at each other through a Plexiglas panel and spoke by telephone. He could sit down with his lawyers at a conference table but was not allowed to touch me. I longed to put my arms around him, to feel the strength of his arms around me. It wasn't going to happen.

Conner Banks's suggestion that Peter married me because of what I had heard in the chapel was always in the back of my mind. Then, when I saw the way Peter looked at me, the way his face lit up at his first glimpse of me, I was again certain that he loved me and had loved me from the beginning.

But a few hours later, when I was by myself at home, it did not seem impossible that he and Susan might have been quarreling about money in the chapel that afternoon. Peter was in college at that time. What kind of allowance did he get from a father who was a notorious skinflint? If Susan had something on him, was he driven to desperation — perhaps by fear of his father — to keep her quiet?

These questions haunted me, but when visiting day finally came around again, I felt wretched for ever doubting him.

A dozen times during the weeks after the hearing, I took Nicholas Greco's card from my desk and considered calling him. I had this crazy feeling that somehow he could help Peter. But each time I would remind myself that Peter might not have been indicted had Greco not tracked down Maria Valdez, and I always put the card back in the drawer, and slammed the drawer shut.

We were enjoying a mild February, and I started jogging again, running every morning around the estate. I often stopped at the place where they had found my father's remains. This grave seemed more real to me than the one he now shares with my mother in MaryRest Cemetery. The police had dug at least ten feet in every direction around the spot where the dogs had started their frantic barking. That area had been filled in now, but it still stood out from the dormant grass around it, and I knew the dirt would start to sink when the spring thaw began.

I decided I wanted to plant rosebushes here, but then I realized I was too new in my position as Mrs. Peter Carrington to know who attended to the landscaping.

Sometimes I would stand at the fence and look out at the area where Susan's body had been found. I would try to imagine the twenty-year-old Peter thinking that it was safe to put her body there, because the cadaver dogs had already been through the estate. I even called Public Service Electric & Gas Company. One of their employees told me that there was a gas line near the curb of our property beyond the fence, and that PSE&G had a perpetual easement to service or replace the line. He told me that normally they would never have any need to disturb the ground nearly fifty feet from the curb.

"When there's a suspected leak, we move right in without notification," he said. "The day the Althorp girl's body was found, an odor of gas had been reported, and our people went right over. Our detectors bored test holes much closer to your fence than they might ever do again, he told me.

Which might answer why, even if he were guilty, Peter had not looked particularly upset when he saw the emergency crew digging near the curb.

I thought back to what I knew about that night. Elaine claimed she had seen Peter come in at two A.M. There is no question that he drove Susan home at midnight. Would she have had the nerve to sneak out immediately, or would she wait twenty minutes or half an hour to be sure one of her parents didn't look in on her? I asked myself. And where between twelve thirty and two o'clock in the morning — whether in a sleepwalking state or not — would Peter have managed to hide Susan's body?

And if he did do that, then someone had to have been helping him. My suspicion that Gary Barr was involved in all this was becoming stronger and stronger. It would explain why lately Gary had been acting so nervous, and had been trying to eavesdrop. He must be terribly worried that if, out of loyalty, he tried to help Peter, he might still be charged with being an accessory to murder.

Conner Banks gave me a copy of a tape from The Learning Channel showing reenactments of crimes committed in the United States by two men who were sleepwalking at the time. Both are serving life sentences. The same tape shows reenactments of a homicide and an aggravated assault committed by two men in Canada under the same circumstances. They were both acquitted. Watching the tape, I was heartsick. Two of the men had been bewildered when they were woken by the police, and had no memory of what had happened. The other awoke in his car, and drove to the police station himself because he was covered with blood.

One way that I occupied myself — and it was something that I *did* enjoy — was to make some changes around the mansion. From what Peter had told me, Grace hadn't done anything much to the mansion, but had completely redecorated the Fifth Avenue apartment. I'd only been at the apartment a few times during those weeks between the literacy reception and our wedding. Now, I had no desire to go there without Peter. It's silly, but I would have felt like an intruder. If Peter was sent to prison, I knew that a major decision would have to be made about all the property.

In the meantime, however, I began to make some small changes in this home — my home, I reminded myself. I had Gary bring down the crate of Limoges china that I had told Peter about. Jane washed and I dried the plates and cups and saucers and all the wonderful extra dishes that were used at lavish dinner parties in the late nineteenth century. "You don't see anything like this anymore, Mrs. Carrington," Jane marveled.

There was a magnificent eighteenth-century breakfront in the formal dining room. We displayed the Limoges there, and packed away the china that Elaine had chosen. Good riddance, I thought.

In one room on the third floor, I found a heavy chest filled with blackened antique table silver. When Jane and Gary had polished it, we found that all the pieces were monogrammed. "Whose initials are ASC?" I asked Peter during one of my visits.

"ASC? That's probably my great-great-, whatever she is, grandmother. Her name was Adelaide Stuart when she married my great-great-, whatever, grandfather in 1820. I remember my mother telling me that Adelaide claimed some remote relationship to King Charles, and never let my paternal ancestor forget that she was a cut above him socially. She was the one behind moving the mansion from Wales."

I learned that conversations like this one were the best way to get a smile on Peter's face. He liked the idea that I was putting my own mark on his home. "Do whatever you want, Kay. Some of those rooms are too stiff and formal for my taste. But leave my library just the way it is, and don't even think about recovering my chair."

I also told him that I was going to switch some of the paintings on the walls downstairs with others that I liked better that I'd found on the third floor.

I had Maggie over for dinner a couple of times a week, or else we went out to our pasta restaurant. I knew other diners' eyes followed me when we came in, but I decided I couldn't hide forever, and that eventually, or at least until the trial began, I wouldn't be too much of a curiosity.

I didn't see Elaine for nearly three weeks after her refusal to give the shirt to me, although I did glimpse her car now and then, passing along the driveway. I'd had all the house locks changed so she could not walk in without ringing the bell. Then one evening after the Barrs had left for the day, I was sitting in Peter's chair reading, and the door chimes began crashing frantically.

I rushed to open the door and Elaine flung herself into the mansion, her eyes wild, her ungloved hands curled like claws. For a moment I thought she was going to close them around my neck. "How *dare* you?" she shouted. "How *dare* you ransack my home?"

"Ransack your home!" I think the shock in my voice and what she must have seen on my face made her realize that I didn't know what she was talking about.

Immediately the anger in her face turned to panic. "Kay," she said. "Oh, my God, Kay, it's *gone!* Someone has stolen it!"

I did not have to ask what she meant. Peter's formal dinner shirt with Susan's blood on it, the shirt that would surely brand him a murderer, was missing.

60

Pat Jennings was spending more and more of her time at the Walker Gallery on the telephone because she had absolutely nothing else to do. In the several weeks since the row with his mother in the office, Richard had been around very little. He told Pat that he was selling his apartment and buying a smaller one, and that he was looking for less expensive space for the gallery. "I think the great romance with Gina Black is over," Pat confided to her friend Trish during one of their frequent phone conversations. "She's been leaving messages for him, but Richard told me to tell her he's out of town."

"How about the other one, Alexandra Lloyd?"

"I guess she's given up. She hasn't called for a couple of weeks."

"Has his mother been in again?"

"No, not once. But I think she lost something. This morning Richard came in and, boy, was he having a fit! He went right to the phone and called his mother. I heard him tell her that he hadn't slept for one minute after what she'd told him last night because he was so upset. He never seems to understand that when he raises his voice, I hear every word."

"When was that?" Trish asked.

"About an hour ago."

"What else did he say?"

"Something about the utter stupidity of leaving it in the house, and why didn't she just run it up the flagpole for everyone to see? Anyhow, he hung up on her, and she called back ten minutes later. I could tell she was crying. She said she didn't want to talk to Richard. Instead she told me to tell her son that it was all his fault that she had to pull it out now, and his fault that she had it in the house in the first place, and that he should go to hell.

"She told you *that?*" Trish said breathlessly. "Did you give him that message?"

"I had to, didn't I? He just slammed out of here saying he wouldn't be back today."

"How about that?" Trish exclaimed. "You have the most interesting job, Pat. It's so fascinating to be around people like the Carringtons. What do you think Elaine lost?"

"Oh, jewelry, I guess," Pat surmised. "Unless it's a ticket to the Carrington money. Richard could sure use that."

"Maybe it's the 'wild card,' whatever that is," Trish suggested.

They both laughed heartily.

"Keep me posted!" Trish admonished as she hung up.

61

"Peter made his point in court at the bail hearing, Kay," Conner Banks said, jabbing his finger at me for emphasis as he referred to his notes. "We have a copy of the tape of him getting out of bed in the sleep center. There's a very clear shot of his face, looking directly into the camera. Anyone can see how glassy his eyes look, and that he's totally unfocused. I think that when the jurors view this, some — maybe all — of them will believe that Peter was in a sleepwalking state at the time, and therefore that he is a sleepwalker. But, Kay, even so, that defense just won't work. If you ever want to see Peter walk into this house again, a free man, you have *got* to convince him to let us attack the state's case, and argue that there is reasonable doubt he killed Susan and there is reasonable doubt that he killed your father."

"I absolutely agree," Markinson said, forcefully.

Banks and Markinson were at the mansion again. It had been a week since Peter's shirt had been stolen from Elaine's house. I don't know whether Elaine or I was more distraught over its disappearance.

There were only two people I would suspect of having stolen it: Gary Barr and Vincent Slater. Vincent had guessed immediately that the "object" Elaine was using to blackmail me was probably the shirt, and I am virtually certain that Gary overheard our conversation about it.

I could even imagine Vince trying to retrieve the shirt after Elaine was paid the million dollars, especially when she tried to continue the blackmail, but why not tell me that? I confronted him about it and told him that Elaine's "object" was the missing shirt. He absolutely denied he had taken it. I didn't know whether to believe him or not.

If Gary Barr took it, what was he planning to do with it? Maybe he was holding it as insurance for making a deal with the prosecutor, something along the lines of, "Peter was just a kid. I was sorry for him. I hid the body, then helped him bury it outside the fence."

Of course both Vincent and Gary had easy access to Elaine's house. Gary was around all the time; Vince was in and out of the mansion on a regular basis. The guard at the house was almost always at the front door. He'd walk around to the back from time to time, but it would be easy enough for either one of them to avoid being seen by him.

Prior to finding her house had been ransacked, Elaine had spent four days at her apartment in New York. Whoever took the shirt had plenty of time to thoroughly search for it. In addition to Vincent and Gary, there was another possible suspect that entered my mind, although it did seem remote. Elaine had let it slip, when she was frantically telling me that the shirt was missing, that Richard had known about it, too. Would he have taken it as insurance against his future gambling losses? But Elaine said that he didn't know she hadn't returned it to the safe-deposit box in the bank where it had been hidden for twenty-two years, and that he had been genuinely furious when she told him about the loss.

All of these thoughts were whirling through my mind while I was listening to Conner Banks laying out for me, step by step, the factors that he thought were the basis for a "reasonable doubt" defense.

"Peter and Susan were friends, but no one has ever suggested they were seriously involved," Banks was saying. "The formal shirt was missing, but there wasn't a trace of blood on Peter's dinner jacket or pants or socks or shoes, all of which were accounted for."

"Suppose that shirt shows up somewhere?" I asked. "Suppose, for argument's sake, it was stained with Susan's blood."

Banks and Markinson looked at me as if I had two heads. "If there was even the faintest possibility that could happen, I would be bargaining for two thirty-year concurrent sentences," Banks said. "And feel lucky to get it."

Around and around and around we go, where we stop, nobody knows, I thought. Unknowingly, Banks had given me my answer. If the lawyers knew about the existence of the shirt, they would want to plea-bargain, and Peter would never admit to committing those murders just to get a sentence that would give him a possibility — at best — of getting out of prison when he was seventy-two years old.

Our child will be thirty by then, I thought.

"I will not try to persuade Peter to change his mind about the focus of his defense," I told them. "It's what he wants, and I'll support him."

They pushed back their chairs and stood to leave. "Then you'll have to face the inevitable, Kay," Markinson said. "You're going to raise your child alone."

On his way out of the dining room, Markinson stopped at the breakfront. "Magnificent china," he observed.

"Yes," I said, aware that we were now making polite conversation, that Peter's lawyers had as good as thrown in the towel, emotionally speaking.

Conner Banks was looking at one of the paintings I had brought down from the third floor. "This is outstanding," he said. "It's a Morley, isn't it?"

"I don't know," I confessed. "I'm woefully lacking in my knowledge of art. I just liked it more than the one that was there."

"Then you have a good eye," he said approvingly. "We'll be on our way. We're lining up medical doctors who have treated people who are parasomniacs, and who can testify they are completely unaware of their behavior when they are sleepwalking. If you and Peter insist on this defense, then we'll have to call them as expert witnesses."

It was visiting day at the Bergen County Jail. My waist was thickening and, when I dressed this morning, I had to leave the top button of my slacks open. I had started to wear high-necked sweaters almost all the time; they helped disguise how thin I was, except, of course, for my waistline. I was worried that I was still losing weight, but the obstetrician had told me that that wasn't uncommon in the first few months of pregnancy.

When did it happen that all my nagging doubts about Peter's innocence began to dissolve? I believe it had to do with the file cabinets I started going through on the third floor. I was learning so much about his childhood in what I found in them. His mother had kept a photograph album for each year of his life until she died; he was twelve at the time. I was struck by the fact that his father was in so few of the pictures. Peter had told me that after he was born, his mother stopped accompanying his father on business trips.

She had written notes on some of the pages, loving references to how smart Peter was, how quick to learn, his wonderful disposition, his sense of humor.

I found myself becoming wistful in seeing how very close Peter had been to his mother. At least you had her twelve years, I thought. Then I found a picture taken by the Bergen *Record* photographer the day of her funeral. A devastated twelve-year-old Peter, trying to blink back tears, was walking beside his mother's coffin, his hand resting on it.

His college yearbooks were in one of the

files. In one, the caption about him referred to "grace under pressure," and I realized that he was just beginning his senior year at Princeton when Susan disappeared. In the months that followed, the prosecutor's office was constantly pulling him in for questioning.

When I got to the jail that afternoon and Peter was brought in, he looked at me through the Plexiglas for a long minute without speaking. He was trembling, and his eyes glistened with tears. He picked up the phone on his side of the divider. His voice husky, he said, "Kay, I don't know why, but I had a feeling that you wouldn't come today, or ever again, that you've had as much of this misery as you can take."

I felt for a moment as if I were looking at the face of the twelve-year-old boy at the funeral of the person he loved best in the world. "I will never leave you," I told him. "I love you far too much to leave you. Peter, I don't believe you ever hurt anyone. You couldn't. There's another answer, and, so help me God, I'm going to find it."

That evening, I phoned Nicholas Greco.

62

Jane Barr had made beef barley soup in case the lawyers stayed for lunch, but they were gone by quarter of twelve. She was glad that she'd had a reason to cook — she needed something to distract her. Gary had been asked to stop at the prosecutor's office, and he was there now. Why did they want to talk to him? she worried. After all these years, they're not questioning him about Susan Atthorp, are they?

Please, don't let it be that, she prayed.

Kay Carrington had a cup of soup before she went to visit Peter at the jail. It's funny about her, Jane thought. She didn't come from money, but she has an air about her, not haughty, but knowing. She's perfect for Peter. And I think she's pregnant. She hasn't said so, but I bet she is.

Where was Gary? she wondered, checking the time. What kind of questions were they asking him? How much was he telling?

After lunch, Jane normally went home to the gatehouse for a good part of the afternoon, then would return to the mansion to turn on lights, draw curtains, and prepare dinner. Today when she arrived home, she found Gary there eating a sandwich and having a beer.

"Why didn't you let me know you were home?" she demanded. "I've been a wreck waiting to hear what they wanted."

"They dug up some stuff about me from the time I was a kid," Gary snapped. "I told you about it. I was in a little trouble when I was a teenager, but the records were supposed to be sealed. There was some stuff in the newspapers at the time, though, and I guess they found out about it that way."

Jane collapsed into a chair. "That was so long ago. They're not holding what happened back then against you, are they? Or are they reading more into it now?"

Gary Barr looked at his wife, something approaching contempt in his eyes. "What do you think?" he asked.

Jane had not yet started to unbutton her winter jacket. Now she reached for the top button and slipped it through the buttonhole. Her shoulders sagged. "I've lived in this town all my life," she said. "I never wanted to be anyplace else. We've worked for nice people. Now all that is in jeopardy. What you did was so awful. Did they ask you about it? Do they know about it? *Do* they?"

"No," Gary replied angrily. "They haven't figured out anything, so stop worrying. The statute of limitations means I'm clear now. They can't file charges because too many years have passed. And even if they try to pin something else on me, I've got an offer for them they can't refuse."

"What are you talking about?" Jane asked, her dismay apparent. "There's no statute of limitations on murder!"

Gary Barr sprang up from his chair and threw the sandwich he was eating at his wife. "Don't ever use that word again!" he shouted.

"I'm sorry, Gary. I didn't mean to upset you. I'm sorry." Tears starting to well in her eyes, Jane looked at the smear of mustard on her coat, the broken pieces of rye bread, the slices of ham and tomato on the floor in front of her.

Clenching and unclenching his hands, Barr made a visible effort to control himself. "Okay. All right. Just remember. It was one thing to be there; another thing to kill her. All right. I'll clean up the mess. Anyhow, that sandwich was lousy. Any of that soup left that you were making this morning?"

"Yes. Plenty of it."

"Do me a favor and get me some, will you? I've had a tough day. And I'm sorry I lost my temper. You don't deserve that, Jane. You're a good woman."

63

Nicholas Greco was pleased to receive an unexpected phone call from Assistant Prosecutor Tom Moran. "That was a good tip," Moran told him. "Barr had a juvenile record that was sealed from the public, but we got access to it. He was arrested for bringing marijuana to school and smoking it in the gym. We also found his high school yearbook and located some of his classmates who still live in Poughkeepsie. Barr had a reputation for having a bad temper. Not exactly your friendly teenage-boy-next-door.

"Of course, that's a long time ago," Moran continued. "It's interesting though, that his classmates remember him as someone with a chip on his shoulder, plus an inferiority complex. He didn't study in high school, didn't want to go to college, then years later, at a high school reunion, whined that he never was given the chance to be a success."

"He struck me as a very insecure, dissatisfied man who is angry at the world," Greco said. "What you tell me fits the pattern that I have observed."

"Changing the subject," Moran said. "There's something else I know you'd want to hear. Mrs. Althorp died today."

"I am very, very sorry to hear that, but I think for her it is a blessing."

"From what I understand, there isn't going to be a wake, and the funeral will be private. I guess those were her wishes, and you can understand that the family has had enough media coverage for a lifetime."

"Yes, I can understand that," Nicholas Greco said. "Thank you, Tom."

Greco looked at his watch. It was past five o'clock, but he was not yet ready to start home. He wanted to think quietly, and sometimes it was easier to do that after everyone else had left the office and the phones were quiet. Fortunately, it was the evening Frances met with her book group, so she wouldn't mind if he was late arriving home.

He smiled to himself. At the end of the day, Frances was a woman who wanted his attention, full and undivided. Most of the time I give it to her, too, he thought affectionately, but right now I need to enter a brown study. When he had first used that expression in front of Frances, she'd asked what he was talking about.

"It has passed out of the language for the most part, but in the nineteenth century it was very common," he had told her. "A 'brown study' is defined as a deep, serious absorption in thought, my dear."

"Oh, for heaven's sake, Nick," she had replied, "why not say it straight — you're just trying to figure something out?"

And that's just what I'm trying to do, Greco thought.

Gary Barr was at the top of his list of people and things to consider. Greco sensed that Barr had a chip on his shoulder toward those who, in his mind, had a privileged life. What was his relationship to the Althorp family? he wondered. In the years he and his wife were not working for the Carringtons, they regularly cooked and served dinners for the Althorps. Gary also chauffeured their daughter. How and why did he become Susan's "pal"? I must talk to Susan's friend Sarah again, Greco thought.

The torn page from *People* magazine found in Grace Carrington's pocket was the next thing on the list. It had significance, great significance, of that he was sure. But *why?*

Next was Susan Althorp's evening purse.

Why did Gary Barr have such a clear memory of Peter Carrington asking Vincent Slater to return it to her the next morning, and then remembering also that Peter was startled when it wasn't found in his car? Or was Barr making up that story for his own reasons? Slater had confirmed the conversation, but only to a degree. He claimed that Carrington merely asked him to check and see if the purse was in the car, and return it to Susan if it was.

But Susan was expected for brunch later that day. Besides, the bag was small, and could only have held things like a handkerchief, compact, comb, or lipstick. So why make an issue of returning it to her? Was there something special in it that she had needed? Greco asked himself.

All of these pieces are tied together, Nicholas Greco thought, as he sat with his hands folded, not noticing that it was becoming dark outside. But how?

The phone rang. Somewhat irritated at the intrusion, Greco picked up the receiver and identified himself.

"Mr. Greco, this is Kay Carrington. You gave me your card at the courthouse a few weeks ago."

Greco straightened up in his chair. "Yes, I did, Mrs. Carrington," he said slowly. "I am glad to hear from you."

"Can you come see me tomorrow morning, at my home?"

"Of course. What time is convenient for you?"

"Eleven o'clock? Is that all right for you?"

"That would be fine."

"Do you know where I live?"

"Yes, I do. I will be there at eleven."

"Thank you."

Greco heard the click of the receiver being replaced, then hung up himself. Still deep in thought, he got up and walked down the hall to the coat closet. At the last minute, he remembered to leave a note on his receptionist's desk: "Will be in New Jersey tomorrow morning."

64

I hadn't yet told Maggie about the baby because I was sure that she would confide it to several of her friends, and then I'd be reading about it in the tabloids. Maggie categorically *cannot* keep a secret. But I thought I'd been spotted at the obstetrician's office by people who knew me, and since I didn't want Maggie to hear a rumor about it from someone else, I knew I had to tell her.

After I phoned Nicholas Greco and made the appointment, I collected Maggie and brought her back to the house for dinner. Jane had prepared a roast chicken and wanted to serve us, but I had told her to go ahead home, that we'd serve ourselves. The last thing I needed was to have Gary Barr overhear our conversation. I think Jane was getting worried by now about whether or not they were going to lose their jobs, and she started to protest. But then she stopped and very pleasantly wished us a good evening.

The kitchen is large and accommodates a refectory table and benches where the servants used to eat when there was a large staff. Maggie wanted us to have dinner there, but I vetoed the idea. The chairs in the small dining room are infinitely more comfortable. Besides, I know she feels intimidated by the mansion, and I wanted her to get over that.

When we were settled at the table, I told Maggie about the baby. She was absolutely delighted with my news, but then, of course, immediately started worrying about me. "Oh, Kay, it's such a tragedy that your baby's father will never be around to see the little one grow up."

"Maggie," I said, "his name is Peter, and I haven't given up hope. He did *not* kill Susan Althorp, and he certainly did not kill my father. But please, let's talk about something else. Daddy was fired only a few weeks after Susan disappeared. Peter told me Elaine Carrington got rid of him because he wasn't interested in her overtures to him."

"You told me that, Kay." Maggie said contritely. I knew she now regretted that she had jumped to the assumption that the firing had been the result of a drinking problem.

"What was Daddy going to do? Did he have any job offers?"

"I don't know, Kay. It was only a few weeks after he was fired that we thought he had committed suicide. The last time I saw him was on September thirtieth, twenty-two and a half years ago. We've talked about this."

"Let's talk about it again."

"On September thirtieth, your dad phoned me around five o'clock and asked me to keep you overnight. He said he had an appointment with somebody. You were kind of unhappy about having to come over because he'd promised that the two of you would try some new recipe for dinner that evening. He promised he'd make it up to you. But the next day he didn't come for you and didn't call, and then the police reported his car had been found on the cliff above the river, and that his wallet was on the seat."

"Did they ever investigate to see who he might have been planning to see on September thirtieth?"

"At the time, the police assumed that he'd just made up that story as an excuse to drop you off."

I could tell we were going nowhere with this conversation. I kept hoping that maybe some fragment of a forgotten memory might surface in Maggie's consciousness, but it just wasn't happening.

Over a cup of tea, I decided it was time to

finally tell Maggie about the time, all those years ago, that I had crept into this house because I was so curious to see the chapel.

Her reaction, as expected, was that I was always too adventurous for my own good. Unexpectedly, she let it go at that.

Probably because of her reaction, I ended up telling her that I overheard a quarrel between a woman and a man she seemed to be blackmailing, something I had planned to keep to myself. "That's why I knew what the man was whistling, even though it was only one line," I told her, "because you used to hum it for me when you told me about my mother singing it in the school play."

Maggie gave me a look that I couldn't interpret.

"What is it?" I asked her.

"Kay," she exclaimed, "you should have told that to your father! When he and your mother began to date, I told him about the school play and bragged about how well she sang that song. He made her sing it for him. From then on, he called it 'their song.' They even chose it for their first dance at their wedding. You know that."

"Maggie, I knew about the play. But I don't think I remember your telling about Daddy calling it 'their song,' or dancing to it at the wedding," I protested.

"It doesn't matter. But after your father came running over here with you to fix those lights the afternoon of that party, he dropped you off at my house. I remember distinctly how really down he looked. He told me that he had heard someone whistling that song when he was here, and had talked with him. I guess your dad told whoever it was why he was nostalgic about it."

"Did he say who that person was?" I demanded.

"Yes, but I don't remember."

"Maggie, it's so important. Think about it. Please try to remember."

"I'll try, Kay. I'll really try."

There was a question I had to ask. "Maggie, could it have been Peter?"

"No. Positively not," Maggie said firmly. "I'd have remembered if it was Peter Carrington. He was the young prince around here. That's why I was so disappointed to think he killed that poor girl. No, I'm absolutely sure he wasn't the one your dad mentioned!"

She looked at me. "Kay, what's the matter?" she asked. "Why are you crying?"

It wasn't Peter, I thought with relief. It wasn't Peter! It was some other man being blackmailed that day in the chapel. But, dear

God, if I had only told Daddy what I heard that day, and he had reported it to the police, maybe he'd still be alive, and Peter wouldn't be in jail, accused of murder.

65

Vincent Slater was convinced that Gary Barr had stolen Peter's dress shirt from Elaine Carrington's house. For a week he had mulled over in his mind the best way to get it back.

The need to recover the shirt had been made even more acute by a call late one evening from Conner Banks, urging him to try to convince Peter to allow his legal team to change the strategy of his defense.

"Vincent," Banks said, "we are more and more convinced that we would have a good chance of a hung jury, and maybe even a shot at an acquittal, if our defense is based on reasonable doubt. An acquittal means that Peter comes home for good. A hung jury means we can argue strenuously for bail, and Peter would probably get to spend at least some time with his child before a second trial. If we got another hung jury at a second trial, the prosecutor would probably give up and drop the charges."

"What would happen if Peter's formal shirt turned up and it had Susan's blood on it?" Slater asked.

"What's going on here? Kay Carrington asked me that same question." There was a long silence; then Conner Banks said quietly, "As I told Kay, if that shirt turns up with Susan's blood on it, Peter had better be willing to plea-bargain."

"I see." It was nine o'clock, not too late to phone Kay, Slater decided. When she answered, she told him she had just driven her grandmother home.

"Kay, my bet is that Gary Barr stole the shirt," he said. "We've got to get it back. There's a set of master keys in a drawer in the kitchen. The gatehouse key is on it. I'll stop by for it at seven thirty, before Jane comes in. Then, I'll phone you at nine as though I'm in New York and ask you to send Gary into the city to help bring some of Peter's private papers home. I'll make sure my people there keep him busy for a while. You just make sure Jane doesn't go home early."

"Vince, I don't know what to think about this."

"I do. I'm not going to leave that shirt in Gary Barr's hands. Let's just pray that he's got it hidden somewhere in the gatehouse or in his SUV. That's something else: I'll tell him that one of our executives may be coming back with him to visit you, so he must be driving one of the family cars."

"As I say, at this point, I don't know what to think, but I'll go along with you," Kay said. "Vince, I might as well tell you, I have an appointment with Nicholas Greco, the investigator. He's coming here at eleven o'clock tomorrow morning."

Vincent Slater then said something he would never have dreamed he could say to his employer's wife: "The more fool you, Kay. I thought you loved your husband!"

66

Retired ambassador Charles Althorp sat in his late wife's study, a cup of coffee in his hand, an untouched breakfast tray beside him. Already the physical reality of Gladys's death had brought about changes in the house. The hospital bed, oxygen tent, IVs, and seemingly endless medical supplies were all gone. Brenda, the housekeeper, tears flowing, had aired and vacuumed Gladys's bedroom last night.

He had caught the sullen look in Brenda's eyes when she served him breakfast that morning and hoped she had an inkling that she'd better be looking for another job.

His sons had phoned, sad that their mother had died, but glad that all the suffering she had endured was over. "If there's a museum in heaven, Mom and Susan are probably debating the merits of a painting," his younger son, Blake, had said.

Althorp knew his sons disliked him. After

college, they both had chosen to accept jobs far away, giving them an excuse to show up at home only about twice a year. Now they would be back for the second time in a few months. The first had been to attend the funeral of their sister; now it was their mother.

Gladys's body was in the funeral parlor. There would be no wake, but the funeral would not be until Friday, to accommodate his older son, whose daughter had just had an emergency appendectomy. The parents didn't want to leave her.

Neighbors had been calling to express their regrets; he had told Brenda to take messages. But at a quarter of nine, she came into the study and hesitantly told him that a Mr. Greco was on the phone, and insisted on speaking with him.

Althorp was about to refuse, then wondered if Gladys had still owed the man money. It was possible. According to the nurse, the man had been to see her very recently. He picked up the phone. "Charles Althorp." He knew his voice was intimidating. He took pride in that fact.

"Ambassador Althorp," Nicholas Greco began, "let me first express my sincere condolences at the loss of your wife. Mrs. Althorp was a gracious and brave lady, and set in motion the wheels that I think will soon bring a killer to justice."

"What are you talking about? Carrington is in jail."

"That's exactly what I'm talking about, Ambassador. Peter Carrington is in jail. But should he be? Or, to put it another way, should not someone else perhaps be sharing his jail cell? This is a dreadful time to intrude, but may I stop by for a few minutes later today? I have an eleven o'clock appointment with Mrs. Kay Carrington. Would it be possible to call on you at twelve thirty?"

"Be here at noon. I'll give you fifteen minutes." Althorp slammed the phone into the cradle, put down his coffee cup, and stood up. He walked over to the desk where there were pictures of his wife and their daughter.

"I'm so sorry, Gladys," he said aloud. "I'm so sorry, Susan."

67

I was in the kitchen when Vince stopped by for the gatehouse key at seven thirty. Then, as planned, he phoned at nine o'clock. Gary Barr was vacunning upstairs, and, on cue, I relayed the message to him. "Mr. Slater needs you to drive into the city and get some records from Peter's office," I told him. "There's a possibility that one of the company executives will drive back with you, so take the Mercedes. Mr. Slater will tell you where in the garage to park."

If Barr was suspicious, he didn't show it. He got on one of the extensions and confirmed the parking arrangements with Vincent. A few minutes later, from an upstairs window, I watched Barr drive the Mercedes past the gatehouse and out onto the road.

Vincent must have been watching for him to leave, because almost immediately, his Cadillac pulled onto the driveway and turned left. I guessed he would be parking behind the gatehouse in a spot that couldn't be seen from the mansion. Now it was my job to keep Jane from darting back home for some reason before her usual after-lunch break.

There was a simple way to do it. I told her that I had a headache and would she please answer the phone and take messages, except if Mr. Greco called.

"Mr. Greco?"

I heard the alarm in her voice and remembered that I had been told that after Mrs. Althorp had first hired Greco, he had talked to Gary Barr.

"Yes," I said. "I have an appointment with him at eleven o'clock."

The poor woman looked both frightened and confused. I felt very sure that if Vince was right, and Gary had stolen the shirt from Elaine's home, Jane had no part in that theft. But then I also remembered that she had sworn Gary was home in bed the night Susan disappeared. Had she been lying? By now, I was almost certain that she had.

For the next hour and a half, I was too restless to settle down, so I spent my time on the third floor. I hadn't been through even half the rooms because it took time to untie and remove the covers off the furniture that was stored up there. I was looking specifically for baby furniture, and finally found an antique wooden cradle. It was too heavy to pick up, so I squatted on the floor, rocking it to see if it was steady. It was exquisitely carved, and I checked to see if it had been signed. It had been, by someone named Eli Fallow, and the date was 1821.

I was sure the cradle must have been ordered by Adelaide Stuart, the posh lady who married a Carrington in 1820. I made a mental note to look up Eli Fallow and find out if he had a reputation as a craftsman. I was finding it fascinating to uncover these treasures, and it at least provided a diversion from my constant worrying about Peter.

That kind of exploring, however, is a dusty business. At 10:30, I went down to the suite and washed my face and hands, then changed into a fresh sweater and slacks. I was barely ready when the doorbell rang promptly at eleven o'clock, and Nicholas Greco entered the house.

The first time I met him had been at Maggie's house, and I had resented his suggestion that my father might have staged his own suicide. He'd even hinted there might be a connection between him and Susan Althorp's disappearance. When Greco spoke to me in the courthouse hallway after the bail hearing, I was so upset that I barely noticed him. But now, as I looked straight at him, I felt that I could detect both warmth and sympathy in his eyes. I shook his hand and led him back to Peter's library.

"What a wonderful room this is," Greco commented as we entered.

"That was my impression the first time I saw it," I told him. Trying to overcome my sudden attack of nerves, brought on by the radical move I was making in meeting this man, I added, "I came here begging the chance to have a literacy cocktail party in the mansion. Peter was sitting in his chair." I pointed to it. "I felt nervous, and not properly dressed. It was a windy day in October, and I was wearing a light summer suit. As I pleaded my case, I was taking in this room and loving it."

"As well you might," Greco said.

I sat behind Peter's desk and Greco pulled up a chair across from it. "You told me you could be of service to me," I told him. "Now explain to me how you would do that."

"I can serve you best by trying to ascertain the entire truth of what has happened. As you are certainly aware, your husband is facing a strong probability that he will spend the rest of his life in prison. It may give him some personal vindication if the world comes to believe that he is innocent — and now I quote — 'owing to the act being a noninsane automatism.' That is what might have happened if all this was taking place in Canada, but of course it is not."

"I do not believe that my husband, sleep-walking or not, committed any of those crimes," I said. "Last night I received what to me is convincing proof that he did not."

I had already decided that I wanted to hire Nicholas Greco. I told him that, and then I unburdened myself, starting with my visit to the chapel when I was six years old. "It never occurred to me that I might have overheard Susan Althorp that day," I said. "I mean, why would she need to beg or threaten to get money from anyone? Her family was wealthy. I've heard also that she had a sub-stantial trust fund."

"It would be interesting to establish ex-actly how much money she had at her dis-posal," Greco said. "Not too many eighteen-year-olds have access to their trust funds, and Susan's friends tell us that her father had been very angry at her the night of the dinner party."

He asked about the time Peter had jumped bail and been found kneeling on the Al-thorps' lawn.

"Peter was sleepwalking and doesn't know why he went there, but he thinks it was the same sleepwalking dream that made him try to get out of the hospital room. That second time he thought Gary Barr was in the room watching him," I explained.

I told Greco that I had begun to think that Peter might have been the one who was being blackmailed in the chapel. "Last night, I found out that wasn't true," I said, and, trying not to get emotional, repeated for him what Maggie had told me.

Greco's expression became grave. "Mrs. Carrington," he said, "I have been concerned for you ever since I heard you had gone to see Susan Althorp's friend, Sarah North. Let us presume that your husband is innocent of these crimes. If so, then the guilty person is still around, and I believe — and fear — that person is in close proximity to you."

"Have you any suggestion as to how I can draw out that person?" I asked, aware my frustration was showing. "Mr. Greco, I know I was only six years old at the time, but if I had told my father about being in the chapel, and had recounted what I heard there, he might have gone to the police when Susan disappeared. The same man I heard in the chapel has to have been the man my father heard whistling outside shortly afterwards. Don't you think that knowledge is

401

torturing me?"

" 'When I was a child, I thought as a child,' " Greco said, his voice gentle. "Mrs. Carrington, do not be so hard on yourself. This information opens up new avenues, but I beg you, do *not* share with anyone else what your grandmother told you last night, and please tell *her* not to repeat it. Someone might begin to fear both her memory and yours."

He looked at his watch. "I must leave you in a few minutes. I asked Ambassador Althorp to spare me a little time today, and I suggested twelve thirty. Unfortunately, he told me to be there at noon. Is there anything else that you think would be helpful in my investigation?"

I didn't know until that moment that I was going to tell him about Peter's shirt, but then I decided I had to go for broke. "If I told you something that could seriously hurt Peter's defense, would you feel it necessary to go to the prosecutor with that information?" I asked him.

"What you tell me is hearsay, and I would not be allowed to testify to it," he said.

"All these years, Elaine Carrington has had Peter's formal dress shirt with some stains that appear to be blood on it. A few days ago, she sold it to me for one million dollars, then, after she was paid, refused to give it to me. Since then it has been stolen from her home here on the estate. Vincent Slater believes Gary Barr is the one who took it, and right now he is searching the gatehouse, looking for it."

If Nicholas Greco was astonished at that information, he did not show it. Instead, he asked me how Elaine got the shirt, and how sure I was that it had bloodstains on it.

" 'Stains' is too strong a word," I said. "From what I could see, it was more like a smudge, right here." I touched my sweater just above my heart. "Elaine said she saw Peter come home in a sleepwalking state at two o'clock that morning, and while she claims she had no idea what may have happened, she recognized that it was a bloodstain on his shirt and didn't want the maid to see it in the morning."

"So now she uses the shirt to blackmail you, then reneges on the deal. Why did she come forward at this time?"

"Because her son Richard is a compulsive gambler, and she's always bailing him out. This time he apparently needed more money than she could come up with, at least in time to keep him from getting in trouble."

"I see." Greco got up to leave. "You have given me a great deal to think about, Mrs.

Carrington. Tell me something. If somebody were to leave something in this house, a personal item of some sort, and your husband thought it might be needed, what do you think he would do?"

"Return it," I said, "and right away. I can give you an example. One night in December, Peter dropped me off at my apartment, then started driving home. He got over the bridge and realized I had left my wool scarf in the car. Can you believe he turned around and brought it back to me? I told him he was crazy, but he said that it was cold, and I had a walk to my car in the morning, and he thought I should have it." I saw what Greco was driving at. "Susan's evening purse," I said. "Do you think that when Peter was sleepwalking that night, he was trying to return her purse?"

"I don't know, Mrs. Carrington. It is one of the many possibilities I shall consider, but it would explain your husband's surprise and distress the next morning when the purse was not in his car, wouldn't it?"

He did not wait for my answer, but instead opened his briefcase, pulled out a sheet of paper, and handed it to me. It was a copy of a page from *People* magazine. "Does this have any significance to you?" he asked.

"Oh, that's an article about Marian Howley," I said. "She's the most wonderful actress. I never miss one of her plays."

"Apparently Grace Carrington shared your enthusiasm for this actress. She tore this page out of the magazine; it was in her pocket when her body was found in the pool."

I started to hand the paper back to Greco, but he waved it away. "No, I downloaded several copies when I got a back issue of the magazine. Please keep this one. Perhaps you could show it to Mr. Carrington."

The telephone rang. I reached for it, then remembered that Jane Barr was supposed to be taking messages. Moments later, as Greco and I were leaving the library, she came running down the hall. "It's Mr. Slater, Mrs. Carrington," she said, "He said it's important."

Greco waited while I went back to the desk and picked up the receiver.

"Kay, I didn't find it," Vince said. "He must have hidden it somewhere else."

There was something in his voice that made me feel sure he was lying. "I don't believe you," I told him.

The phone clicked in my ear.

"Vince Slater claims he didn't find Peter's shirt," I told Nicholas Greco. "I don't believe him. He has it. I'd stake my life on it."

"Does Vincent Slater have a key to this house?" Greco asked me.

"I changed all the locks and gave him a key only to the door that goes from the terrace into his private office. But you can get into the house from the office."

"Then he does have a key, Mrs. Carrington. Have that lock changed immediately. I believe that Vincent Slater may be a very dangerous man."

68

"I've decided to close the gallery at the end of the week," Richard Walker told Pat Jennings. "I know it's short notice, but the building owner has someone who wants the space right away and will pay a bonus to get it."

Jennings looked at him, dumbfounded. "Can you get other space yourself that fast?" she asked.

"No, I mean I'm going to close the gallery *permanently*. As I'm sure you're aware, I'm too fond of horse racing for my own good. I'd like to try a complete change of scenery. I have an elderly friend who has a small but most interesting gallery in London, and he'd very much like to have me go in with him."

"That sounds wonderful," Jennings said, trying to sound sincere. I wonder if Mama has pulled the plug on bailing him out, she thought. I wouldn't blame her. And maybe he's right. It would be a lot better to get away from all the bookies who supply him with all those hot tips. "What does your mother think of all this?" she asked. "I'm sure she'll miss you."

"Even with the Concorde gone, England is just a hop, skip, and jump away, and she has many friends there."

Pat Jennings realized that she was going to not only miss her salary, but also the flexible hours she had here — they dovetailed perfectly with her kids' school schedule. And it had been fun to see Trish regularly, to say nothing about having a seat on the fifty yard line of the Carrington family saga.

She decided to go for one more tidbit before it was too late. "How is Mrs. Peter Carrington doing?" she asked Richard, trying to sound concerned but not overly interested.

"How nice of you to ask! I haven't seen Kay in several weeks, but my mother tells me they've been in close touch, and we'll be having dinner together before I leave for England."

With a dismissive smile, as if he realized he was being pumped for information, Richard Walker turned to go into his private office. The phone rang. When Pat Jennings answered it, an angry voice snapped, "This is Alexandra Lloyd. Is Richard there?"

Without even asking, Pat knew the answer

to give, only this time, she made it more elaborate. "Mr. Walker is on his way to London, Ms. Lloyd. May I take a message?"

"Oh, indeed you can. Tell Mr. Walker that I am very disappointed in him, and he knows what I mean."

This is one message I don't want to give him, Pat thought. I had believed all along that this lady with the fancy name was an artist. Now I'm beginning to think she's a bookie.

It was three o'clock, time to get uptown and pick up the kids. Richard's door was closed, but she could hear the murmur of his voice, which meant he was on the phone. Pat wrote out Alexandra Lloyd's message word for word, and, not happy with the way it looked on paper, tapped on Richard's door, walked in, and placed it on the desk in front of him.

Then, with the haste of someone who knows that a firecracker might explode at her feet at any moment, she grabbed her coat and left.

69

When Nicholas Greco was escorted by the housekeeper into the study where previously he had met with Gladys Althorp, he felt protectively annoyed that her husband had so quickly commandeered the space that so recently had been hers. He saw that her shawl was missing from the chair, and that the blinds were no longer tilted. Sunlight that hinted of an early spring was pouring into the room, destroying the dim and quiet intimacy he had experienced there.

"The ambassador will be with you shortly," the housekeeper said.

Is this a power play? Greco wondered. I asked to come at 12:30; he insisted I be here at noon. Now is he going to keep me waiting?

Greco remembered how concerned the housekeeper had been about Gladys Althorp. What was her name? he asked himself, then remembered it. "Brenda, I witnessed how solicitous you were of Mrs. Althorp. I am sure you were a great comfort to her."

"I hope I was. I haven't been here that long, but I was very fond of her. And I do know she died happy, knowing that the man who killed her daughter was finally going to pay for his crime. Mrs. Althorp told me that the day she was in court watching Peter Carrington in chains was something she'd prayed for every single day for twenty-two years."

Charles Althorp had come into the room while she was speaking, and had overheard her. "We're delighted to have your opinion, Brenda," he said sarcastically. "You may go now."

Greco took an instant dislike to Althorp. Humiliating his housekeeper in front of another person was probably indicative of the employer-employee relationship that existed in this house, and given Althorp's attitude on the phone, he expected nothing more.

Brenda reacted as though she had been slapped. Her body stiffened. Then, with quiet dignity, she turned and left the room.

Althorp indicated a chair for Greco and sat down himself. "I have a luncheon engagement," he said, "so you do understand that fifteen minutes means fifteen minutes."

"I am aware of the time constraints,"

Greco said. Deliberately avoiding the use of Althorp's courtesy title, he began, "Mr. Althorp, you were very angry at your daughter, Susan, that last evening. It was noticed and remarked upon by a number of people. Why were you so upset with her?"

"I don't even remember, and it isn't important. Naturally, I have always felt terrible that my last contact with Susan was under those circumstances."

"You and Mrs. Althorp left the dinner party early the night Susan disappeared."

"We left shortly after dinner. As had become usual, Gladys was not feeling well."

"Before you left, you ordered your daughter to be home by midnight. The party, from what I understand, lasted well over an hour after that. Why the curfew?"

"Susan was overtired. I was concerned about her. I wanted her to leave with us. The dancing had just begun. Peter asked if she could stay for a little while; he offered to escort her home."

"You liked Peter."

"Very much, at that time."

"Mr. Althorp, I will ask you again: why were you concerned about your daughter?"

"That is none of your business, Mr. Greco."

"Oh, but I think it is. If what I believe is

correct, it is the reason Susan is dead."

Greco watched as Althorp's face turned crimson. Rage or fear? Greco asked himself.

"When Mrs. Kay Carrington was a six-year-old child, she was sitting outside the Carrington mansion waiting for her father, Jonathan Lansing, who, as you know, was the landscaper there. It was the same day as the party. He was attending to a problem concerning the lighting. Kay had heard about the chapel, and, being a typically curious child, went into the house to look at it. While she was there, she heard the chapel door opening and hid between the pews. She did not see the people who entered, but she heard the words they exchanged. It was a couple, and the woman was demanding money from the man."

Greco paused, then, his tone bitingly cold, said, "I believe that the woman in the chapel was your daughter, Susan. I believe that she had developed a drug problem, and that she needed money because she needed more drugs. I believe that you knew of the problem, but wanted to control it your own way, by making sure she had no money, and by keeping such a close watch on her that she would not have access to whoever was her supplier."

"No wonder you have such a fine reputation as an investigator, Mr. Greco. But even if this were true, what does it prove? Why does it matter now?" Althorp's voice was equally cold.

"Oh, I would say it matters very much, Mr. Althorp. If you had sought professional help for Susan, she might still be alive today."

"When she disappeared, I thought she had run away with her dealer. I thought she'd show up again someday," Althorp replied.

"And, thinking that, you committed the unpardonable sin of letting Peter Carrington be a suspect in her disappearance? Despite the fact that you actually thought there was a possibility she might still be alive?"

"I simply didn't know. I couldn't have opened up that possibility. It would have killed my wife," Althorp said. "Susan's mother thought she was a perfect child. The idea that Susan was a drug addict would have destroyed her."

"When did you first suspect that Susan was using drugs?"

"Shortly after she returned from her freshman year at college. There was something different about her that last summer. She'd get irritable, or cry easily, and that was totally unlike her. I didn't know what to believe, but then one evening when she was out, I passed her room and saw that she'd left all the lights on. I went in to turn them off, and spotted something on the floor. It was tinfoil and there was some white powder in it. It appeared to be cocaine. I knew then what was going on. When Susan came home, I confronted her and demanded to know where she was getting the drugs. She wouldn't tell me. That was about a month before she disappeared."

"If you had told the police about Susan's problem, it would have immediately changed the nature of the investigation, and her dealer might have been apprehended. Why did your wife hire me six months ago? It was to find something that could bring your daughter's presumed killer, Peter Carrington, to trial. The arrest and imprisonment of Susan's killer surely would have brought her peace and closure." Greco heard his voice rising. "Was it better to let your wife suffer every day of her life as she did? Was that your idea of being merciful? That is a comfortable excuse for your silence, isn't it? Isn't it true that you hoped to be appointed to another ambassadorship and didn't want any hint of scandal attached to your name? The beautiful debutante presumed to have been murdered by a wealthy young man engendered public sympathy for the family. You were content to leave it at that."

"That is your opinion and I will not dignify it by responding," Althorp said. "Why are you here, Mr. Greco? What difference does any of this make now? It won't bring Susan back, and as my son pointed out to me yesterday, if there is an art museum in heaven, Susan and her mother are there, discussing paintings. It is a scenario in which I find comfort."

"You may find comfort in your scenario, but do you really have the nerve to ask what difference it would make if the truth were told now? Didn't it ever occur to you that Susan may have been murdered by the drug dealer, and not by Peter Carrington?"

"Peter's shirt was missing. I thought that he might have had an argument with Susan that got out of hand."

"It was either a drug dealer or Peter who took her life, and you are content with either answer! I have another theory, Mr. Althorp. You may have heard Susan trying to sneak out that night. You may have been angry enough to harm her yourself. It was noon the next day before anyone realized that she was not in her room. You had plenty of time to hide the body until you could dispose of it permanently."

Charles Althorp gripped the arms of his

chair. "That is absolutely preposterous, Mr. Greco! And insulting. Your fifteen minutes are up. Get out!"

"I am going to leave now, Ambassador Althorp," Greco said, emphasizing the title with contempt in his voice. "But I will be back," he said. "I assure you, I will be back."

70

I spoke to Maggie a couple of times in the next few days, and I knew she was concentrating on trying to remember the name of the man my father had heard whistling the tune that was so nostalgic to him. Then something occurred to me. "Maggie, you said that Daddy was down in the dumps when he told you about it. His car was found so soon afterward, and you thought he had committed suicide, do you think you might have talked about that incident to your friends?"

"We certainly talked about how much he missed your mother. I probably did tell them about it. It was an example of how much he missed her."

"Then there's always a chance that you mentioned the man's name, because you said Daddy mentioned it to you."

"I may have, but, Kay, that was over twenty-two years ago. If I can't remember, how do you expect anyone else would?"

"I really don't. But it's just one of those things that are easy for you to do, and may be so helpful to us. I want you to talk about Daddy to your friends. Tell them that, in a way, it's been good for me to know that he didn't willingly leave me. Then you can remind them of that story, and say that it's been annoying you that you can't come up with the name of the man who was whistling that song the day of the party. But talk about it *only* to your friends, please."

"Kay, it's really unlikely that someone will come up with a name after all these years, but I'd do anything to help. It's a visiting day at the jail, isn't it?"

"Yes, it is."

"Will you congratulate your husband — I mean Peter — about the baby?"

"Thank you, Maggie. He'll appreciate that."

Two hours later, I was in the visiting room of the Bergen County Jail, looking at Peter through the Plexiglas. I wanted so much to touch him, to link my fingers with his. I wanted to bring him home and close the door on the rest of the world. I wanted our life back.

But, of course, to say any of that now would only make it harder for him. There were so many things I couldn't say. I couldn't talk about the shirt that I thought Gary Barr had stolen from Elaine, only to have it stolen again by Vincent Slater. Vince had continued to deny he found it when he searched the gatehouse and the SUV, but I didn't believe him.

I couldn't talk to him about the money I'd paid Elaine, and I certainly couldn't tell Peter that I'd hired Nicholas Greco.

Instead I told Peter about finding the antique cradle, and how I was going to look up Eli Fallow, the craftsman, and see if I could learn anything about him. "The third floor is like a treasure hunt, Peter."

Small talk. Unsatisfactory. The kind you make with a patient in the hospital when you know you really can't talk about important things because it would be too upsetting. Peter's face lit up at any reference to the baby, but that was followed by worry about me. He noticed my weight loss, and I assured him that the obstetrician said that in the first trimester it was not unusual.

He asked if I saw much of Elaine and Richard. I hedged by saying how shocked I had been when Elaine told me that Richard was pulling up stakes and moving to London. "I gather he's facing his gambling problems, and also the fact that his own gallery is always losing money," I said.

"I think that's a solid direction for him to take," Peter said. "As far back as when Elaine and my father were dating, Richard was into the horses, which, if you knew my father, was absolutely unforgivable. I think one of the reasons my father demanded to see every bill that came into the house during the big decorating siege was because he wanted to make sure Elaine wasn't supporting her son's gambling habit, at least with his money. I think it would be nice if you had Elaine and Richard and Vince for dinner before Richard leaves, Kay."

I couldn't say that was the last thing I wanted to do. Instead I ignored the suggestion and asked, "What kind of allowance did you have as a kid? Was your father generous with you?"

Peter could look so boyish when he smiled. "Actually, he was okay. Fortunately for our relationship, I never went the route of the rich man's spoiled son. I liked to go into the office during the summer and on school holidays. I'm fascinated with the financial world. I'm good at it. That pleased my father. And he honestly had a soft heart for anyone in genuine need, which is why the check he gave Maria Valdez was exactly the sort of gesture he would make, and *did* make to many people."

Then Peter's expression darkened. "And try to convince anyone of that," he added softly.

I knew I only had a few minutes left. I was holding the phone. "Guessing game," I said, and hummed the melody of the song I had heard in the chapel. "Do you recognize this tune?" I asked.

"I don't think so. In fact, I'd say that I don't."

"I had a friend who was a good whistler. Nobody does that anymore. Did you ever know anyone who whistles, I mean, some-one, maybe like Vince?"

Peter actually laughed. I realized it was the first time I'd heard him laugh since we came back from our honeymoon.

"Kay, I can as easily imagine Vince whistling as I can see him being a circus barker. Buttoned-up Vincent Slater, whistling a tune for anyone to hear? Come on!"

The guard was approaching me. Our visiting time was up. Peter and I pressed our lips against the glass that separated us, and, as usual, I tried not to cry. "How do I love thee?" I asked him.

"Let me count the ways," he whispered. It had become our way of saying good-bye after a visit.

But then he added, "Kay, have a dinner for Richard before he leaves for London. I'd like that. He's always had his problems, but he *is* my stepbrother, and Elaine has always been kind to me."

71

The more I learn, the less I know, Nicholas Greco thought as he drove into the grounds of the Carrington estate. The guard had been told to expect him and gave a casual salute as Greco turned onto the driveway of the gatehouse.

He had phoned yesterday to request this appointment with Gary Barr, and had made it clear that he did not want to have it in Jane's presence.

"I am not aware of how much your wife knows of your activities," he had told Barr, "but unless you have shared all your experiences with her, I suggest you find a reason to schedule our meeting when she is not around."

"I'll be out doing errands until about noon," Barr told him. "Jane is always at the mansion then." In a tone of voice that was both hostile and worried, he'd added: "I don't know why you want to bother with me.

424

I've already told everything I know about that girl's death, and I wasn't even working here around the time the landscaper disappeared."

I hope my strategy to unsettle him by giving him time to worry about the reason for our appointment is working, Greco thought as he parked the car and walked up the path to the gatehouse.

It was a narrow stone structure with leaded pane windows. When Gary Barr answered the door and grudgingly invited him in, Greco was surprised and impressed by the interior of the dwelling. The limited space had been maximized by having the first floor turned into one large room with kitchen, dining, and sitting area flowing together harmoniously. The handsome stone fireplace and high-beamed ceiling imparted a sense of timelessness. How many generations of people have lived here in the four hundred years since it was built in Wales? he wondered.

A comfortable residence for a housekeeping couple, he decided — far more pleasant than the quarters most employees enjoy. He noticed that it was spotlessly clean. In his experience as an investigator, he had sometimes come across housekeepers whose own homes were hardly models of cleanliness.

Without being invited, he selected a

straight-backed chair near the couch, sat down, and with a deliberately cool tone, said, "Mr. Barr, I think that we should not waste each other's time this morning. Let's get to the point: You were dealing drugs to Susan Althorp."

"That's a lie!"

"Is it? When you were chauffeuring those young women around, and Susan sat in front with you, you made it your business to become her 'pal.' But there were three other girls in the back. One of them, Sarah Kennedy, was Susan's closest friend. Do you seriously suppose that Susan didn't confide in her?"

It was the kind of tricky question Greco liked to ask, the kind that often brought out a truthful response.

Gary Barr did not respond, but looked around nervously as if afraid someone might overhear their conversation. *A chronic eavesdropper is always afraid of someone eavesdropping on* him, Greco thought with contempt.

"You and your wife worked quite regularly for the Althorps during the years you were not employed by the Carringtons. I have witnessed Ambassador Althorp's attitude toward his employees. You must have resented that very much, didn't you, Mr. Barr? What a sweet revenge it must have been for you to entice the young daughter of the family into drugs, then refuse to give them to her unless she paid for them immediately. After she returned home that last night, she slipped out again because you were going to meet her. Isn't that what happened?"

Gary Barr impatiently brushed away the perspiration that was glistening on his forehead. "Don't you come here and try to scare me. I know the law. Even if I *did* sell her a little cocaine, that was over twenty-two years ago. The statute of limitations ran out a long time ago. Look it up."

"I don't have to look it up, Mr. Barr. I am quite aware of the statute of limitations, and you are right. Unfortunately, you cannot be prosecuted for selling drugs to that poor girl, but, as I hope you are also aware, there is no statute of limitations for murder."

"*Murder*? You've got to be kidding. I didn't —"

Greco interrupted him. "If I go to the prosecutor and tell what I know, they will undoubtedly open another grand jury investigation. You will be subpoenaed, and you can't take the Fifth Amendment. You can't refuse to testify, because they can't prosecute you. But you can and will be charged with perjury if you lie to the grand jury about your involvement with Susan and anything else you know about her disappearance, so you had better come clean."

"All right! I was there," Barr said, his voice hoarse and hesitant. "It's like you said. She wanted some stuff and I told her I had to have the money up front, and she said she'd have it for me. I told her I'd be outside at quarter of two and to be on time."

"Peter Carrington left Susan at her home at twelve o'clock. Why so late?"

"She wanted to be sure her father was asleep."

"Why didn't you give her the cocaine at the party?"

"She didn't have the cash for me when she left the party. Otherwise I would have given it to her then."

Greco looked at Barr with loathing and disgust. By not giving her what she needed, you signed her death warrant, he thought. Somebody else was going to meet her, supposedly with the money.

"I left here at one thirty and walked over to the Althorps'," Barr said. "I cut across the lawn of the neighbors who live behind their house, and waited under the big tree in the side yard. No one could see me there. She didn't show up at quarter of two. Then, about ten minutes later, I heard a car coming. I waited to find out what was going on, figuring it was someone bringing her the cash, getting there late."

Barr stood up, walked over to the sink, and poured himself a glass of water. He gulped half of it, set the glass down, and came back. "I recognized the car. It was Peter Carrington's. He got out, came around and opened the passenger door, and took something out of it."

"You could see him clearly enough to see what he was doing?"

"There's a streetlight right on the curb in front of the Althorps' house. That's why I was meeting Susan at the side of the house."

"Go on."

"Peter got out of the car and walked across the lawn. Then he knelt down. I kind of crept forward, and I could see he was bending over something. There was just enough light that I could make out that something — maybe even someone — was lying on the ground. Then Peter got back in his car and drove away. I didn't know what was up, but I got out of there and came home."

"You didn't check to see if anyone needed help?"

"Carrington drove away. *He* didn't help anyone."

"And you saw no one else?"

"No."

"Are you sure you didn't meet Susan, have an argument because she didn't have the money, and perhaps, she even threatened to tell her father about you if you didn't give her the cocaine? You strangled her, then heard Peter's car coming and hid. When he drove off, you disposed of the body. Didn't it happen that way, Mr. Barr?"

"No, it didn't. I'll take a lie detector test if you want. I was home at twenty after two. I even woke up my wife and said that I didn't feel so good."

"You mean you wanted a witness, just in case. You're a very self-serving individual, Mr. Barr. I remember your wife offered to take a lie detector test to swear that you were home all night."

"She thought I was."

"We'll leave it at that. By the way, did Mr. Slater find the bloodstained dress shirt after he lured you into New York and searched this house, Mr. Barr?"

It was a satisfaction to Greco to see the dumbfounded look on Gary Barr's face.

"So, *he's* the one who did it," Barr said heavily. "I might have known."

72

Richard was leaving for London on Sunday night. I scheduled the farewell dinner for Saturday evening, more to honor Peter's wishes than to honor Richard, but I did go all out preparing for it. I'm a good cook and I worked with Jane to plan some really special dishes: asparagus with warm cheese as an appetizer, Dover sole, a watercress salad with apples, followed by raspberry sorbet and then an assortment of cheeses with a dessert wine.

"We'll have cocktails in the living room, then after dinner have coffee in Mr. Carrington's library," I told Jane.

"I'll have Gary build a fire in the library," she promised.

Gary Barr was being uncomfortably solicitous toward me, and I knew that before much longer I was going to give him his walking papers. I was very sorry that it would mean letting Jane go, too, but I knew

I had no choice, and I was sure she could see the handwriting on the wall.

I had spoken to Nicholas Greco several times, and he had said that my suspicions were totally correct about the missing dress shirt. He told me that Barr had stolen it from Elaine, and Slater had then found it in the gatehouse, and presumably still had it. He warned me that I was not to say or do anything that would indicate *I* was aware of the shirt having been recovered.

"But I was the one who put Gary on the phone with Vincent," I protested. "I set him up for that trip to New York."

"My guess is that Barr is probably thinking that Slater tricked you for his own purposes," Greco said. "You must act as if Gary Barr is still your trusted employee, and I would suggest that when you speak with Mr. Slater, you apologize for doubting his word about the shirt. Certainly Gary Barr would not dare to challenge him on the subject."

Whenever I spoke to Greco on the phone, he continued to warn me: "You must be very careful around both Slater and Barr. We may still find an unholy alliance there. Elaine Carrington is a blackmailer, and her son is always desperate for money. Throw that into the mix and you have a potentially explosive situation."

I told him that Richard was going to live in London.

"I doubt that distance will solve his problems," Greco said. "The problem is not in the location; it's in the man."

Greco asked if I had brought the page from *People* magazine to show Peter. I confessed that I had not. "I'm sure he did not see Grace showing her guests that magazine," I said. "Everyone agrees he went straight upstairs after that scene with her."

"I understand your wishing not to cause your husband any further distress, but Mrs. Carrington, someone took that magazine that night. I believe it was taken because that person didn't realize Grace had already torn out the page featuring an article about that actress. It *is* important. Trust my instincts. It is very important."

"I will show it to Peter next time I visit him," I promised. Then I asked Greco if he was making any progress in proving Peter's innocence. His answer did not encourage me: "I am learning why this tragedy was set in motion," he said. "Now it is up to me to put the rest of the story together. It's far too soon and most unfair to offer you unfounded hope."

I didn't want double-talk. "Is there any hope that you can find new evidence so that

Peter can be acquitted when he comes to trial?"

"There may be hope, Mrs. Carrington," Greco said. "But until I can offer proof that would stand up in court, it would be impossible to offer you more than just that."

For now I had to be content with that. The problem was, I was missing Peter so acutely that I needed some kind of reassurance that he would come home, even if it would take a miracle.

Planning the farewell dinner for Richard was a diversion, and as I made my selections in the cheese shop, I forced myself to believe that someday soon I would be buying Peter's favorite cheese for him.

I spent time that week having Gary Barr move furniture around in the living room. My first impression of that room had been wholly favorable — it was a beautiful room. But I had come to realize it also was a reflection of Elaine's taste — she had chosen everything in it, and as I got used to being there, I began to feel uncomfortable. Everything seemed too formal, too precise. The room lacked the lived-in feeling necessary to give it comfort and warmth.

I began to exchange the lamps Elaine had chosen with lovely porcelain antique lamps I found on the third floor. According to Jane Barr, Elaine had banished them when she redecorated the mansion. I set framed family pictures on the mantel, and placed photograph albums dating back one hundred years on top of the grand piano.

I once heard a prominent journalist say that in her home, books were the interior decoration. The bookcases by the fireplace in the living room contained expensive but modern tchotchkes. I packed many of them away and replaced them with some of my books which I had shipped to the mansion before the wedding. Peter and I joked that those boxes constituted my dowry. When Elaine came to the house on Saturday, it would be her first visit since I had made my changes. I would be watching for her reaction.

I had told the guests for Richard's dinner to arrive at seven o'clock. It seemed like years had passed since Peter and I had dinner with these same guests the week after we returned from our honeymoon. I decided to wear the same silk shirt and velvet slacks that I'd worn that night. I could tell I wouldn't be wearing those slacks again until after the baby was born. Then I let my hair fall loose on my shoulders. I knew I was dressing for my husband, not these people.

I had left that page from *People* magazine on top of my dresser, hoping that if I kept looking at it I would find the information Greco was sure was there. When I was about to go downstairs, I impulsively picked up that page and took it with me. I placed it on top of Peter's desk in his library, where it would be easy to see when we were having coffee. I had said I wanted to draw out the real killer — if he or she was in that small group. If there really *was* significance to that page, then maybe one of them would react to it. Frankly, I thought Greco was putting far too much weight on it.

At precisely seven, the chimes sounded, and the first of my guests arrived.

73

"Go easy, Richard," Elaine Carrington cautioned as she watched her son pour a second vodka for himself. "We'll be having cocktails at the mansion, and then wine at dinner."

"I would never have guessed that," Richard said.

Elaine eyed her son anxiously. He'd been on edge ever since he arrived, which meant he probably had placed some bets after getting a few more of his hot tips. But maybe not, she thought, trying to reassure herself. He knows I can't cover his losses anymore.

"What do you think will happen after Peter is convicted?" Richard asked abruptly. "Will Kay just rattle around in the mansion all by herself?"

"She's having a baby," Elaine replied sharply. "She won't be alone for long."

"You didn't tell me that."

"Kay didn't tell me that. I found out because Linda Hauser's daughter ran into Kay at Dr. Silver's office."

"That doesn't prove she's pregnant."

"Trust me. She is. In fact, I'm going to ask her tonight, and I'll bet she'll admit it."

"So we have an heir to the Carrington fortune," Richard said with a sneer. "Isn't *that* wonderful?"

"Don't worry. I plan to be the ultimate stepgrandmother. Kay already understands that I hid that shirt to save Peter, and she's grateful for that. Not giving it to her was a big mistake — she'd have been forever in my debt. Now she sees me as a blackmailer who didn't deliver."

"Which you are." Richard said.

Elaine slammed down the glass of wine she had been sipping. "Don't you dare talk to me like that! If it weren't for you, I'd be living on the interest of ten million dollars as well as a million a year. Between your gambling and your lousy investments, you've drained me dry, Richard, and you know it. You've put me through the tortures of the damned, and now you insult me! Go to hell, Richard! Go to hell!"

Her face crumbled as her son crossed the room in two strides. "Hey, none of that," he said soothingly. "It's you and me against the world — including the whole damn bunch of Carringtons. Right, Mommy?" His voice became teasing. "Come on, Momma-mia, make up with me."

"Oh, Richard," Elaine said with a heavy sigh. "You remind me so much of your father. Turn on the charm, let's make up. That was his routine."

"You were crazy about my father. I remember that."

"Yes, I was," Elaine said quietly. "But even when you're crazy about someone, at some point you can have enough. Remember that, Richard. And forget that second vodka. Have another at the mansion. It's time to go. We're due at seven."

74

Vincent Slater was the first to arrive for the dinner. As usual, he parked in the driveway behind the mansion and took out his key, planning to enter through the French doors that opened into his office.

The key did not turn — the lock had been changed.

Damn her, he thought, *damn* her! Kay Lansing, the landscaper's daughter — she's now making Peter Carrington's home off-limits to the one person who has protected Peter from the time he was a young boy. And continues to protect him, Slater thought grimly. If she only knew!

If I'd given her the shirt, she would have showed it to that detective, and that would have been it. She puts on an act of being so crazy about Peter, but the way it's going, this will end up with him rotting in prison while she enjoys the Carrington fortune.

Maybe. But then again, maybe not,

he thought.

His anger rising with every step, Slater walked around the mansion, nodded curtly to the guard on duty, and went to the front door. For the first time in nearly thirty years, he pressed his finger on the doorbell and waited to be invited inside.

75

"It was Slater," Gary Barr told his wife as he entered the kitchen. "You can count on him being Johnny-on-the-spot. The clock chimes seven, and there he is, ringing the doorbell."

"Why are you so mad at him? He's always been nice to you." Jane Barr was putting cheese puffs in the oven. She closed the oven door and turned to her husband. "You need to change your attitude, Gary, although it may be too late. I can tell Mrs. Carrington isn't comfortable with you around. That's why most nights she's been telling us not to wait to serve dinner."

"She was the one who got Slater on the phone to tell me to run that fool's errand in New York. She was in on searching the house. She even had you answer the phone so she'd be sure you wouldn't run over there for any reason." Too late, Gary Barr realized that he had said too much. Jane knew nothing about Peter Carrington's dress shirt, nor did she realize that their home had been searched.

"What are you talking about?" Jane demanded. "Who searched what? Why?"

The doorbell rang again. Saved by the bell, Gary Barr thought as he rushed to answer. This time it was Elaine Carrington and her son Richard.

"Good evening, Mrs. Carrington, Mr. Walker."

Elaine ignored him and brushed by as she headed inside.

Walker paused: "I would suggest that, for your own good, you return what you took from my mother's home. I know more about you than you think I know, and I'm not afraid to use it."

76

Barbara Krause and Tom Moran had stayed in the office long after the rest of the prosecutor's staff had said good night and scurried away for the weekend. After Barbara received the phone call, she told Moran to get out the Susan Althorp file so that they could review the statements Ambassador Althorp had made at the time of his daughter's disappearance.

The ambassador had phoned Barbara, asked for the appointment, and said it was necessary to make it that late because his lawyer would be accompanying him.

"We always considered it possible that he was the one who did it," Moran said, "although it seemed only remotely possible. But now that his wife is dead, maybe he needs to come clean. Otherwise, why would he bother to bring a lawyer with him?"

Promptly at eight o'clock, Althorp and his lawyer were escorted into the prosecutor's office. Krause's first impression of Althorp was that he looked sick. The ruddy complexion she had remembered when she last saw him was now pasty, and his face had become jowly.

He looks like a guy who just suffered a blow to the solar plexus, she thought.

"My wife has been buried," Ambassador Althorp began abruptly. "I cannot protect her any longer. After the funeral, I told my sons something that I have kept secret for twenty-two years. In turn, one of them then told me something that Susan had confided to him the Christmas before her death, and this new information changes everything. I believe that there has been a terrible miscarriage of justice, and I share responsibility for it."

Krause and Moran stared at him in stunned silence.

"Ambassador Althorp wishes to make a statement," his lawyer said. "Are you prepared to take it?"

77

Elaine did not comment on the changes I had made in the living room, which I interpreted to mean that she was not pleased with them. She carried it off well, although I could understand how she must be feeling. Six months ago she knew nothing of my existence. She had lived in this house for the five years she was married to Peter's father, and after his death had stayed on, running the place until Peter married Grace Meredith. Now it was mine.

"That was when things changed. Mrs. Elaine moved into the other house, and Peter invited us to come back," Jane Barr had confided to me. "Mrs. Grace Carrington took the people on the staff that she especially liked and shifted them to the apartment. That's where she really lived and did her entertaining, so even though there was a new mistress in the house, Mrs. Elaine pretty much had the run of the mansion, even though she didn't actually live here anymore."

In the years following Grace's death, Elaine had become a kind of de facto lady of the house. Then I had come along to spoil it.

I was aware that without me in the picture, she was the closest thing to a relative that Peter had, and it would have been only natural for him to turn to her for comfort if he went to prison. And Peter was generous.

Vincent Slater was either acting very cool to me, or he was afraid of me. I wasn't sure which it was. I couldn't decide whether he felt I had betrayed Peter by hiring Nicholas Greco, or was afraid that Greco would find out something that would incriminate him. Greco had suggested the possibility of an "unholy alliance," as he had put it, between Vince and Barr. I really hadn't had time to give that possibility much thought.

I will say in Richard Walker's behalf that he was the one who made the evening. He told anecdotes about the years he had spent working at Sotheby's when he was in his early twenties, and told us about the elderly art connoisseur in London who had hired him now. "He's quite a delightful guy," Richard said, "and it's a perfect time to make the move. I can get out of my lease for the gallery and even get a bonus in giving up the space. My apartment is in the hands of the broker, and we already have offers on it."

For a little while we avoided talking about Peter, but then at dinner it became impossible to ignore the fact that we were here, dining in his home, while he was in a jail cell. "I did give him some good news," I said. "I told him we were having a baby."

"I guessed it!" Elaine said triumphantly. "I told Richard only a couple of hours ago that I was going to ask — I had my suspicions."

Both Elaine and Richard gave me big, seemingly heartfelt hugs.

That left my other guest, Vincent Slater. Our eyes met, and I saw an expression in his that frightened me. I couldn't read it, but for an instant the image of Peter's other pregnant wife, floating in the pool, flashed through my mind.

By nine o'clock, we were having coffee in the library. By then we had run out of things to say to one another, and there was a kind of forced attitude of civility. I felt so much hostility in the room that I resolved I would never bring these people into Peter's special space again. I could tell that all three of them despised Gary Barr. I knew Elaine suspected him of stealing Peter's shirt. Greco had confirmed that Barr admitted to the theft, and we knew that Vincent had then found it and taken it himself.

I could not be sure if any of them, including Barr, had noticed the page from *People* magazine lying on the corner of Peter's desk. I had placed it in such a way that it was hard to miss. I still didn't understand how it could be important, but if it drew a reaction from one of my guests, then I might have a clue.

At nine thirty, they all got up to go. By then, the stress of the evening had begun to exhaust me. If any of these men was the one I heard being threatened by Susan Althorp all those years ago in the chapel, I was not going to find out about it tonight.

We stood by the front door for a few minutes as Vincent and I wished Richard all good luck in London. He told me that if possible, he would be back for Peter's trial, to lend moral support. "I love that guy, Kay," Richard said. "I always have. And I know he loves you."

Long ago, Maggie had told me that you can love a person without loving everything about that person. "Monsignor Fulton Sheen was a great speaker who had a television program about fifty years ago," she had reminisced. "One day he said something that really impressed me. He said, 'I hate communism, but I love the communist.'"

I think that was a good comparison to the

way Peter felt about Richard. He loved the person and despised his weakness.

After I closed the door behind Elaine and Richard and Vincent, I walked back to the kitchen. The Barrs were about to leave. "The cups are all washed and put away, Mrs. Carrington," Jane said anxiously.

"Mrs. Carrington, if you need anything during the night, you know we'll be there in a minute for you," Gary Barr said.

I ignored his remark, but did say that I thought everyone had enjoyed the dinner very much. I bid them good night and they left by the kitchen door; I double-locked it behind them.

It had become my habit at the end of the day to sit for a while in Peter's library. It made me feel close to him. I could relive the moment I walked into this room for the first time and saw him sitting in his chair. I could smile as I remembered the way his reading glasses slipped from his face when he stood up to greet me.

But tonight I didn't stay there long. I was exhausted, both emotionally and physically. I was beginning to fear that Nicholas Greco would not be able to come up with anything that would help in Peter's defense. He was so cautious when I asked him about what he had learned. Maybe he was even finding information that would *hurt* Peter.

I got up from the chair and walked over to the desk. I wanted to be sure to take the page from *People* magazine upstairs with me. I didn't want to forget it. Greco had been so insistent that I show it to Peter on the next visiting day.

I had anchored the page with Peter's handsome antique magnifying glass, and it was covering a section of the background in the picture of Marian Howley.

Part of the section magnified included a painting on the wall behind Howley. I lifted the magnifying glass and studied the painting intently. It was a pastoral scene, identical to the one I had replaced in the dining room. Taking the page and magnifying glass with me, I ran upstairs to the third floor. I had changed a number of the paintings, and had to dig it out from within a stack I had placed on the floor, each painting covered and carefully wrapped.

The frame was heavy, and I was cautious not to overdo the pulling and lifting, but finally I got it out. I propped it against the wall and then sat cross-legged on the floor in front of it. Using the magnifying glass, I slowly began to examine it.

I'm not an art expert, so the fact that this painting did not in any way stir me was not a test of its value. It was signed in the corner — Morley — with the same flourish as the one now hanging in the dining room. The two paintings were essentially identical in content. But the other one compelled attention; this one did not. The date on this one was 1920.

In 1920, had Morley painted this scene and then gone on to create other similar scenes, only with greater skill? It was possible. But then I saw what could only be visible by careful examination: There was another name under Morley's signature.

"What do you think you're doing, Kay?"

I whirled around. Vincent Slater was standing in the doorway, staring at me, his face white, his lips a thin hard line. He began walking across the room to me, and I shrank away from him.

"What do you think you are doing?" he asked again.

78

In Barbara Krause's office, a court stenographer had been summoned to take down the statement given by Ambassador Charles Althorp. More composed now than he had been when he entered the office, Althorp's voice was steady when he began to speak again.

"At the time of her disappearance, I did not reveal that I had learned my daughter, Susan, had developed an addiction to cocaine. As investigator Nicholas Greco pointed out to me the other day, had I told that to the police when Susan disappeared, the investigation might have moved in another direction."

He looked down at his folded hands as if contemplating them. "I thought that by keeping a tight rein on Susan, and cutting off her allowance, I would force her to stop using drugs. Of course, I was wrong. Greco told me that the afternoon of the party in the

Carrington mansion, the present Mrs. Carrington, who was then six years old, overheard a woman blackmailing a man because she needed money. Greco believes — and now I do as well — that it was Susan she heard. Hours later, Susan disappeared.

"For years I have kept the secret of Susan's addiction. I told my sons about it as we stood next to their mother's grave. Had I revealed it earlier, a great injustice might have been avoided." Althorp closed his eyes and shook his head. "I should have . . ." His voice trailed off.

"What exactly *did* you tell your sons, Ambassador?" Tom Moran asked.

"I told them that I believed Susan started taking drugs when she returned from college the beginning of the last summer she was alive, and that she may have been blackmailing someone to get the money she needed. My confession prompted them to open up in turn, telling me things they knew about their sister, things that take on new meaning in context with recent developments.

"My son David had come home for a visit the Christmas before Susan disappeared. Susan had been spending a lot of time at the Carrington mansion. David told me that she confided to him she had noticed that several of the paintings downstairs in the Carrington mansion had been replaced with copies. She was studying art, you know, and knew a lot about the subject. She was sure she knew who was doing the copying, because on one occasion that person invited a young artist to a party in the house, and Susan saw her taking photographs of several paintings.

"David advised Susan to forget what she had discovered and not breathe a word of it to anyone. He said he knew what would happen if Mr. Carrington Sr. found out about it. It would end up as a very messy court case, and Susan might have to testify. David told her that our family had had enough grief with that family because of my earlier affair with Elaine Carrington."

"So Susan did as David suggested, but that summer, when she needed money, she may have used her knowledge of the theft of the art to try to get it," Krause suggested.

"I believe that's exactly what she did," Althorp confirmed.

"Was it Peter Carrington, Ambassador?" Moran asked. "Was he stealing from his own father?"

"No, of course not. Don't you see why this is tormenting me? Peter is in jail right now, accused of killing Susan. He had no reason to kill her. David told me that he believes if Susan had asked Peter for the money, he would have given it to her without question, and then would have tried to get her help. But Susan would never have asked Peter because she was in love with him. David said that my silence has been a curse on Peter. When I spoke to David this afternoon, he said that if I didn't come here tonight, he would never speak to me again."

"Then who was stealing the paintings?"

"Elaine Carrington's son, Richard Walker."

79

Pat Jennings put down the book she was reading, picked up the television remote control, and flipped on the ten o'clock news. "Have to see what's going on in the world," she told her husband, who was dozing over a magazine. Not expecting a response, she turned her attention to the screen.

"We have a breaking news story," the Fox News anchor was saying. "The body of forty-six-year-old Alexandra Lloyd has been found floating in the East River. The victim had been stabbed numerous times. A neighbor and close friend described her as an art teacher who had recently lost her job at a local high school because of budget cuts. Anyone with information should phone the tipster line, 212-555-7000."

"Alexandra Lloyd!" Pat exclaimed, just as the phone rang.

It was Trish. "Pat, I was just watching the news, and —"

"I know," Pat said, "I was watching it, too."

"Are you going to call that tip line and tell them about her calls to Richard Walker?"

"You bet I am, and right now."

"That poor woman. That's so awful, to be stabbed and dumped in the river. My God, do you think he did it?"

"I don't know, but that's for the police to figure out."

"Keep me posted," Trish urged as she hung up.

80

After Charles Althorp had completed his statement and departed with his lawyer, Barbara Krause and Tom Moran stayed in her office, discussing the impact of what they had heard, and assessing how it affected their case against Peter Carrington.

"Even if Walker was stealing good paintings and substituting copies, it doesn't mean that he killed Susan. And much of what Althorp told us is hearsay," Barbara Krause said, flatly.

"And it doesn't answer why Carrington hid his dress shirt that night and why his father handed Maria Valdez a check for five thousand dollars," Moran pointed out. "Anyhow, the statute of limitations has run out on prosecuting Walker for theft, even if we can prove that he was an art crook."

Barbara Krause stood up. "I'm tired. Let's give it a rest."

Her phone rang. "My family probably

thinks I ran off with you," she told Moran as she picked up the phone. Then, as she listened, her expression changed, and she began to pepper the caller with questions: "When did you find her? . . . The secretary is sure she was threatening him? . . . He's leaving for London tomorrow? . . . Okay. Thanks."

She hung up and looked at Moran. "Richard Walker's name has turned up again. The body of a woman who frequently called Walker at work, and who left an angry, almost threatening message a few days ago, has been found floating in the East River. Her name was Alexandra Lloyd. The information about Lloyd calling Walker came from his secretary. My God, I wonder if the two stepbrothers are both killers."

"How did she die?" Moran asked.

"She was stabbed at least a dozen times," Krause said.

"Walker's mother, Elaine Carrington, lives in a house on that estate. He may be there now," Moran said.

"We'll alert the Englewood cops and have them send a squad car over there immediately," Krause replied, a worried tone in her voice. "I know they have some private security outside the estate, but Kay Carrington is alone in that house at night."

81

"What are you doing here?" I asked Vincent Slater as I scrambled to get up from where I had been sitting on the floor. "How did you get in?"

"How did I get in? I cannot describe to you the indignity of your asking how I got in. After thirty years of having a key to my own office in this house, after all the years I have spent protecting Peter, including protecting him from prosecution, I arrived here earlier this evening to find that the locks had been changed."

"What do you mean, protecting Peter from prosecution?" I screamed. *"Peter is innocent!"*

"No, he is not. He was sleepwalking the night Susan disappeared. He didn't know what he was doing. I'm sure of that."

"You believe that!"

"His father must have known what happened," Vincent replied. "That's why he paid off the maid. I have the shirt; it has blood on it. That's why I know that he must have done it. You know, Kay, you really had me fooled. At first I thought you really loved Peter, and that you would be good for him. But then you hired Greco, the very man who had located Maria Valdez, whose testimony about a bribe from Peter's father will put another nail in Peter's coffin. Weren't you really hoping that Greco would dig up more evidence, so you could bury Peter once and for all? I know you would have given the shirt to Greco, so that's why I kept it. Admit it. You married Peter to get your hands on his money. Now that you're carrying his child, you've got a lock on it. Or, is it really Peter's child?"

I was too dumbfounded to even respond.

"Or is it the child of the man to whom you've given a key to my office? I just saw someone coming into the house through my office. He left the door open, and that is how I came in. I came back for two reasons: one, because I had to tell you what I thought about your humiliating me by changing the locks, without even a warning."

"And the second reason?" I asked scornfully.

"The second reason," he replied with equal scorn, "is that, if by some remote possibility, I am wrong about Peter having killed Susan, you were inviting disaster this evening by flaunting that page from *People* magazine in the library. I just can't fathom why you did that. I don't know what significance that page has, but I suspect it must have some. Why else would Grace have kept it?"

"Vince, you just told me you saw a man come into this house through your office. Who was it? That door should have been locked."

"It was dark, and I couldn't tell who it was. But I think you know damn well who it was. Where is he now — in your bedroom?"

"No, I'm right here. Kay, you shouldn't have left the new keys in the kitchen drawer."

Startled, we both turned and looked in the direction from which the voice had come. Richard Walker was moving toward us, a pistol in his hand.

82

Deciding not to use the patrol car's overhead lights or sirens that would alert Richard Walker if he was at the Carrington estate, Englewood police officer Steven Hausenstock pulled his squad car up to the gate and spoke to the guard. "Do you know if Richard Walker is here?" he asked.

"He arrived around five o'clock," the guard replied. "He's still here. He sometimes stays overnight at his mother's house."

"Who else is here?"

"Mr. Carrington's assistant, Mr. Slater, left about half an hour ago, but then came back in the last few minutes."

"All right. I need to check on Mrs. Kay Carrington."

"You can drive up to the front door and ring the bell. If she doesn't answer, the other guard is stationed there and has a key. He can let you in."

The officer drove up to the front entrance.

He could see that the only lights visible in the house were on the third floor.

"Is Mrs. Kay Carrington home?" the officer asked the guard.

"Yes, she is," the guard answered. "She had dinner guests earlier. They all left about half an hour ago."

"Who was here?" the officer asked.

"Mrs. Elaine Carrington, her son Richard Walker, and Vincent Slater. Mr. Slater just returned and went around to the back of the house where his office is. He usually enters there."

"Where did Richard Walker go when he left?" the officer asked.

"He walked with his mother toward her house," the guard said, pointing in that direction. "He must still be there, because I haven't seen him. His car is parked outside her house."

Officer Hausenstock got on his car radio. "Richard Walker is here," he said. "The guard last saw him a half hour ago, walking toward his mother's house on the grounds. Send backup units, but don't use sirens or lights. Hopefully he hasn't spotted me yet." Still holding the radio in his hand, the officer asked the guard, "Does Slater's office lead into the interior of the house?"

"Yes," the guard replied.

The officer continued to talk into his radio as he walked. "I'm going around to the back of the house to see if Carrington's assistant, a guy named Slater, is there. If he is, I'll get into the house that way and check it out. I don't want to ring the doorbell in case Walker has somehow gotten back into the house without the guard seeing him."

Officer Hausenstock turned back to the guard. "Richard Walker may be dangerous, and he may be armed. More police officers will be here soon. If you see Walker, try to avoid any contact with him, and alert the other officers as soon as they get here. He may try to drive out. Tell the guard at the gate what is happening and make sure he closes the gates as soon as the other police arrive."

83

I stood virtually frozen with fear as Richard Walker moved toward us, but then stopped far enough away so that neither of us would have a chance to grab the gun away from him. Vince stepped in front of me; I knew he was attempting to shield me. Richard was pointing the gun directly at us.

"Richard, don't do anything stupid," Vince said calmly. "What is this all about?"

"What is it *about?*" Walker's voice was choked with emotion. "I'll *tell* you what it's all about. It's about the fact that, in the very short time that the present Mrs. Peter Carrington has been here, my life has been destroyed. My mother, for all these years, has protected Peter by hiding that shirt. She saw him wearing it when he came home that night. She could see the bloodstains on it, and she believed he had gotten into some kind of trouble. If she had turned it over to the police the next day, when everybody realized that Susan was missing, Peter would have spent the last twenty-two years in prison."

The telephone on the table at the bottom of the stairs leading to the third floor began to ring. Walker made a gesture to us to be quiet so that he could hear if a message was left on the answering machine.

I had put the volume on high that afternoon so that I could hear any messages while I was on the third floor. A moment later, Maggie's voice, sounding anxious and frightened, said, "Kay, it's late. Where are you? I just remembered who it was your father told me he'd heard whistling that song. It was Richard Walker, Elaine's son. Kay, wasn't he going to be at your house for dinner tonight? Kay, please be careful. I'm so worried about you. Call me back as soon as you get this message."

I could sense that Richard knew that it was all over for him. I stepped away from Vincent. Whatever was going to happen, I wanted to confront Richard. "It was *you* who killed Susan Althorp," I said, my calm tone masking the fear I felt. "It was you and Susan that I heard in the chapel that afternoon, wasn't it?"

I pointed to the painting I had been examining. "You're the art dealer with the gambling problem. I think you're the one who switched this painting — and God knows how many others. Peter told me that the best art was on the walls downstairs. Well, this one was hung in the dining room, but it's only a copy. The real one can be seen on the wall behind Marian Howley in that *People* magazine article. That one actually belongs in this house, doesn't it, Richard? Grace was on to you, just as Susan had been years before. Susan knew a lot about art. She confronted you about the theft, didn't she? I don't know why Susan would blackmail you instead of telling Peter's father, but she did."

"Don't say anything more, Kay," Vince warned. I realized that Vince was concerned that Richard might lose control and shoot, but I was determined to finish what I had begun.

"Your mother wasn't protecting Peter," I said. "She was protecting *you*. And there's a lot more. My father prepared a landscaping design for the other side of the fence, the area where you had buried Susan. He sent it to Peter so he could pass it on to his father, but Peter was away at school and didn't see it. But I think that your mother did see it, and then she showed it to you. You both realized then that you had to get rid of my father. It wasn't enough that you had already fired him. You were afraid that he might still communicate with Peter's father about the design, and you couldn't let that happen. You made his death look like a suicide, and then you buried my father here on the grounds, because you thought they'd never search these grounds again."

Vince had grasped my arm; I could tell he was frantic to stop me. Richard's hand was shaking. Even though I knew he would probably shoot us, I had to keep going. I was overwhelmed by the emotion of all the years of desperately missing my father, and, even worse, believing that he had abandoned me. I was tortured by the weeks of watching my husband shackled and chained, and it was all because of this man.

In that moment, I became aware of a shadow moving in the hallway behind Richard. I wondered suddenly if it could be Elaine Carrington or Gary Barr, coming to help Richard. Even if Maggie had decided to call the police when I didn't answer the phone, it was probably too soon for them to have arrived here. Whoever it was out in the hallway, I wanted that person to hear what I had to say to Richard Walker.

"You not only killed Susan and my father, you killed Grace, too," I continued. "She had that page from the magazine in her pocket when they found her in the pool. She must have realized that the original Morley painting belonged in this house. And Richard, you might be interested to know that the person you had copy it for you was so proud of her work that she actually signed her own name under the forged Morley signature."

I pointed again to the painting I had been examining. "Tell me, Richard, who is Alexandra Lloyd?"

With a sigh of resignation, a weak smile crossed Richard's face. His hand stopped trembling. "As a matter of fact, Alexandra Lloyd was an artist, but now she's dead. I just heard on the news that her body has been fished out of the East River. Like Susan, the charming young lady who was also a drug addict, Alexandra didn't understand that blackmailing me was a very stupid move. You have also made some serious mistakes, Kay, and now I must deal with you as I dealt with them."

Richard then looked at Vince, and spoke directly to him. "I am sorry, Vince. I did not come here intending to harm you. You have always been decent to me and to my mother. But, unfortunately, you showed up at the wrong time. It's over for me. My luck has run out. The police will eventually connect me to Alexandra, and then they'll figure out the rest of it. I still have a small chance of escaping, though, and so I can't leave you here to notify the police."

Richard turned to me. "But if they do get me, I'll have the satisfaction of knowing, when I'm sitting in prison, that you won't be enjoying yourself on the Carrington money." He aimed the pistol toward my head. "Ladies first, Kay."

As I whispered Peter's name, the shadow I had seen in the hallway became a cop who burst into the room, knocked the weapon from Richard's hand, and tackled him to the floor. "Police!" he shouted to Richard. "Stay down, stay down!"

As the police officer struggled with Richard, Vincent kicked the pistol across the room and then fell onto Richard, trying to help the officer subdue him. Moments later, there was a pounding of feet on the stairs and two more police officers raced into the room. When he saw them, Richard stopped struggling and began to sob.

As if in a trance, I watched as Richard was handcuffed and pulled to his feet. One of the officers retrieved the pistol, and the officer who had been out in the hall turned to me. "I heard everything, Mrs. Carrington," he said. "Be assured, I heard everything."

84

At 1:30 P.M. the next day, my husband, shackled and wearing a bright-orange jumpsuit, was brought before Judge Smith. Once again, Barbara Krause would speak for the state, and Conner Banks would stand beside Peter. Once again, the courtroom was jammed with spectators and media. Once again, I sat in the front row. Vince Slater sat on one side of me, and Nick Greco was next to him. Maggie sat on the other side of me, clutching my hand.

Prosecutor Krause addressed the court. "Your Honor, extraordinary events have taken place over the last fifteen hours. Richard Walker, the son of Elaine Carrington, has confessed to the murders of Susan Althorp, Jonathan Lansing, and Grace Carrington. My office has formally charged Mr. Walker with these crimes, and he will be arraigned before Your Honor tomorrow. He has also confessed to the murder three days ago of Alexandra Lloyd, whose body was discovered in the East River in New York City. The New York Police Department has filed a criminal complaint charging him in that case.

"Your Honor — and may I also address Mr. Carrington — we have profound regret that this gross miscarriage of justice has occurred. Our only comfort is that it was discovered before any further harm was done. We are moving to dismiss the indictment that the grand jury returned against Mr. Carrington. That indictment charged him with the murders of Susan Althorp and Jonathan Lansing. We are also, in the interest of justice, moving to dismiss the bail jumping charges that were recently filed. I note that we had not yet formally charged Mr. Carrington with the homicide of Grace Carrington. Your Honor, the only charge that could possibly remain would be the assault on the police officer when Mr. Carrington returned to the Althorp property, apparently in a sleepwalking state. I have personally spoken to the officer involved, and he has asked me to request the dismissal of that charge, too. He is profoundly sympathetic, as are we, to Mr. Carrington; we believe that he has suffered enough. I move that that complaint be dismissed also."

Judge Smith then motioned toward Conner Banks. "Is there anything that you or Mr. Carrington wish to say?"

Banks and Peter looked at each other, and Peter shook his head. "Your Honor," he said, extending his manacled hands, "please tell them to take these things off me. I just want to go home with my wife."

Judge Smith, visibly moved, said, "I am granting the prosecutor's motion to dismiss all of the charges. Mr. Carrington, I rarely make personal comments, but then, I rarely witness anything like this. I am so sorry that you have been a victim of this tragedy. You will be released immediately."

As the courtroom erupted in applause, I ran to Peter and threw my arms around him. I was too emotional to speak, but he did: "It's over, my love, it's over," he said. "Let's go home."

EPILOGUE

One Year Later

It has been a year since Peter stood in the courtroom and heard the prosecutor ask that the charges against him be dismissed. The wheels of justice have continued to turn for the people responsible for putting Peter through this ordeal.

Richard Walker pleaded guilty to the murders of Susan Althorp, my father, Grace Carrington, and Alexandra Lloyd. He was sentenced to life in prison in both New Jersey and New York. The prosecutor's office has assured me that he will never be released.

Vince Slater turned Peter's dress shirt over to the prosecutor's office. The bloodstain on it was determined to be consistent with Richard's admission of what had happened to Susan the night of the dinner party. He had promised to meet her outside her house at 1:30 A.M. She wanted it to be that late to be sure her father was asleep. When he met her, she assured him that she was going to quit using drugs and that this would be the last time she would come to him for money. But he didn't believe her. Frightened that she would reveal his theft of the art, Richard decided he had to kill her. To keep her from screaming, he punched her in the mouth, causing her to bleed onto the front of her gown. Then he strangled her. Before he could move the body to the trunk of his car, Richard saw Peter's car pulling up to the curb in front of the Althorp property.

Panicked, Richard had hidden behind the shrubbery, and had watched as Peter got out of the car, retrieved something from the passenger seat, and then walked across the lawn to where Susan was lying. He was wearing his formal dress shirt but no jacket. Richard saw Peter drop an object — which turned out to be a purse — and then kneel down and lay his head against Susan's chest, apparently to listen for a heartbeat. That is when the transfer of blood to his shirt occurred. Peter then returned to his car and drove away.

Richard admitted that during all this, Peter had seemed to be in a daze consistent with sleepwalking.

Elaine Carrington denied any prior knowledge that Richard was going to harm Susan Althorp, but she did admit that he had told her what he had done within hours of its happening. His explanation to her was that he had snapped and killed Susan because she had resisted his advances, even though she had slipped out of her house to meet him.

Elaine confessed that she had advised Richard to hide the body at his fishing cottage in upstate New York, then later helped him to bury it on the property beyond the fence after they were sure that the police searches were over. She also admitted that it had been her idea to have Richard, using a different name, lure my father to an estate that was for sale in upstate New York on the pretext of hiring him as a landscaper.

After Richard murdered my father, Elaine once again helped him bury the body on the grounds. Richard drove my father's car to where it was found near the Hudson River, and Elaine had followed in her own car. She then drove him home.

Elaine denied any involvement in the deaths of Grace Carrington or Alexandra Lloyd. She also claimed to have no knowledge of the art thefts.

Gary and Jane Barr are now divorced, and

I am very pleased that Jane has continued to work for our family.

Nicholas Greco has become a regular crime commentator on the Fox News network. I am forever in his debt for his perseverance in helping us to find the truth.

Vince Slater and I have realized that, in very different ways, we were both desperately trying to protect Peter. I shall never forget how he stood in front of me as Richard pointed the gun at us. Vince continues to be Peter's most trusted aide, and has become my dear friend.

The newest Peter Carrington is now six months old. I can't say "Junior," because he is really Peter Carrington the Fifth. He is the image of his father, and the light of our lives.

Maggie delights in her role as great-grandmother. She and Peter are now very close. She has even convinced herself that in her heart, she had always believed that he was innocent.

Peter is once again the chairman and CEO of Carrington Enterprises, and the company continues to prosper. He will always require medication to prevent sleepwalking, but there have been no further episodes.

A major factor in sleepwalking is stress, and I see it as my job to make our home a safe haven for Peter in every way. When he walks through the door at night and finds the baby and me waiting for him, I can see by the look that comes into his eyes and the smile that lights his face that I am succeeding.

AUTHOR'S NOTE

To sleep: perchance to dream: ay, there's the rub . . .

To sleep: perchance to *sleepwalk:* ay, there's the rub . . .

With apologies to Shakespeare for paraphrasing him, the concept of writing a story about a person who is a chronic sleepwalker and may have committed crimes while in that condition intrigued me so much that it became a reality.

My gratitude to nurse Jane O'Rourke for her kindness in showing me through the Pascack Valley Hospital Sleep Disorders Center and explaining its services. I am also grateful to the magazines and Web sites that offer so much information about sleepwalking and particularly to the following authors of articles on the subject: Marion Howard; Rosalind Cartwright, Ph.D.; and Fumiko Konno.

We hope you have enjoyed this Large Print book. Other Thorndike, Wheeler, and Chivers Press Large Print books are available at your library or directly from the publishers.

For information about current and upcoming titles, please call or write, without obligation, to:

Publisher
Thorndike Press
295 Kennedy Memorial Drive
Waterville, ME 04901
Tel. (800) 223-1244

or visit our Web site at:

www.gale.com/thorndike
www.gale.com/wheeler

OR

Chivers Large Print
published by BBC Audiobooks Ltd
St. James House, The Square
Lower Bristol Road
Bath BA2 3SB
England
Tel. +44(0) 800 136919
email: bbcaudiobooksbbc.co.uk
www.bbcaudiobooks.co.uk

All our Large Print titles are designed for easy reading, and all our books are made to last.